T0114848

FRATERNITY ROW

THE PLEDGE

JAMES JACKSON

authorHOUSE

AuthorHouse™
1663 Liberty Drive
Bloomington, IN 47403
www.authorhouse.com
Phone: 833-262-8899

Published by AuthorHouse 03/05/2021

ISBN: 978-1-6655-1829-1 (sc)
ISBN: 978-1-6655-1830-7 (e)

Library of Congress Control Number: 2021903910

Print information available on the last page.

CHAPTER 1

ALPHA MORE GRADUATION PARTY

German

THERE WE WERE again, another party. Summer was here, and school was over. A part of me was really excited because my biological brother, Paris, had graduated and was leaving our Fraternity house. I walked through the back so no one would know I hadn't been there the whole time. Paris would have killed me if he knew I'd snuck off. I walked in, The music was loud, and the place was crowded. This was a party thrown by Paris Rigen, but it was Chaotic.

"Hey, G, come here!" Paris said as he walked across the room to me. He had a huge grin on his face. I thought he was about to throw me in the cross fire for leaving, but he didn't.

"What's up?" I asked. He put his arm around me and suprisingly said nothing as we walked through the party with people acknowledging his very existence. That made me sick, but hey, three months from then, I wouldn't have to worry about this; I'd be running Alpha More, our fraternity house, with my own crew.

Paris saw a beautiful brunette in the corner, so he walked over to her, and I headed to the kitchen. I knew my boys would be there. My crew was Justin Baker, the quiet yet personable one, and Adam Banks, the sensitive

1

yet creative one. And of course, every crew had one who was egotistical but sweet, and ours was my best friend, Donnie Diamante. The four of us were officially sophomores at Pendleton University, and we were going to rule Alpha More.

When I walked into the kitchen, I saw Donnie mixing drinks, Adam preparing pinwheel sandwiches, and Justin putting them on a platter.

"Hey, G! Where you been?" Donnie asked.

"I had a Biology final," I said as I began helping Justin.

"I thought that final exam was tomorrow?" Adam asked.

"Do you really think I'm going to make it tomorrow with this crazy party going on?" I asked.

"*Please!* This party sucks. I think the only reason people even came is because of the food," said Donnie.

I told you that the parties Paris threw were very boring not to mention they weren't what we stood for as Alpha More.

"You wouldn't be able to tell. I mean, Paris has gotten hit on by every girl and guy here," said Justin.

Justin was being truthful. Part of being the little brother of Paris Rigen was that I had always lived in his shadow in the fraternity house, on campus, and even in our childhood home. My dad was surprised I had even been chosen to be in Alpha More considering Paris and I couldn't be more different. My dad had also been a member of Alpha More; he was one of the biggest legacies of the house. I'll tell you more about my dad soon. But for now, time to enjoy the festivities of a really boring party.

"Well, boys, before we have to go out in the crazy, let's have a toast," said Donnie. He poured silver tequila into our shot glasses. "This party kicks off our sophomore year. I'm excited that we made it through freshman year with the pranks, the parties, the classes, and my favorite of all, the ladies. Let's toast to running Alpha More sophomore year, and screw the new seniors!" Donnie said as he raises his shot glass.

"I agree," I said as I raised mine.

"Alpha More … *Hoot, hoot, hoot!*" we yelled and downed the tequila. The burn reaction we all had was priceless.

The door flew open, and some guy stormed in. He looked at us as if he had walked into a murder scene. "I'm sorry," the guy said. He began to shake.

"Who the hell are you?" Donnie asked. That scared the guy even more.

"I'm Ben Klovis," he said in a nervous tone. "I want to pledge Alpha More this year."

"Are you sure?" Justin asked sarcastically. We all looked at Ben.

"Sure! Alpha More has to be the best house in the whole Greek system. You guys throw the best parties, and it seems like a real brotherhood living here."

He wasn't wrong. I would have taken a bullet for any of these three, which is how loyal I was to them.

"That's real sweet, man. In fact, I know how we can make it official," Donnie said convincingly. I looked at Donnie as if he had lost his mind.

"You do?" Ben asked enthusiastically.

"Sure! Follow us," Donnie said smiling.

I knew Donnie was going to prank this kid so bad. However, he was right. Once they leave, graduating seniors appoint a member of each class to pick a pledge to have an automatic vote in. I knew for sure I was going to win because Paris had chosen me. Donnie knew exactly what he was doing, and he convinced this poor kid to engage in a silly prank. We all walked out of the kitchen, and we got in my Range Rover and drove off.

Adam

I had a full-sour stomach riding in the car sitting next to this kid who had no idea what he was in for. We drove to Bresha Lake, which was in the middle of the woods. I saw Donnie looking in the rearview mirror at Ben. I couldn't quite see Ben's face, but I imagined he was about to shit himself. Who wouldn't have?

Donnie pulled up along the ditch.

"Really, Donnie? I just bought new tires," German said as he looked out the window.

"I promise it'll be fine," Donnie said with a smile as he put the car in park. When I realized where we were, I knew exactly the prank Donnie was going to pull. I hoped this kid could swim well because this challenge sucked when we'd had to do it. Donnie and Justin led Ben to the location while German and I stayed back a distance to talk.

3

"Where the hell is Donnie going?" German asked.

"You had Greek immunity when we had to do this challenge. But just to let you know, this is going to suck," I answered with a disappointed tone.

We approached the lake, and the four of us crowded around Ben, which made him very nervous. "Well, Ben, my boy, this is called Sunkin' Lake. A part of the commitment to Alpha More is to always wear your Greek letters," Donnie said. He was referring to the Greek letters we all wore around our necks. Donnie took off his letters and held them up. "The challenge will be to rescue these from the bottom of the lake."

I saw German shaking his head, not agreeing to any of this.

"If I do this, I'm in?" Ben asked in an anxious tone.

Donnie threw his letters into the water. Losing your letters was a highly disrespectful matter, and intentionally throwing them into the water was a crazy move even for Donnie.

"Will you rescue our Greek letters?" asked Donnie.

Ben looked very concerned, and I was unsure if he would jump in the water. Ben looked at the lake as we all gave him room to jump. "Well, are you going to rescue our letters?" Donnie asked again with a huge grin.

Ben looked at Donnie with all seriousness. It was as if he knew how important the Greek letters were to us. He took off his shirt, which Justin picked up. "I'll hold this for you," Justin said. Ben gave him a nod, did a small jog in place, and then did an impressive dive into the water.

"He did it! He actually jumped in!" Donnie shouted.

"Did you think he wouldn't?" German asked in irritation.

"Come on, G. I didn't think he would actually jump in." Donnie looked at the lake.

"I'm going to wait in my car. This is ridiculous," German said. He began to walk away. I noticed that it had been a little bit of time and Ben hadn't come up for air. I started to get concerned. Unless Ben was a great swimmer, he would have come up for air.

"Damn, he's great swimmer," Donnie said, reading my mind.

"Shine the flashlight in the water, Donnie," Justin said in concern. Donnie flashed the light in the water, and the three of us looked. "Guys, I don't see him," Justin said. We continued to watch for him. I never saw Donnie get nervous; his ego wouldn't let him. "Man, something's wrong," Justin shouted as he began to take off his shirt.

German ran back to us. "What happened?"

"He hasn't come up yet," said Donnie. German took his phone and keys out of his pocket and jumped in with Justin. Donnie and I looked around to be sure Ben wasn't floating.

"Man, I can't believe this is happening," Donnie said. He was very nervous.

German and Justin rose out of the water. "He's stuck!" German yelled. He and Justin went back down. I looked at Donnie. His nervous look had turned into complete worry.

Justin

In the water, I noticed that Ben's foot was caught, and he wasn't responding to German and me. I grabbed German, and we rose to the surface.

"What's going on?" Donnie asked as he flashed the light on us.

"Looks like his leg's stuck somehow," German said.

"G, come up," Adam said as he jumped into the water with the flashlight.

When Adam pointed the light at Ben, we saw the branch he was caught on. I swam next to Adam and pulled on the branch, which let Ben's foot free. We got Ben to the surface, and Donnie helped us get him out of the water.

"What do we do?" Donnie asked.

"We have to give him CPR," German said.

"How're we supposed to do that?" Donnie asked. Though this kid was unconscious and in bad condition, I thought it was funny to see Donnie scared because his ego was so big that it would stomp on any human emotions he had.

"Move! I'll do it," German said as he got on the ground. "Justin, level his head for me," he told me, and I folded his shirt to make a pillow. "Donnie, call the police. Tell them we need an ambulance."

We heard a branch break and thought that we weren't alone. Everyone looked into the woods.

"What was that?" asked Adam.

"Hello?" Donnie yelled. It became very silent as we continued to look.

"Do you guys think that was someone?" asked Donnie.

"No, it probably was an animal. Let's do this," German said.

Donnie called the police and an ambulance as German propped Ben's mouth open to give him CPR as Adam pumped his heart. Adam counted backward from ten, but Ben didn't respond. "G, do it again," Adam said as G gave Ben air again and Adam continued to pump.

Donnie came back. "Paramedics are on the way."

"He's not responding," G said.

"Is he dead?" asked Donnie as we looked at each other in disbelief.

The paramedics and the police arrived. I didn't know what to do. We watched them take Ben away. The police approached us.

"Gentlemen, I'm Officer Jenkins, and this is Officer Varon. What happened?"

"He jumped in the water, and his foot got stuck on a branch down below," German said as if he weren't nervous.

"Why did he jump in the water?" Varon asked. We were all silent. The officers looked at us. "I asked the four of you a question."

"It was supposed to be a prank," Donnie said.

"A prank?" Jenkins asked

That was the moment I knew the four of us were in deep trouble. I couldn't believe this had happened. If I could go back, I would have told Ben just to enjoy the party.

"Yes," Adam said.

"Hang tight," Jenkins said as he and Varon walked off to converse.

Another car pulled up, and a well-dressed gentlemen got out and approached us smirking all the way. "Gentlemen, I'm Detective Darren Drake. I'm here to investigate what happened and get your side of the story."

Drake asked us routine questions to get an idea of how Ben had drowned, but he didn't seem to buy our stories about what had happened, and I saw that that irritated German.

"You four are telling me that his foot got caught in a branch underwater and you believe he was underwater for more than three minutes?" Drake asked.

"I said it was approximately three minutes," German said.

"This question may seem a little unethical, but it doesn't hurt to ask. Did you know Ben Klovis prior to this incident?"

We were thrown off balance by that. We looked at each other, and we all said that we had just met him at the party. Drake walked off to talk with the officers. I looked at them wondering if they were talking about arresting us and charging us with murder. I wanted to go home. The longer we waited, the more anxious I became.

Drake walked back to us with that smirk of his. "Gentlemen, at this point, I don't have anything to hold you on as I don't have an autopsy report to suggest anything other than accidental death. I'll be in touch with you after I have the report. You're free to go."

We walked to German's car. "What do you think's going to happen?" Adam asked.

"We're going to be charged with reckless endangerment. We could receive five years since it resulted in an accidental death, and we might be discharged from Alpha More," German said.

Hearing those words made me worry even more. I didn't know how I'd overcome this.

Drake

The next morning, I received a call from Monty Clark, the toxicologist, and an invite to his lab. I went there and gloved up.

"Good morning, Monty," I said as I walked up to the examining table.

"Good morning, Detective Drake."

"I'm hoping you have something for me."

"I do. Cause of death is drowning. I did find a scar on the left ankle," Monty said as he lifted the left leg up. "There was a struggle, which may indicate he got stuck on something at the bottom of the lake. I wrote it all in my report."

He provided me with all the details to charge the four boys with reckless endangerment. I was going to place his report in my report and charge those boys to fullest extent of the law in Maine.

CHAPTER 2

RETURNING

Adam

THREE MONTHS LATER, I was driving back to Pendleton. The four of us had been charged with reckless endangerment. German found an amazing lawyer to represent us; we spent the summer doing community service but all separately, so I hadn't seen Donnie, Justin, or German the entire summer. I missed them despite the trauma of Ben's death.

Driving back to Pendleton was rough mainly because I had to drive past Bresha Lake to get to campus. I was having flashbacks of that night.

I drove up Concord Street, where the Alpha More house and five other fraternity houses were. The street behind us was Lexington Street, where the sorority houses were. Alpha More was at the end of the street. I had a designated parking spot in the lot next to the house, so I was able to avoid parking on the street.

I didn't see Donnie's, Justin's, or German's cars, which made me nervous. I started to think that they had changed their minds about coming back to the house. I walked up to the house avoiding the freshmen. When I opened the door, I heard a very familiar voice.

"Yeah baby! Touchdown! Oh yeah!" Donnie yelled. "Twenty bucks right now!" he told a frat brother. "Adam!" Donnie yelled when he spotted me.

"Couldn't wait to get back," I said smiling.

"Are you kidding me? The last three months have been hell!" Donnie said, and we laughed. "It's really good to see you, bro. I missed you!"

The door opened, and in walked Justin with a beautiful girl, who was five-one to Justin's six-six. "Bros!" Justin shouted and then hugged Donnie and then me. The girl smiled seeing Justin in his element. "Guys, I want to introduce Pip, my girlfriend." She smiled and extended her hand. "Pip, this is Donnie and Adam."

Donnie smiled but seemed a little hesitant. "You look familiar," Donnie told her.

She smiled. "I just transferred here from Columbia, so unless you spent any time there, I don't think you'd know me."

"Where's G?" asked Justin.

"He hasn't shown up yet," Donnie said; we were all wondering the same thing.

German

That summer was horrible. My dad tormented me the whole time about what had happened. I decided to go to Bresha Lake before I went to Alpha More. I hadn't told the rest of the guys, but I'd gone to Ben's funeral. What can I tell you is his family was in such disbelief about what had happened. I walked to where we had pulled him out of the water and began questioning everything. I knew I was dwelling on it. My feelings of guilt for this kid's death haunted me more than anyone knew.

My phone vibrated. It was a text from Donnie: "G, where are you?" As much as I wanted to respond, I didn't, but I knew that I had to get to Alpha More to check in. Another text: "G, come on, please respond." We had court in a couple of hours; I decided to meet them there. I just needed a moment.

In the court hallway, I saw my den father, Mr. Alves.

"German, how are you?" he asked as we hugged.

"I'm OK."

"You didn't show up at the house. I still need you to sign your contract," he said as he looked at me with concern.

"I need a couple of days," I said hoping he would understand. I didn't want to tell him I was having second thoughts about rejoining Alpha More because the guilt was haunting me.

"We'll talk later. Your case is about to begin," he said as he opened the courtroom door. I walked in and saw Donnie, Justin, and Adam in the front on the defendants' side. I walked to their row and joined them.

"I texted you. Why didn't you answer?" Donnie asked me.

"Sorry. My dad gave me the third degree all summer. I needed a moment to myself," I said hoping Donnie would accept that.

The doors opened, and the four of us turned and saw what looked like Ben Klovis walking into the courtroom.

"What the hell?" Donnie asked.

"That's not who I think it is …" Justin said.

"It's not," I said. "That's Brandon Klovis, Ben's twin."

"All rise. Court is now in session. The honorable Judge Hostead Crowly presiding."

We all rose. I looked at Brandon, who was looking at us and smiling.

The four of us walked out of the courthouse. "I'm free!" Donnie said as he extended his arms up.

The judge had mercy on us; he dismissed our probation since we all had been consistent with our community service.

"It turned out a lot better that I could've imagined," Adam said.

I knew they would ask why I hadn't shown up at Alpha More, so brought it up myself. "Guys, I don't think I'm coming back," I said, and they gave me shocked looks. "I have a lot going on, and I don't know if I can rejoin the house with all that's happened."

"G, we've all had a horrible time with this, but you know it won't be the same without you," Justin said.

Donnie was staring at something behind us. "Guys, look," he said.

We turned and saw Mr. Alves and Brandon talking.

"Get in my car so we're not seen," I said, and we all got in. We saw Brandon looking at a paper and Mr. Alves handing him a pen.

"What do you think he's signing?" Adam asked.

"All of this is strange, G. How did you know Ben had a twin?" Donnie asked.

"I went to Ben's funeral, and by the looks of it, we might be in way over our heads in this new situation," I said.

Justin

I'd found out that Donnie would be my roommate that year. I knew Sharing a room with him would be interesting; Adam, who had roomed with him last year, said that Donnie had a different girl at least twice a week and had a gumball machine literally filled with condoms. I'd be lying if I said I wasn't excited to see that because I was, but I had a girlfriend and was going to do my best to be faithful to her.

A knock at the door … I walk over to answer it. It's Pip, who said, "Hey, babe," with a smile.

"Hi," I responded, and we kissed. I invited her in and closed the door.

She looked around and said, "This room is really spacious!"

"Yeah, a lot bigger than my room at home."

"Is your roommate here?"

"Yeah, Donnie. You met him earlier."

"He's kind of different," she said. "I guess fraternity men always have a certain exterior to them, but Donnie's quite the mystery."

I began setting up the place slightly because there was a house meeting in about an hour to go over the house rules. "Want to give me a hand setting up?" I asked.

"Sure." Pip smiled and began hanging my clothes in the closet. A piece of paper fell out of the closet, which Pip picked up. I walked over quietly and quickly so she wouldn't read it. "What's that?" Pip asked.

"Nothing," I answered hoping she wouldn't ask any more questions. I hadn't spoke to Pip on why I had been charged with reckless endangerment, and luckily, she was a transfer to Pendleton, so the word about my criminal past hadn't reached her. I knew that it was unfair to keep her in the blind about that part of my life, but I wanted to forget it had happened to me.

Pip was organizing my closet when the door opened.

"Yo, bro! I'm super excited you're my roomie," Donnie said as he paused seeing Pip.

"Hi," Pip said.

"Hey," Donnie said and looked at me. "Awkward … I'm going to put this on my bed and leave," Donnie said.

"No, actually, I'm going to take off," Pip said. She gave me a kiss. "Call me?"

"Sure," I said.

Pip left, and I shut the door. Regretfully, I looked at Donnie, who was shaking his head.

"You know this isn't going to work, right?" he asked.

"What's not going to work?" I asked knowing he was talking about Pip.

"This whole relationship thing. You know, Alpha More men are single to smash."

"Who says I won't be smashing?"

"I didn't say you wouldn't be smashing, but it's a lot better to be single and smashing."

I shook my head. Throughout all of this, I was glad Donnie hadn't lost his ego.

After he and I finished setting up our room, we walked out into the hallway and saw Adam come out of his room. "Hey, man, how's your room?" I asked; he looked bummed out.

"My roommate is Brody Brockett," Adam said as we walked to the stairs.

"Dude, that sucks. Brody's as annoying as hell," Donnie said.

"What sucks more is that G was supposed to be my roommate, but since he hasn't decided to come back, I got stuck with Brody," Adam said.

We all looked at each other. "Somehow, we need to convince G to come back," Donnie said.

"How? I don't want him to feel we're badgering him to come back," I said.

"I know how to get G to come back," Donnie said as German quietly came up to us.

"Get me to come back where?" German asked.

"Come back here, G. You know this house wouldn't be the same without you," Donnie said.

Before German could respond, Brody came up to us and said, "Hey, guys, house meeting in five minutes," he said as we rolled our eyes.

"I can tell this is going to be a long year," Adam said shaking his head.

We made our way to the conference room, where all fifty of us were going to have a discussion with our den father, Alves.

Donnie

The house meeting was a circus. The seniors were seated to the right of the podium, and behind them were the juniors. The sophomores were to the left of the podium, and the freshmen were behind them. Adam, Justin, German, and I sat in the front row to make sure the house knew we were taking over.

"Hello, Alpha More," Alves said. "We're back for another year of a successful college adventure. If you're sitting here, that means you're a member of Alpha More. There are forty-nine of you here, which means we're missing one."

"Mr. Alves?" Brody asked.

"Yes, Brody?"

"I noticed that German's name isn't on our sophomore roster. Is he still in Alpha More?"

If I'd been sitting next to Brody, I would've backhanded him in his nose even though I knew that because of our actions, we were on thin ice.

"Unless German resigns from Alpha More, he's still considered a member," Alves said. He looked to his left and said, "I would like to introduce you to the fiftieth member of the house, Brandon Klovis."

We were stunned when Brandon walked up to the podium, waved, and said, "Thank you for having me." Everyone clapped.

"Gentleman, we are all aware that this is Ben Klovis's brother and that Ben was going to pledge our fraternity this year. Pledge week has been cancelled, and freshmen were selected based on interviews I conducted. Brandon, please join the freshmen section," Alves said. Brandon walked past us with his creepy smile.

After the meeting, we all went to Justin's and my room, and Justin closed the door.

"Well, this confirms what we saw at the courthouse," Adam said.

"This is strange. Like, why would you join the very fraternity that was responsible for your brother's death?" Justin asked.

"Yeah. Could this day be any worse?" I asked sarcastically.

A knock on the door ... The door opened. Brody appeared. "Hey, guys, you have a visitor in the living room," he said as I became more annoyed.

We headed downstairs not sure who this visitor could be. "Hopefully, it's the mayor issuing an apology letter to us," I said. The guys laughed as we walked into the room, but our visitor was Detective Drake. The surprised look on our faces made left field look right. "Well, well, Justin Baker, Adam Banks, Donnie Diamante, and German Rigen. Welcome back," Drake said. I'd thought we would never see this jerk ever again, but I'd thought wrong.

"I understand you boys have a party to prepare for, so I won't be long," Drake said making us nervous.

"May I ask why you're here?" German asked sounding irritated.

"Sure. Ben Klovis's case has been reopened. Apparently, there was certain circumstantial evidence that has surfaced over the last several months."

"I read the autopsy report," German said with confidence. "Ben's death was determined to be due to accidental drowning. There was a bruise on his left foot indicating that he had been trapped underwater, which is what two out of the four of us said at our trial for reckless endangerment."

"His parents are requesting a second autopsy, which is within their rights, something you should be aware of since you're a prelaw major, Mr. Rigen," Drake said smiling. "Have a great party." The detective left.

CHAPTER 3

THE PARTY S JUST BEGUN

Justin

AFTER DRAKE'S SURPRISE visit, we all agreed that the party was more important and that we wouldn't dwell on what he had said about the investigation. But I was scared and wasn't sure if I was in the mood to party.

The sophomores were in charge of the school scare party. Donnie had the brilliant idea to turn our house into a haunted maze. The four of us and Adam's roommate, Brody, and five sophomores—Petey, Jonesy, Otto, Brian, and Dunbar—planned it.

"Guys, it's real simple. We start with the entrance. The first scare will be the door slamming. We'll have the first costume move them into the east wing, to the kitchen, to upstairs, and then to the conference room, from where we'll move them to the real party in the backyard," said Donnie as he pointed to a map.

"What if someone gets hurt?" Brody asked to Donnie's annoyance.

"We still have those liability forms from the Halloween party the seniors threw last year. We can make copies and get everyone to sign them," Donnie said.

Donnie was really good at organizing parties; he had every detail down as if we were opening a business.

"I have costumes for all of you. They're upstairs. Make sure you come to my room when we're done setting up," Donnie said as he looked around. "All right, guys, hands in!"

We made a circle with our fists and yelled, "Alpha More! *Hoot hoot hoot!*"

Donnie, German, and I were in charge of the setup. Adam, Brody, and Otto were in charge of the food. Petey, Jonesy, Brian, and Dunbar were in charge of the drinks. Donnie made the freshmen hang the decorations throughout the house while the juniors and seniors set things up in the backyard.

Donnie, German, and I walked to the front door, where the maze began. Donnie had thought it would be a good idea to install a hydraulic pump on the front door, and the engineer was almost finished with that. Mr. Alves walked up as the engineer explained how the door would work.

"All right, gentlemen, this how this works. When you're in a clear zone, you push the button and the door will slam shut at twenty miles per hour." He pressed the button and the door slammed shut scaring everyone.

Donnie chuckled. "This is so awesome!"

"Donnie, this seems very dangerous," Alves said.

"Mr. Alves, please. I'll make sure that everyone is safely inside before I punch the button," Donnie said.

"OK, fine. Make sure everyone signs a copy of the forms."

"Yes sir," Donnie said.

"All right, and here's the bill," the engineer said."

"And here's the guy who'll be paying," Donnie said as he pointed to German.

German took the contract and scanned it. "Two thousand?"

"I take all major credit cards," said the engineer.

Donnie smiled and nodded at German, who gave the man his credit card.

Donnie went to make copies of the waivers, and German and I went to the kitchen to check on Adam, who was there alone and multitasking. "Hey, guys, grab an apron. I'm desperate!" he said.

"Where are Otto and Brody?" I asked.

"I sent them to the grocery store. Nobody went shopping yet."

"I thought the seniors were supposed to do that," German said.

"They obviously didn't," Adam said.

The stove bell rang. "G, can you get those?" Adam asked.

When German was putting on oven mitts, Donnie walked in. "All right, I made two hundred copies of the waiver and why does it smell like ass in here?"

The smell coming from the tray German was putting on the counter was indeed very odd.

"Those are my Cajun baked tuna balls," Adam said as he put some on a plate.

We all gave Adam looks of disgust.

"What? All we had in the pantry were cans of tuna. Try one?" Adam asked.

We each took one. I ate mine first as Donnie and German watched me. "It's actually really good," I said to Donnie and German.

"Good. Here's mine," Donnie said as he and German gave me their tuna balls.

"I'm going to order pizzas. I'll meet you guys upstairs," German said.

"If all else fails, Adam, I'll eat your tuna balls," I said to make Adam feel better.

Donnie

The first party of the year was always the toughest in a frat house. I looked on my phone to see that over two hundred had RSVP'd. Not bad considering I'd posted that only an hour earlier.

"Hey, Donnie?" Brandon said approaching me.

"Yeah?" I asked not seeming interested.

"I'm all settled in. I was wanting to help out, and everyone said I should talk to you." Brandon said not getting the clue.

"You're a freshman, right?"

"Yeah."

"Freshmen are in charge of setting up and cleaning up. I think they're finished, so you can just get ready for the party."

Brandon nodded and left. It felt weird being in the same house as this kid. I walked into the office, where German was working on the computer.

"That guy is really creepy," I said.

"Who?" G asked.

"Brandon," I said confirming German's suspicion. I could always tell when German was up to something. Who doesn't know his best friend? "What are you up to?"

"I'm on Ben Klovis's Facebook profile," German said as he looked through Ben's pictures.

"Why?" I asked.

"I don't know. The fact that the investigation is being reopened concerns me."

"G, c'mon. That detective jerk is full of it. They're not going to find anything different from what they found before," I said as I watched German scroll through the pictures rapidly. "Wait! Go back!" I said, and German went back a few pictures. "Stop! Right there," I said. He and I looked at a photo of Ben with Pip. I knew all hell was going to break loose. I couldn't hide my smile.

"Who's that?" German asked.

"Come on. You don't recognize her?" I asked not knowing if German had met Pip.

"No."

"That's Justin's girlfriend, G."

"The new one?"

"Yes," I said. "You think Ben and Pip dated?"

"Let's see if there are any more pictures," German said as he scrolled through some more, and we saw some pictures of Ben and pip that looked like they had been taken a few days before his death.

"Wait. Go to that picture," I said pointing at one, and German clicked on it.

"That's what he was wearing the night he died," German said as he pulled up the date of the picture, which was indeed the night of the party. German clicked on the next picture, which showed them at our house for the graduation party. German and I were shocked.

"No way," I said.

"She was here the night of the party. Do you think she knows that he left with us?" German asked.

"Don't know," I said as I selected print on the computer to get a copy of the picture.

"What are you doing?" German asked.

"Saving this for Justin."

"We have to tell him!"

"No, not now," I said.

"Donnie, we can't just sit here and allow this."

"I know, but how would you feel if you were him?"

"I'd want you to tell me."

"I agree. This may be everything or maybe nothing. Either way, we owe it to Justin to tell him. After the party, we'll meet in your car and tell him. For now, let's get ready for the party."

German agreed to that.

Adam, Justin, German, and I were in my room about to pull our costumes out of the bags. Justin opened his first. "Cool. I'm Leatherface!" he said.

Adam opened his bag. "I'm Jigsaw. Nice!"

We all looked at German. I grinned hugely because I knew German was going to kill me.

He opened his bag and pulled his costume out. "Chucky? Donnie! What the hell!"

He punched me, which cracked Justin, Adam, and me up. "Sorry, G, but I couldn't help it. You're five-five, short, and cute, and so is Chucky at times," I said as I laughed.

"What are you dressing up as, Donnie?" Adam asked.

"The Sorcerer, the Greek god himself."

"How fitting!" German said sarcastically.

I was right next to Justin's phone when it rang. I saw it was Pip.

"Donnie, hand me my phone please," he said, and I pitched his phone to him. He said, "Guys, I'll be right back," and he walked out.

The looks German and I gave each other made Adam suspicious. "What's wrong?" he asked.

I peeked out of the room to see how far away Justin was—at the end of the hallway. I closed the door quietly and nodded to German.

"Look, Adam," German said. "We're about to show you something, but you can't tell Justin about this just yet."

I gave the print to Adam, whose eyes went as large as saucers. "That's—"

"We know, Adam. Pip and Ben the night of the graduation party, the night he died," I said.

"Where'd you get this?"

"Ben's Facebook page," said German.

"You going to tell him?"

"Tell me what?" Justin asked as he walked back in. We all thought we'd been caught.

"G didn't order enough pizzas," I said as I snatched the picture out of Adam's hand.

"Oh, no worries, G. I like Adam's tuna balls, so I'll just eat them," Justin said.

"Cool! Let's party!" I said.

Adam

I looked out the window and saw that the line for the party was really long. Word had gotten out that we were having a maze in the house. Freshmen always ruined the surprises.

"Hey," German said.

"Have you looked outside?" I asked.

"Yeah. They set up six tables, which means twelve people are coming in at a time. It would take forever to let them in the front door, so some freshmen are letting people in the side entrance," German said.

German looked concerned. "Donnie and I said we're going to tell Justin at the end of the party. We're going to meet in my car."

I nodded as we put our masks on and I powered on my Jigsaw laugh, which got everyone's attention. "Nice. OK, guys, listen up. Operation Scare Maze is now in full effect, so we're going to do this in shifts. The seniors will take the eight o'clock shift. We have ten minutes until it's seven. Any questions?" Donnie asked us ten sophomores. "All right, let's get moving."

The first twelve people entered. The room was dark. We had black lights and red arrows pointing at the door, which had a sign that read Dead End. I looked at the people who walked in and saw Pip among them. Donnie made sure that the door was clear and then pressed the button;

the slamming door made everyone scream. Justin opened the Dead End door and started his chainsaw. Pip, who was in front of the door fell and screamed. Justin pulled her to her feet, and she stared running.

"Babe! Wait!" Justin said as an excited Donnie stopped him from chasing her.

The crew was coming my way. When the first person crossed the line, a red light came on and activated my Jigsaw laugh. Pip was directly in front of me and was terrified. The arrow pointed the crew to the conference room, a very large room where German was. I watched German scare them, and Donnie was right—German played a great Chucky. He led them to the backyard, and I signaled Donnie to let the next crew in.

The first walk-through of the maze had been awesome. I saw Justin walking toward me.

"Hey, Otto," Justin said as Otto ran up to him.

"What's up?" I asked Justin as he was taking off his costume.

"I scared Pip really bad. I need to make sure she's OK," Justin said as he gave his costume to Otto, who put it on and ran to get behind the Dead End door. "I'll be right back," Justin said.

"OK, guys, get ready," Donnie shouted.

I continued to scare the guests for our hour-long shift. The seniors came in the same costumes except for Donnie's; his ego wouldn't permit anyone else to be in the same costume.

Donnie, German, and I walked outside. The entire campus was at our house.

"Where did Justin go?" Donnie asked.

"He said Pip was really scared. He wanted to check on her," I said.

"Really?" Donnie asked in an annoyed tone.

"Donnie, come on. She's still his girlfriend regardless of what we found out," German said.

"Listen. That girl is shady. I'm starting to think she's dating Justin for insight," said Donnie.

"Insight on what?" I asked.

"Think about it. Why is this case being reopened? Why would she date a guy knowing we killed her boyfriend?" Donnie asked.

"We didn't kill him. He drowned," I said.

German looked as if he had just had an epiphany. "Suppose Justin words it exactly like Donnie just did? That would be considered a confession, which would add her as a character witness if she's working with Drake," German said as Donnie nodded.

"We have to find Justin," I said.

Donnie was staring to the right. "Who the hell is that?"

German and I looked in the same direction and saw someone in the same Sorcerer costume Donnie had on and holding a medieval axe that looked real.

"Did you buy someone else that costume, Donnie?" I asked.

"Hell no. Why would I do that?" Donnie asked.

Donnie started walking to whoever it was, and German and I followed. The Greek god pointed the axe at us, which made Donnie charge him. The music started, which caused the crowd to get up and dance. By the time we made our way through the crowd, the Greek god had disappeared.

"You see him?" Donnie asked, and we all looked around.

I saw Justin hugging Pip outside. "No, but there's Justin," I said and pointed.

We walked to Justin, who gave Pip a kiss after which she walked off.

"Hey, guys. What's up?" he asked.

"Where's Pip going?" Donnie asked.

"Home. Her anxiety level's through the roof. I scared her pretty bad."

Justin looked quite suspicious as he looked behind us. "Donnie, someone has your same costume."

We all turned to where Justin was looking.

"Let's get him!" Donnie said when the Greek god ran into the house. The four us ran into the house not sure if anyone else had noticed the guy. We saw him run upstairs, which led to twenty rooms on two levels. Donnie led the way up, Justin followed him, and I followed German. Once we arrived at the second level, Donnie stopped.

"Adam, G, you two take the second level. Justin and I'll go to the third level," Donnie said, and we split up. On the top level were juniors and seniors while freshmen and sophomores were on the second. I figured this would be quite a chase.

German

Chasing some idiot in the Greek god costume was stupid. For all we knew, it could have been an upperclassman playing a prank. Adam and I walked down the hall slowly.

"Who do you think this is?" Adam asked.

"It could be anybody. This is all Donnie and his ego because someone wore the same costume," I said.

I noticed that Justin's and Donnie's room door was cracked while all the others down the hallway were closed. I tapped Adam's shoulder and pointed at the door. Adam held his finger to his lips to shush me. We walked even slower just in case he was in there. I pulled out my phone to text Donnie and Justin to come to their room. I heard Donnie's ringer, so I knew they were close.

Adam peeked in the door as Donnie and Justin came down. Donnie got in front of Adam and flashed his fingers one, two, and three; we shoved the door open and barged in. The room was empty. The window was open. We rushed to the window but didn't see anyone outside.

"Hey, guys," Justin said. He pointed to our Greek letters hanging from the top of a mirror. "Donnie, is that yours?"

"No. I'm wearing mine," Donnie said as he took the letter necklace down. He looked lost.

"What's wrong?" I asked.

"Guys, this is the same one I threw into the lake that night," Donnie said.

"No way that's the same one," Adam said.

Donnie paced the room as Adam and Justin looked at the necklace.

"Donnie, are you sure that's it?" I asked thinking it would have been impossible for it to have surfaced.

"Justin, read the name on it," Donnie said.

Our names had been engraved on our letters when we joined the fraternity.

"Clear Gold Jewelry," he said.

"Donnie, that doesn't prove anything," said Adam.

"Adam's right. This could have been made by anyone," I said.

"That's where you're wrong, G. Only five of us knew what was thrown in the water that night, and one is dead," Donnie said.

"Donnie has a point, G. Unless one of us told someone about what we did, how could someone know where Donnie got that from and plant it in the room?" Justin asked.

Adam looked guilty as we all looked at him, Adam looked at all of us as it was a struggle for him to speak,

"I told Detective Drake about the Greek Letters." Adam said.

"So Drake was the only other person that knew, it would make sense why it would reappear."

"You think he bought another replica?" Donnie asked

"Let's find out," I answered.

In the hallway, we saw a door open and Brandon step out. He gave us a smile and headed for the stairs.

The guys followed me out to my car. Justin got in the front seat. "Are we going someplace?" Justin asked as we were quiet.

"No. We need talk to you about something first," I said.

"About what?"

"About Pip," said Donnie.

"Pip?" Justin asked.

I gave Justin the picture of Pip and Ben not knowing how he would react.

He looked at the picture in disbelief. "What the hell is this?"

"I went on Ben's Facebook profile and found pictures of him and Pip. That picture was the night of the graduation party," I said.

Justin started to shake a little.

"Justin!" Donnie said as Justin opened the door and slammed it.

"That went well," I told Donnie and Adam.

"Do you guys think we should have done this?" Adam asked.

"Suppose he found out another way, or worse, suppose he found out we knew and hadn't told him?" Donnie asked.

Adam and I went back to the party. We saw Justin alone on a bench and went over to him. He looked very angry. "How long have you guys known about this?" he asked.

"We just found out today," said Donnie.

"What do I do now?" Justin asked.

"Either talk to Pip about it or go on Facebook to see if maybe we were wrong about the relationship," Adam said.

"That's not a bad idea," Donnie said. "Maybe he should look at the profile. Maybe we all should. Something might be there."

We walked into the office as the party was going on.

"I can't believe we're missing the first party of the year," Donnie said as Adam was helping Justin on Facebook and I helped Donnie find out more about the Greek letters.

"What do you want to search?" asked Donnie.

"Go to the website where you bought the replica. We'll start there," I said.

"Guys, look at this," Justin said, and we gathered around the computer. Pip had a timeline post about how she couldn't believe that the love of her life was gone; it was dated a week after Ben's death.

"Damn, Justin. I know that's hard to read," said Adam.

"I don't know if I can face her right now," Justin said.

Donnie and I went back to the other computer.

"This is it," Donnie said as he pulled up some contact info.

"The place is in Boston," I said as I wrote down the address.

"What do you want to do?" asked Donnie.

"Let's go there tomorrow after cleanup. We'll see if we can get more info about who bought the necklace so we can know how serious we need to take this," I said.

CHAPTER 4

THE GRAND ATTACK

Donnie

T HE DAY AFTER the Alpha More party we had to clean up the huge mess. We had just finished doing that, and Justin and I were waiting for Adam and German to come downstairs. Justin really looked down.

"What's wrong, man? You look like you lost your big brother," I said.

"I don't know what to do, man." Justin said.

I moved closer to comfort him. I knew he needed a friend.

"It'll pass," said Brandon, who had just walked up. "Whatever you're feeling, it'll pass."

He left the room just as German and Adam came downstairs.

"What was that all about?" German asked.

"Who knows? That kid is strange. Ready?" I asked as we walked out to German's car.

"I called my lawyer," G said. "He's going to look into the case being reopened."

"What do you think he'll find?" asked Adam.

"I think he'll find out that the Klovis family will try to sue us," said German.

"Maybe we should call our parents," I said.

"No. If they try to file a civil suit, I'll settle with them out of court. I'll pay for that myself if it comes to that," said German.

What most people didn't know about German Rigen was that he was loaded, I mean, well paid. I wouldn't want him to lose his money over something that had been an accident.

"What if Brandon put the necklace in our room?" Justin asked.

"One thing's for sure. If Brandon did it, we'll find out," I said.

We parked in front of the Clear Gold Jewelry store and went it.

"Good morning, gentlemen. How can I help you?" the jeweler asked.

"Mr. Keegan, I was hoping you could answer some questions," German said.

"Online, it says you can make replicas of necklaces. I've had one made that looks like this," I said. I showed Mr. Keegan the replica.

He examined it. "Yes, this is definitely mine," he said.

"Do you mark them accordingly?" asked German.

"Maybe. What's it to you?"

"Anyone can come in and buy this to replicate our fraternity house symbol," said Adam. "If you look closely at mine, you can see the engraving. It was made by a manufacturer in New York," Adam said.

"Still don't see what this would have to do with you," said Keegan.

"What if I buy that replica and information on the person who bought it?" German asked.

"The price would be too high for you, way more than what this is worth."

"What's your price?" asked German.

Keegan smiled at German not knowing that there wasn't a price he could give German that he wouldn't be able to put on the table. "Five hundred," Keegan said.

German pulled out his wallet and counted out five hundreds. "Five hundred clear and easy, and here's an extra hundred for you if you get me that information right now."

Keegan scooped up the bills and went to his back room. Adam and Justin looked at German in shock. Keegan came back with an index card he handed to German, who read it and smiled.

"Pleasure doing business with you, sir," said German as he took the necklace from Keegan and walked out. We all followed him. "G, I hope that was worth six hundred," Justin said.

German smiled. "Trust me. I would have paid six million for this card." He handed the card to Justin, and we gathered around. We read the name Darren Drake. Our shock was apparent.

We headed back to Pendleton. I looked at the card with Detective Drake's name, address, and phone number on it. "What do you think this means?" I asked.

"It means Drake's working the other side of the spectrum," German said.

"Why would he plant this in our room?" asked Justin.

"At this point, I don't know, but we know we can't trust him," German said. "Guys, look. This card is about to open a Pandora's box. All we can do is to keep the same story. I'm going to get my lawyer involved more, and we'll make it out of this."

"Do we even know what this is?" I asked.

"Look. The outcome of this might be nothing, but it's all we have at this minute, and maybe it's all we'll need."

I wasn't sure how the others felt, but all of what was happening was strange—Brandon joining Alpha More, Klovis's case reopening, Drake planting the necklace, and whoever that was in the Greek god costume. I believed we were coming back to anything but a normal school year. I believed we were stepping into a full-fledged revenge plot. I believed that the number of people we could trust outside the four of us needed to be very limited.

Adam

We got back from our long drive to Boston, and I went upstairs as Donnie, Justin, and German socialized with our frat brothers in the main hall. What we had found out had really made me sick to my stomach. I couldn't believe that one silly little prank was causing all of this. I walked into my room and saw Brody as his desk playing a computer game. I didn't want him to notice that I'd walked in; I quietly shut the door.

"Hey, Adam. I was looking for you. You got mail on your desk," he said.

On my desk was a letter from Pendleton University. I opened unable to guess what it was about. Brody turned off his computer as I began reading my letter.

"Hey, I'm going downstairs. You want anything to eat or drink?" he asked.

"Ummm, no. I'm good. Thanks," I said as Brody gave me a strange look.

"*Are* you good?" Brody asked.

"Yeah, I'm fine," I said.

Brody left. The letter said that my mom hadn't submitted her portion of my financial aid application. If the application didn't arrive soon, I'd be dropped from my classes, which were starting in a few days, and that would mean I'd have to terminate my contract with Alpha More. I called her, but it went straight to voice mail: "Hi. You've reached Lana Banks. I'm not here to take your call. Please leave a brief message and I'll be sure to call you back."

"Mom, it's me. I need you to call. It's very important. Bye."

What a day it had been. When I heard a knock, I shoved the letter under my pillow. German walked in and said, "Hey. Seems Mr. Alves is throwing a BBQ later." He noted that I seemed down. "What's wrong?"

Out of the three guys, I trusted German the most. I pulled the letter from under my pillow and gave it to him.

German read it and looked at me. "When did you find out about this?"

"A few minutes before you walked in," I said.

"I'll pay."

"G, No! I can't let you," I said.

"You're not letting me do anything. I can't let you leave the house. This is the only way I know for sure you'll stay."

"Let me call my mom. I'll take care it," I said.

German looked at me and for once didn't fight me on this. "OK," he said as he patted me on the leg and left.

The next morning, I called my mom again but got no answer. I went to the financial aid office to see if I could get an extension on my tuition payment. Nancy, the advisor, asked, "Hello, sir. How can I help you?"

"My name's Adam Banks. I got a letter from your office that my mother hasn't submitted her part of the application. I need an extension on that." I gave her my ID.

"How long will you need?" she asked.

"I'm from Hoboken, so I can get this handled by next week," I said.

She nodded, which put me at ease. "OK, Mr. Banks, I'll extend your enrollment for a week from Monday so you can start on schedule." She gave me my ID back.

"Thank you," I said and took a step back. I heard a book drop. I realized I'd bumped into someone, and I turned around. "I'm so sorry," I said as I saw Brandon and an older woman.

"No worries," Brandon said as he smiled and picked up his book. "Adam, this is my mom. Mom, this Adam. He's part of Alpha More."

His mom extended her hand. "Hi. I'm Katheryn Klovis. It's nice to meet you."

"I'll see you at the house, Adam," Brandon said.

I got back to Alpha More and went to Justin's and Donnie's room. "What's up, man? Your text was urgent," Donnie said.

"I just met Brandon's mom," I said.

"So what? He's a transfer student. Maybe he needed something from her," Justin said.

"Wouldn't a mom be angry if she saw the person responsible for her son's death and You guys don't think it's strange that Ben's case reopened as she's in town?" I asked.

"I already called my lawyer. He'll get more information," German said.

"Did she say anything?" asked Donnie.

"No," I said.

"OK, let's say she had a hand in reopening the case. Like German said, all she can do is file a civil lawsuit against us," Justin said, and I threw my hands up.

"She can try, but she won't be too successful," German said.

"I can't believe you guys are taking this so lightly," I said.

"Adam, I get what you're saying. Let's say it's true. They can't prove that Ben was murdered. They can't prove that it was premeditated reckless endangerment. There's nothing," said German. "I have to talk to Mr. Alves. I'll see you guys later."

"You're staying?" Donnie asked with a huge smile.

"Yes, Alpha More for life," German said. Donnie and Justin gave him big hugs.

"That's great, G," Justin said.

German turned to me. "Look, bro, everything will be fine, I promise." We hugged it out. German left, and Donnie and Justin smiled with excitement.

German

What Adam saw today was important, but I needed her to be seen with someone of more stature such as Detective Drake. Once I saw that, everything would make more sense. I walked to Mr. Alves's office to let him know that I wanted to sign my contract. I knocked on the door.

"Come in," he said. I did. "German, please close the door." I did and sat across from him. "What can I do for you?"

"I'm ready to sign my contract," I said, and he was excited.

"Excellent! What made you consider coming back?"

"No matter how much I fight it, this is home and will always be. Plus, my dad would never let me live it down if I left. All I'd hear is, 'Paris didn't leave the house! Paris was MVP!'" I said.

Alves smiled. "Paris was great, but in all the years I've been den father of Alpha More, I've never met anyone who had the integrity of an oak tree."

"What do you mean?" I asked.

"You stand tall for what you believe in. You don't let life just happen to you without making sure it gives you an explanation," Alves said as he laid the housing contract in front of me.

That made me feel great. My father didn't see half of what Mr. Alves saw in me. Without hesitation, I signed the contract and pushed it over to Alves.

"It's my honor and privilege to say, 'Welcome back to Alpha More,'" he said as he and I shook hands.

"Thank you, Mr. Alves," I said as I got a text message: Drake would be leaving the precinct in thirty minutes I learned.

"Everything OK?" asked Alves.

"Yes. I just have an overdue book," I said.

"Oh well, let me just assign you your room. You'll be in two A, the single. You're welcome by the way."

"My dad's and Paris's old room?" I asked not that excited.

"Yeah. I figured it would continue a tradition."

"Thanks. I appreciate it," I said as I attempted to walk out.

"German?" asked Alves. I turned around. "Have a great time." I smiled and left.

I decided to see Drake without the guys because I knew that my lawyer had called Drake and that he would be inclined to tell me the truth. At least I hoped so.

I pulled into the alley behind the precinct station on Seventh Street and parked right behind his car so he would have no choice but to see me when he walked out. I got out of my car and counted down thirty seconds. Drake opened the door right on time and spotted me.

"Mr. Rigen, to what do I owe this pleasure?"

"I came to ask you some questions. I hope your answers won't be cringe-worthy."

"You're here to ask me questions?" Drake folded his arms.

"Correct," I said.

"OK, let's hear them," Drake said smirking.

"Who reopened the Klovis case?" I asked.

"That's not public information," Drake said.

I threw a folder at him, and he stumbled trying to catch it. "I know the answer to that question. Open the file," I said.

Drake did, looked at the file, and asked, "How did you get this?"

"Let's make something clear, Detective Drake. I'm not one to play your little games. Honesty is going to be the key," I said.

"Next question. Why did you buy this?" I asked as I held up the replica necklace.

"I don't know what that is," Drake said.

I pulled the receipt out of my pocket and put in his hands. "Drake, if you lie to me again, I'll make sure that this case never sees the light of day," I said.

"I planted it to see if one of you would confess that maybe something else had happened," Drake said.

"So it was you who wore the Greek god costume?" I asked.

"I don't know what that is. Should I count that as your third question?" asked Drake.

I showed him the Sorcerer costume on my phone. He looked at it and then at me. "That wasn't me."

"What is Katheryn Klovis's motive for working with the DA on this case?" I asked not sure if he would be honest with me.

"She believes that her son was murdered and that his drowning was a coverup," Drake said confirming my suspicion.

"Thank you, Detective," I said as I turned around.

"Hey, wait a second. Let me ask you a question. Why are you threatened by this case? Is there something you're hiding?"

"Detective Drake, I'm in no way threatened by anything. I think it's foolish of Mrs. Klovis and you to even want to reopen this case, but go ahead. The next toxicologist will find what the first one had found, which is that he drowned accidently. That's my story and I'm sticking to it. Have a nice day," I said.

I returned to Alpha More with my suitcases, and Brandon approached me "You need help?"

"Sure, thanks," I said.

Room 2A had a queen-sized bed, a desk, and a flat screen TV.

"Whoa, nice room," Brandon said.

"Yeah. This was my father's and my brother's room."

"I didn't realize your family had a legacy here," Brandon said.

"Yep. It's quite a legacy. My father played pro football for twenty-five years. He retired when I started here," I said.

Brandon nodded. I started to get comfortable with Brandon. I was about to ask him why he had joined Alpha More when I heard a knock and Donnie, Justin, and Adam barged in and looked surprised to see Brandon.

"I'll leave you guys," Brandon said.

"Thanks, Brandon," I said. Brandon nodded and left.

"What the hell was that all about?" asked Donnie.

"He helped me with my bags. Before you three barged in, I was going to ask why he was here."

"Oh well," said Donnie as he lay on my bed.

"G, I was looking for you earlier. Where were you?" Adam asked.

I wanted to lie, but I knew that would come back to bite me on my ass, so I told them. "I went to meet with Drake."

"You did what?" Donnie asked.

"Katheryn Klovis and the DA requested that the case be reopened according to my lawyer, and Drake confirmed that. She thinks it was murder."

The news shocked them. I knew they had a lot of questions. I was more than prepared to answer them.

Justin

I can't say that I was surprised that German had gone to question Drake. That was classic German Rigen. He always got to the bottom of things.

"Did Drake say why he'd bought the necklace?" Adam asked.

"He thought that planting it in the room would trigger one of us to confess that maybe Ben hadn't accidently drowned, that we'd killed him," German said.

"That makes no sense," said Donnie.

"Exactly," said German.

"So he willingly gave you this information?" I asked.

"No. I had to blackmail him into giving it to me," German said.

"Blackmail? What would you possibly have on him that would make him give you that information?" asked Donnie.

"Enough to make this case go away," said German.

My phone rang. Pip texted that she was on her way over. "Guys, it's Pip. Gotta go," I said.

"You going to confront her with what we found?" Donnie asked.

"I don't know," I said.

"Justin, you have to. I mean, right now we have a case open, and she could be a material witness to it all," said German.

"You just said you had enough dirt on Drake to make sure this case gets closed," I said.

"I know what I said, but you never play your trump cards first unless you know for sure you'll win. She's standing in the way of this if she's working with Klovis. We need to know where she stands," said German.

"I agree with G. Having dirt on Drake is one thing, but we need to know if Pip's an informant," Donnie said.

"This is my girlfriend we're talking about, not a Russian spy," I said.

"The girlfriend who never mentioned she'd dated the guy we're being accused of murdering?" Donnie asked rhetorically.

I started to get annoyed with Donnie and German because I didn't believe Pip had ulterior motives when it came to our relationship.

"Justin, at least ask her why she never told you about her past with Ben. She owes you that much at least," said Adam.

I felt like it was three against one. I didn't respond. I just left the room and went outside the house to clear my head. My phone rang again. I pulled it out, and I heard a loud noise as if someone had kicked a rock. I stood and looked in the direction the noise had come from. "Hello?" I asked.

I looked up at German's room. I sent a group text telling them to look out the window. The window to German's room opened, and I saw him, Donnie, and Adam looking out.

"What's wrong?" Donnie yelled.

"I heard a noise. You guys see anything from up there?" I asked.

They looked around. "I don't see anything," said Donnie.

"Me neither," said German.

I looked at the far left corner of the house and saw the Greek god guy pointing his medieval axe at me. I began to run to the front door, but he cut me off; he raised his axe and swung it at me, but I lunged forward and made him miss. I tackled him, and we tussled. He elbowed me in the head and stood. I tried to stand, but he hit me with the axe and knocked me back down. Things got blurry, but I saw Donnie and Adam tackle him and German come up to make sure I was OK.

"Justin! Oh wow! You're cut pretty bad," said German. He took off his shirt and pressed it to my wound. He pulled out his phone and called the paramedics and the police. I heard Donnie say that the guy had gotten away.

"Hang in there, Justin!" Adam said. I was in so much pain. I heard the sirens. Pretty soon, I was being picked up and put on a gurney. At that point, I knew that this was more serious than a mom wanting a case reopened. This was for revenge.

I woke up in a hospital bed and saw Adam, German, Donnie, and Mr. Alves.

"Justin, are you all right?" Alves asked.

"What happened?" I asked.

"That's what we're going to figure out. Two detectives are waiting outside. I'll get them," Alves said.

"Look, guys. We can't tell them everything," German said.

"I agree. Let's keep it to a minimum," Donnie said.

Alves walked in followed by two detectives. "Fellas, you know Detective Drake. Joining him is Detective Bradshaw. They'll be asking you four some questions. Justin, I'm going to call your parents, so excuse me." Alves left.

"Hello again, gentlemen. Mr. Baker, I'm sorry to hear about your attack. We'll do our best to bring justice to this case," Drake said, and German chuckled. "Did you say something, Mr. Rigen?" Drake asked.

"No. Please continue," German said.

"Gentlemen, my name is Detective Marsha Bradshaw. I'll be assisting Detective Drake in the investigation. Mr. Baker, I understand you're in a lot of pain, but I need to know what happened."

"I was attacked," I responded.

"Did you see your attacker?"

"No. He was wearing a Greek god costume," I said.

"A what?"

"It's a costume inspired by the Sorcerer. The Greek system wears it on graduation day. It's supposed to symbolize the power of the Greek god," German said.

"So this may be someone in the Greek system?" asked Bradshaw.

"No one we can think of," said Adam.

"Detective Drake, would you know of anyone who would want to hurt us considering the Klovis case is reopening?" German asked prompting Drake to give him an evil look.

The door opened. Pip walked in. "Justin!" she yelled as she rushed over to me.

"And it's getting more interesting by the minute," said Donnie as we all looked at Pip.

CHAPTER 5

WOMAN OF THE HOUR

Adam

ETECTIVES BRADSHAW AND Drake decided to interrogate Justin alone, so Donnie, German, Pip, and I went to the waiting room. When Pip went to get some coffee, Donnie said, "I say we confront her with the Ben thing."

"Have you lost your damn mind?" German asked.

"You know as well as I do that Justin isn't going to ask her about this situation, and I'm starting to think she's involved," Donnie said.

"Donnie," said German.

"Don't tell me the thought has not crossed your mind either of you," Donnie said.

"Yes, the thought had crossed my mind," I said.

"G, c'mon. I know you," Donnie said smiling at German.

"Of course, but Donnie, Justin will kill us if we ask her about this after all he's been through," German said.

"Which is more reason to ask her," Donnie said.

When he headed over to Pip, German and I followed.

She turned to us and asked, "Can I help you?"

"What are you doing?" Donnie asked.

"Excuse me?" asked Pip.

"Playing dumb is not attractive," said Donnie.

"Donnie!" yelled German.

"Where's this coming from?" Pip asked.

Donnie pulled out his phone and showed her the picture of her and Ben.

Pip took a deep breath and looked very guilty. "Not here," she said.

"Give us a date, time, and location and we'll be there," Donnie said.

"You can't tell Justin what I'm about to tell you," she said.

"Why?" German asked.

"Despite what you three think of me, I do like him and want our relationship to work."

"Girl, first off, this is shady. How the hell can you stand here and tell us that you want your relationship with Justin when you haven't even told him the truth?" Donnie asked.

Pip gave him a dirty look and shook her head. "Meet me at Pendleton Coffee and Cake at five today. I'll tell you all that I know," she said.

We watched her walk back into Justin's room.

"You think she'll tell us?" I asked.

"If she were smart, she'd tell Justin first," said Donnie as Bradshaw came out and approached us.

"Hello, gentlemen. Detective Drake is finishing up with your friend. You'll be able to see him shortly."

"Thank you," said German as Bradshaw gave him a peculiar look.

"Can I ask you question?" she asked.

"Me?" asked G.

"Yes," she said.

"You were the one who asked Drake those questions. What exactly were you looking for?"

"That doesn't concern you, and it doesn't pertain to this situation," German said.

"I asked you a question," said Bradshaw in a demanding tone.

"And I have a right to remain silent," German said as Drake came out of the room.

"Detective, we're done here," said Drake.

I was really confused about what had just happened. Bradshaw and Drake walked away. Donnie looked at German. "You want to tell us what the hell that was all about?" Donnie asked.

"She was trying to intimidate me and do Drake's dirty work. Neither has a clue about how I got access to the DA's information about the case," German said.

"What do you think will happen now?" I asked.

German shrugged; he didn't have an answer. I felt, however, that the detectives would retaliate and that it wouldn't be pretty.

Donnie

We arrived at Pendleton Coffee and Cake. German parked and turned to me and Adam. "So how are we going to do this?" he asked.

"Just let me do all the talking," I said.

"Oh no, Donnie. I know you. You aren't going to play fair. Let me ask," German said.

"Forget it," I said as I attempted to exit the car.

"Donnie, wait," Adam said. "G's right. We can't just attack her with this information."

"I don't know about you two, but I have a strong feeling that Pip had something to do with Justin's attack," I said.

"Why would she be involved in Justin's attack? And why would she want it to happen?" Adam asked.

"I can think of one reason," I said as I held up the picture of Pip and Ben.

Adam and German remained silent. We got out of the car and went into the café looking around for Pip. It was pretty crowded, so I wasn't sure if this was where I wanted to ask questions.

"Guys, I don't see her," Adam said.

"That's because you beat me here," said Pip, who walked in.

German, Justin, and I followed her to a table and sat across from her.

"Before I tell you guys about Ben and me, we need to agree that this conversation stays between us," she said.

"You must be out of your mind if you think I'm going to keep this from my friend," I said.

"Donnie!" said German.

"Forget it," said Pip as she stood.

"No! Sit down!" I yelled.

People were looking at us. "Way to bring attention to this table," she said as she sat.

"Believe me, I can get a whole lot worse," I said.

"Why do you want us to keep this from Justin?" Adam asked.

"I don't want this to ruin my relationship with him," she said.

"So lying is better than telling your boyfriend the truth?" I asked.

Pip remained quiet as I looked at Adam and German.

"You and Ben were at the Alpha More senior party the night he died," German said.

"Yes we were," Pip said.

"Did Ben tell you that he was leaving the party at any time?" asked Adam.

"Yes. He said that he'd met some frat members in the kitchen and that they were taking him somewhere. I kissed him goodnight and went home," said Pip.

"So that night was the last night you spoke with him?" I asked.

"Yes," Pip said.

Adam, German, and I looked at each other.

"Did he ever mention where he ended up that night?" asked German.

"No, he didn't. I tried to call him the day after the party, but he never answered. A few days later, I saw on the news that he had accidentally drowned."

"What are you hiding that you don't want to come out?" asked German.

Pip looked at German as his question was valid. "I'm not over Ben, OK!" Pip said.

"I'll give you twenty-four hours to tell Justin about this. If you don't tell him, I will," I said.

"You're the devil!" Pip said as she got up and walked away.

"That went well," said Adam.

When German, Adam, and I got back to Alpha More, we saw a banner above the house. I saw Boomer, a junior, and asked, "Boomer, what the hell is this?" I asked.

"We got tagged by Theta Monroe," he said.

Getting tagged by a sorority house meant we had to compete with them in a ritual duel for the annual back-to-school carnival. Our frat house had been in charge of it for the last ten years, so there was no way we were losing.

"All right, so it's off to Theta Monroe to accept the challenge," I said, and the three of us headed there.

Theta Monroe was basically the Alpha More of sororities; just like our house, they threw the best parties. It was at the end of Lexington Street. We got there and rang the doorbell. Mrs. Mack, the den mother, answered the door. "Hello Donnie, Adam, German. To what do I owe the pleasure of this visit?"

"They're here because we just challenged them," said Ginger.

Virginia May Magnolia was a southern belle. She went by Ginger, which was odd because she was blond, not redheaded. Ginger and I had a history. Let's just say that she was my first and a reoccurring love affair there.

"Hey, fellas, so what's it gonna be?" she asked.

"Challenge accepted," I said.

Ginger smiled as Mrs. Mack left the door. I looked at German and Adam. "Guys, I'll see you back at the house," I said. Adam and German waved goodbye to Ginger.

"It's been a while," said Ginger.

"I know. We should go upstairs and catch up," I said with a smile.

My smile was many ladies' weakness.

"I don't think so," she said.

"Really? You're saying no to all of this?" I asked.

"As hard as that is, I can't," she said. "Freshman year was amazing, but I just don't want to be a booty call my entire college experience."

"So now you want to change the rules?" I asked.

Ginger grabbed my arms to pull me in, and we kissed. I smiled at her, and she smiled back.

"I hate you," said Ginger as she pulled me into the house.

She couldn't resist me. Ever.

Justin

My back hurt like hell. I wanted to reach the button to call the nurse.

"Mr. Baker, my shift is almost over. Can I get you anything?" she asked.

"I'm feeling more pain. Is there anything else I can have?" I asked as I adjusted my posture.

"I can have Dr. Mixster take a look at your chart?"

"Yes please," I said.

I looked at my phone and saw a message from German: "Theta Monroe tagged us on the battle for the Pendleton Carnival, Donnie and Ginger are hitting the sheets. I'll be there in about an hour. Do you want me to bring you anything?"

"Candy please," was my reply.

The door opened, and Pip walked in. "Hey, babe! How are you feeling?" she asked as she came over to comfort me.

"I'm in pain waiting for the doctor to come in. G's going to be here later," I said. "Where were you?"

"I had something to take care of," she said.

I was very suspicious, but I was in so much pain; I was glad that she had come.

The doctor walked in. "Mr. Baker, how are you feeling?"

"I'm feeling a lot of back pain," I said as the doctor checked my wounds.

"Just making sure your bandage is not seeping, your medication will put you out for sometime. I will be right back."

The doctor left, and Pip began to rub my head. "There's something I need to tell you," she said. "It's hard for me to say this, but I want you to hear it from me. Ben and I were a couple."

I was quiet. Pip looked at me on the verge of tears. "Say something, please," she said.

"Why are you telling me this?" I asked.

"Your friends found out first and told me that if I didn't tell you, they would. Donnie, Adam, and German found a Facebook photo of Ben and me and confronted me with it."

"They already showed me the picture. The question now remains is were you ever going to tell me that you and Ben were a couple?" I asked.

"So you knew this the entire time?"

"Don't try to turn this on me," I said.

"I didn't think it would ever come up. When he died, I buried it along with him."

I was still in shock even after she explained it to me. Nothing about it made sense. I was thinking, *You were OK with being in a relationship with the one responsible for Ben's death?* "I need to be alone right now," I said, and Pip began to cry. She didn't try to plead with me. She picked up her bag, gave me a long look, and left.

Pip and Ben had been in a relationship? I began questioning everything, Did she really love me? Is what Donnie and German said true?.

The door opened. German walked in. "Hey, man, I bought you a Snickers bar."

I was angry that none of them had told me about this. I was silent.

German knew I was mad. "You OK?" he asked.

"You can stand there as my friend and not tell me that you confronted Pip about the picture? All three of you?" I asked.

"I can't defend confronting her without your being present, but we needed to know. We felt you weren't going to ask her."

"I told you guys that I would ask her, and I did just before you got here," I said.

"I'm glad. It's not our story to tell."

"I know, but G, come on. You of all people know how I feel about what happened," I said.

"Would you have made a rational decision in this state of mind?"

"Just leave, G," I said.

"You sure?"

"Yeah! Get the hell out now!" I yelled.

German nodded and left. I felt bad for having yelled at him, but I was really angry at what they had done. I fell asleep.

Whatever the doctor had given me hit me hard; I woke up with blurry vision and saw someone who looked like Adam. "Get out!" I said. As the person came closer, I saw it was Brandon. "What are you doing here?" I asked.

"I heard about your attack. I wanted to see how you were doing."

"I need water," I said as I attempted to reach for it.

"Here, let me," said Brandon.

Brandon poured a cup of water and lifted my head so I could drink some. "Drink a little more," he said. "There you go, bud." He set the cup down and sat across from me.

"Thank you," I said.

"Anytime," he said with a smile. "I know this may be weird, but I don't want you to get the wrong idea about me."

"What do you mean?" I asked.

"I mean about my brother and what happened. I wasn't very close to him, and though I'm very sad that he's gone, I'm not angry with any of you."

"Why'd you join the fraternity?" I asked.

"Mr. Alves reached out to my parents asking if I was interested in joining."

"Mr. Alves asked you to join?" I asked.

"Yeah. I figured it was for the university's reputation, you know, doing some damage control."

"Why did you agree to it?" I asked.

"Not sure yet, but once I find out, you'll be the first to know."

The nurse walked in. "Excuse me, Mr. Klovis, but visiting hours are over."

"I was just leaving. I'll see you at home. Take care," he said, and he left.

Brandon really confused me. I was second-guessing the idea that he had been my attacker.

German

I pulled into the lot and saw Ginger and Donnie kissing as they were saying goodbye. Donnie walked over and got in. Ginger waved at me, and I waved back. Donnie was smiling as if he'd just won the lottery. He said, "Man, that girl knows she's the best I've had in college." He looked at me. "What's wrong?"

"She told him," I said.

"Let me guess. Justin took it all wrong," said Donnie.

"How did you expect him to take it?" I asked.

We saw a car pull up. "Hopefully, that's Adam. I'm starving," I said.

"No, that's not Adam," said Donnie.

The car stopped, and Detective Drake got out.

"What the hell's he doing here?" asked Donnie.

"Probably to mess with us some more," I said.

Brody walked out of the house, and Drake handed him an envelope.

"Well, well, well, I wonder what that's about" said Donnie.

Drake drove off, and we get out of the car and walk up to Brody.

"Hey, Brody, what the hell was that about?" asked Donnie.

"Nothing," Brody said.

Donnie snatched the envelope from Brody and opened it. "So money is nothing?" he asked.

"Look. I'm not rich like you two, OK? Drake paid me to put a necklace in your room."

"Really?" I asked.

"Yeah, I didn't see any harm in it, so I did."

There was something bigger going on than just a case being reopened. And with Justin getting attacked, we needed more info. I called Adam to meet us at the hospital to tell Justin what we'd found out.

As Donnie and I walked to Justin's room, Adam met us in the hallway looking very confused. "What's going on?" he asked.

"Just come in," said Donnie.

We walked into Justin's room and saw Pip. We paused as we were really surprised to see her there considering how mad Justin was.

"What are you guys doing here?" asked Justin.

"We need to talk," I said.

"Alone," Donnie said abruptly.

"Baby, can you give us a minute please?" Justin asked Pip.

"Sure," Pip said; she left the room.

"Look. I know you're mad at us, but you need to know something," I said.

"I don't need to know anything. I can't believe you three questioned her about her relationship with him," said Justin.

"Oh please. Clearly you're over it. Otherwise, the bitch wouldn't be here," Donnie said.

I whacked his arm. "Donnie! Damn!" I said. I wanted Justin to hear me out. "Brody said that he was the one who put the replica in your room. Drake paid him to do it. However, we can't connect the person in the Greek god costume to Drake or the Klovises. He may be after us for a different reason," I said.

"So what do we do?" asked Justin.

"I think it's best if we watch Mrs. Klovis first to be sure the Greek god has no relationship with her and find out how Detective Drake is involved in all of this," I said.

All of them agreed with my plan, which meant that at that point, we held all the cards and were ready to play them.

CHAPTER 6

LIES AND CONFUSION

German

I DROVE INTO TOWN and made a left on First Avenue. I'd been told that Mrs. Klovis was leasing a store on the street. I pulled up across from it and saw a contractor and her inside talking. I looked up and saw that the restaurant I'd parked in front of had a condo for sale right above it. I called the relator to make an appointment to see the place, and then I drove off. A few blocks down, I spotted Detectives Bradshaw and Drake eating outside a café. I parked and walked over.

"Welcome to the Red Cup Café," a host said. "Will there be anyone joining you?"

"My party's already here on the patio, thank you," I said. I walked over to the detectives' table. "Good afternoon! Is this seat taken?" I asked as Bradshaw and Drake looked at me.

"Have a seat," said Drake.

I sat keeping my eyes on Drake, and he looked at me with the same passion.

"I take it this isn't a coincidence that you're intruding on our lunch," Drake said.

"Correct. I'm here to have some words with you," I said.

"Right now's not the best time," said Bradshaw.

"Oh trust me, You'll want to hear this," I said. "You paid Brody

Brockett to plant the necklace in our room to see if one or all of us would confess to a story different from what we'd told you. I'm starting to believe that your motive for doing that was not to get Ben's case reopened but to blackmail us for Klovis's sake," I said.

Drake looked at me and smiled. I could tell that he felt he'd just been busted. "You know, German, I have to hand it to you. You're very smart, maybe smarter than I thought considering being in a fraternity. I don't need to blackmail you for anything. This case will prove something else happened, and the Klovises will get the justice they deserve."

"I'd be careful about how you involve yourself in this case. I have a feeling you're playing the double spectrum, and I'd hate for that to come out the wrong way. Enjoy your lunch," I said and left.

I got a call from the realtor to look at the condo across from Klovis's place. I met him in the alley so Klovis wouldn't see me.

"Are you Mr. Rigen?" he asked.

"Yes," I said as I shook his hand.

"I'm Brad Douglas. Nice to meet you."

We walked upstairs and entered the condo. "This is a two-bedroom, two-bath condo with a full-sized kitchen and living room, and it's fully furnished," said Brad.

I looked around the condo, which was very nice. I opened the blinds on the front window and had a clear view of Klovis's building across the street. Brad came over and looked out the window. "Do you know what that building will be?" I asked.

"There's word it'll be a flower shop. That building is identical to this one. The restaurant here has an enormous kitchen, and across the street, I think she'll use the space for a sunroom."

"How motivated is the seller?" I asked.

"The seller owns the restaurant and has a new family, so there's no need for the condo. Would you like to make an offer?"

"Tell the owner I'll give him double what he's asking for if I can move in immediately," I said.

"I'll give him a call right away," Brad said and left.

I looked across the street and saw Klovis exiting the building and talking on her phone. I looked at the ceiling and saw a smoke alarm. I knew of a camera that could be implanted in it, the perfect way to collect more information. I pulled out my phone and called someone who could help me with that. "Hey, Vince, German Rigen here. I need a favor, and I need it immediately," I said.

Adam

It was my first day of school, and my mom still had not answered my messages. She was a different kind of mom in that she was unavailable in all aspects. I was an only child, and in reality, I'd raised myself. Joining Alpha More was a huge relief because it prevented me from living in my car. All the students had wireless headphones, fresh clothes, and laptops. I tried calling my mom again, and that time, I was told her voice mail was full. It was unlike my mom not to answer her phone, but if she had a new boyfriend, she would probably check for messages in a few weeks, which meant I was screwed either way.

"Excuse me?" asked a girl with a red backpack.

"Yes?" I asked.

"I'm new here. I'm looking for building J, room two forty-four."

"That's the culinary building. It's on the southeast corner of campus. I'm going there. If you'd like, I can walk you there," I said.

She smiled. "Thank you."

"I'm Adam, Adam Banks." I extended my hand.

"I'm Jessica Caine."

We began walking to the building. "So what are you majoring in?" I asked.

"Baking and pastry arts."

"Nice," I said.

"What about you?" asked Jessica.

"The same, a BA," I said.

"What do you plan to do with that degree?"

"Open my own café, sell pastries, and have an open-mic night. That's my dream," I said.

We had a small pause of awkward smiling and eye contact.

"Room two forty-four is right there," I said pointing.

"Thanks. It was nice meeting you."

"You too," I said.

Jessica walked off to her classroom.

I went to the financial aid office to see if I could get another extension on my tuition payment.

"Can I help you?" asked Nancy, who had helped me earlier.

"Yes. I was here last week to get an extension on my tuition payment, but I still can't get hold of my mom. I may need to look at other options," I said.

"A student loan is an option, but it'll take time for an application to be processed, which means you could be withdrawn from your courses."

"Are payment plans available?" I asked.

"I'd be happy to look into that for you. May I have your ID please?"

I gave her my ID, and she looked me up on the computer. "For this semester, your tuition for all four classes is eight thousand two hundred and eighty-eight dollars. The payment plan we offer is a four-month program. We ask for two hundred and eighty-eight dollars up front, and each month, you'll be charged two thousand."

"Would you excuse me for one sec?" I asked.

"Sure."

I turned to my left and pulled out my phone. I looked up my bank account and saw that I had $290.65 in my checking account. I knew it would be a huge risk, but I had to take it. I walked back to Nancy, who gave me a serious look.

"OK, I'm going to take the payment plan," I said.

"All right, that'll be two hundred and eighty-eight dollars."

I gave her my debit card.

"Please sign for me," Nancy said as I took her pen and signed the receipt.

"Thank you, Mr. Banks. I realize the sacrifice you're making for your education. Your first payment of two thousand will be on the fifth of the next month and three more times on the fifth of subsequent months this semester. Any failure to pay will discharge you from your courses. Any questions?"

"No," I said.

"All right, Mr. Banks, Have a great semester."

I had $2 left in my account and three weeks to come up with $2,000. I wasn't sure what I was going to do, but I had to make sure it happened.

I had about an hour after my first class until my next class. I sat at a table reading the notes I'd taken since I couldn't afford my book. I had a bag of chips and a bottle of water. I was starving, but that was all I could afford.

"Yo, A-dog," said Donnie as he joined me at the table. He had a huge sandwich and a soda.

"What's up?" I asked.

"First day of school is always hell," Donnie said.

"Have you talked to Justin?" I asked.

"No. Mr. Alves said he's being released today. I'm going to sleep in G's room until he calms down."

"I didn't think he was going to react that way to the whole Pip situation," I said.

"Me either. He's whipped." He looked at me. "You seem down, man. What's wrong?"

"I just have a lot on my mind," I said.

"Like what?"

"Can't get in touch with my mom. It's been a few days, and I'm getting worried," I said.

"I'm sure she's fine. Damn. I'm going to be late. You want the other half of my sandwich?"

"Yeah, thanks," I said as Donnie passed his plate to me.

"See you later," Donnie said as he ran off.

I wondered how Donnie had known something was up with me. I knew G would never tell anyone what was going on, but I wasn't sure how long I could keep my situation from my brothers.

Justin

The doctor cleared me to go home. I didn't know what to believe, but I missed my brothers.

The door opened, and Mr. Alves walked in. "Justin, how are you feeling?"

"Better, actually," I said as I got off my bed.

"I'm here to take you home. Your brothers will be happy to see you. I contacted your instructors to make sure they were aware of why you weren't in class today. Here are the syllabuses."

We walked out to his car and drove off.

"I'm a little surprised that Donnie, German, or Adam didn't pick you up. Everything OK with the four of you, Justin?"

"Everything's fine. They had classes today. Didn't want them to be interrupted," I said.

"German didn't have any classes today. He starts tomorrow. Did you know our house has been tagged by Theta Monroe?"

"I heard something about that," I said.

"The ticket sales will determine who'll be in charge of the fall carnival."

We pulled up into the driveway of the frat house, parked, and walked in. I went directly to my room hoping Donnie was not there. When I walked in, I saw Pip. "Hey, I thought you had class," I said as she came up to kiss me.

"I do in about twenty minutes. I wanted to see you first. I'm glad you're home," she said.

I heard a knock. "Come in," I said.

Brandon opened the door. "Hey, Justin, welcome home."

Pip looked at Brandon as if she were seeing a ghost. I was confused that Pip had that reaction considering she'd dated his identical twin.

"I'm sorry. Didn't know you had company. Sorry," Brandon said as he closed the door.

"Pip, are you OK?" I asked.

Pip looked at me and shook her head out the trance she was in. "Yes, I'm fine. I have to go. Get some rest."

She kissed me and left. Her exit made me suspicious of the situation with her and Ben. I couldn't quite figure it out. I sat on my bed and thought about it some more. I heard a knock. "Come in," I said.

Brian, another sophomore, opened the door. "Justin, welcome home. How're you feeling?"

"Good, man, just a little sore," I said.

"You heard about Theta Monroe's challenge? And where are Donnie, Adam, and G?"

"Donnie and Adam have classes today, and G's been running errands," I said.

"I'm glad you're home. If you see those three today, tell them to come see me."

"Will do," I said, and Brian left.

I napped until Donnie woke me up. He said, "Get dressed. We have to meet G in town."

"Why?" I asked.

"Who knows? Meet you in the car in fifteen minutes," Donnie said.

On the way to town, I asked Donnie, "G didn't tell you why he wanted us to come?"

"Nope, but knowing G, it has to be good."

I then knew that the three of them had found out something. I was quiet for the rest of the ride. I couldn't handle another thing about Pip, and having seen her reaction to Brandon, I started to feel very uncomfortable about everything.

"You OK?" Donnie asked.

"No man. I feel the pain again," I said.

"From your injury?"

"Yes. On my side," I said.

"Did you bring your medicine?"

"Yeah, but I haven't eaten anything, so I don't want to take it right now," I said.

Donnie pulled over, parked, got out, and retrieved something from his trunk. He got back in and gave me a protein bar and a bottle of water. "Here. Now you can take it," he said.

I took my medication and let the seat back to relax.

Donnie got to town and parked in front of this café. "What are we doing here?" I asked.

"This is where G said to meet up."

Adam pulled in behind Donnie and got out. "Hey, Justin, how are you feeling?"

"Fine once my meds kick in," I said.

"Where's G?" asked Adam.

"He said meet him here, so we're meeting him here," Donnie said.

"Hey, guys," said German.

"What took you so long?" asked Donnie.

"Sorry I'm late, but I have something to show you. Follow me," he said.

We followed him up some stairs on the right of the restaurant. At the top of the stairs was a short hallway that led to a door. German opened it, and we all walked into a furnished condo. "Guys, welcome to headquarters," German said.

Donnie

"What is this place?" Adam asked.

"It's my new condo, two bedroom, two baths."

"You just randomly bought a condo, G?" asked Justin.

"I had a reason," German said as he went to his double Apple computer monitors. He turned one on, and we saw the inside of a building.

"What are we looking at?" I asked.

"The building right across the street. Mrs. Klovis is renting it," German said.

Adam, Justin, and I looked out the window. "So you're going to spy on her?" Adam asked.

"Because Ben's case is reopened, we need to know each moves she makes. If you look at the camera on the left, there's at least twenty feet of open space. This could be where she meets with Drake," said German.

"G, what happens if she catches you spying on her?" asked Justin.

"She won't find out unless she sets the place on fire."

"What about the Greek god guy?" asked Adam.

"I think we should find out if they're in cahoots first because it could lead us to everything else," said German.

"I don't think Pip's involved," Justin said. "When Brandon came into our room, she froze."

"You don't think they've met before?" I asked

"I don't think so. When Brandon was there, her whole vibe was off. Really strange."

Adam, German, and I looked at each other; we know the real reason Pip was stuck when seeing Brandon. I thought Pip was a part of this. I couldn't figure out what part, but I was sure she was involved somehow.

"So what do we do?" asked Adam.

"We wait and we watch," German said. "Right now, all we know is that Drake and Klovis are coming up with some plan for us. We know that Drake paid Brody to plant that replica necklace, so we can't trust him. At this point, we stick together and don't say anything to anyone."

We waited for two hours, and I began to get hungry. "G, we'd be better off with a record line," I said as German watched the monitors.

"Yeah, I'm with Donnie, G," said Adam. "It's been two hours. Who's to say the plan is that they're coming after us? Maybe they're going after the school."

"It's more than that. I want to know who attacked Justin and who continues to send us subliminal messages about that night," said German.

As much as I hated to admit it, German was right; this was one step forward. But my stomach was taking five steps back. "How about we order a pizza?" I asked.

"Wait a second," German said. We gathered around him and saw the Greek god.

"That's him," said Justin.

From the monitor, we heard the door open. From the angle of the camera, it was hard to tell who it was. The person walked into the view of the camera, and we see Mrs. Klovis walk to him and hear their conversation.

"I heard the boy you attacked, Justin, is out of the hospital," she said. "We have more work to do. Here's the plan," Klovis said as the door opened, which made her pause; he and she looked over to see it was Detective Drake.

"Katheryn, we need to talk," Drake said. He looked at the Greek god. "Who the hell's this?"

"Don't worry about that," Klovis said.

Drake pulled Klovis to the side to talk, and German moved the camera angle so we could hear their conversation.

"We got a problem," Drake said. "I just got the autopsy report. There's no reasonable suspicion that this was manslaughter. This toxicologist said your son died of accidental drowning."

That relieved us.

"We need another plan. There has to be something else," said Klovis.

"You're a parent. File a civil lawsuit under reckless endangerment," said Drake.

"My husband said the same thing, but money won't be enough to make this right. I lost my son. Do you have any idea what that's like? I'm going to take the four of them down. You're with me or against me. You decide."

"At least we know it's personal," said German.

"Is anyone else about to shit on himself?" asked Justin.

"G, we have to take this to the police," said Adam.

"Yeah? How do I explain rigging cameras over there?"

"We need to figure out her plan and beat her at her own game," I said.

Drake

The woman was foolish. If she knew what I knew, she'd back off, but I was in too deep. I sat in my car not knowing what to do. I picked up my radio. "Bradshaw, come in," I said.

"Go ahead Drake," said Bradshaw.

"Meet me at the precinct in twenty," I said.

"Got it. Over."

I drove to the precinct. I remembered German Rigen had been at my car a few days earlier. I wondered if there was something in his background that I could use. My plan was to book a private corner room with no surveillance so I could look up stuff privately. I arrived at the reception desk, where Officer Barrad was working.

"Detective Drake, good evening."

"Good evening, Officer. Room five available?" I asked.

"Officer Mullins was in there ten minutes ago doing reports. It hasn't been cleaned."

"It's fine. I'll wipe up. When Bradshaw comes in, send her in please," I said.

I walked to room five, which had the best Wi-Fi spot in the precinct, and I logged into the computer. I wondered whether this was worth my career. I thought maybe I could get five million instead of one and go rogue. I typed in Rigen's name, and there was one confidential case pending. I was a little stunned but not surprised. The door opened, and Bradshaw came in.

"Hey, what's going on?" she asked.

I put the file that Rigen had given me on the table.

"What's this?"

"The file that could have me indicted," I said.

"Where did you get this?"

"The better question is who gave it to me," I said.

"Why are you looking at a confidential file sealed by the FBI?"

"This is a criminal background report on Rigen. Don't worry. The feds won't know we saw this."

I opened the file. I knew I had struck gold.

Bradshaw was in complete shock. "No way! German Rigen was engaged to Jo-Sally Levinsque? The granddaughter of mob criminal Arthur Levinsque?"

"Yep, the same one who stole billions of dollars in paintings in the Boston Museum heist. We'll find out what happened to our friend German and why he was involved in this crime," I said.

Rigen was a con artist just like his late fiancée. According to the report, Rigen was never convicted after the death of Jo-Sally Levinsque. He also collected the $75 million reward for recovering the stolen paintings estimated at over $50 billion.

Bradshaw looked at me. "We're not dealing with some average Joe."

"I know, but I feel this is a huge payoff for joining forces with Klovis," I said. "After reading this, how much do you think German Rigen is worth?" I asked.

"At least that seventy-five million."

"What if we blackmail him for all of it?"

"How do we blackmail him if he has no criminal record?"

"It's a long shot, but what if we can prove that he was with Jo-Sally when she robbed the museum?" I asked.

"That's a long shot especially since the case is closed and sealed. Think about what could happen if the FBI learns we looked at a file that the Supreme Court had sealed."

Bradshaw was right. I was risking being jailed, but I knew I could get myself off if I did it for the right reasons. "What if we get him to confess that he did it?" I asked.

Bradshaw remained quiet as that would be a huge risk. German was smart, maybe too smart to confess to this, but blackmailing him for that money would be worth it.

CHAPTER 7

WHO S DEDICATED?

Adam

W E'D GOTTEN A text to meet back at Alpha More for a house meeting, so we drove there.

"Remember, don't tell anyone about my condo," German said. "We'll take shifts watching the monitors. I sent a link to all of you so we can watch it from our rooms if we can't be at the condo. Mrs. Klovis left, I'm not sure where she is, but if she goes there, we'll get an alert."

"G, you've taken stalking to a whole other level," said Donnie.

"Shut up, Donnie," German said.

All the brothers were in the podium room; we saw Brandon talking to Alves. "What the hell is that all about?" I asked as Brandon sat up front in the seniors' section.

"You're sitting in the wrong row," Donnie told him, but Brandon just smiled.

Alves said, "Alpha More, thanks for taking this meeting. As you know, each semester, the Greek houses host a fundraiser. We've always hosted a carnival in the town square. Theta Monroe has challenged us to host this semester's event, and we've accepted the challenge. Whichever Greek house sells the most tickets for the carnival will be able to host it and present the check to the fundraiser chosen by the university, the Maine School for the Hearing Impaired in honor of Ben Klovis."

We had not known that Ben was hearing impared.

"The ticket proceeds will go to the foundation along with thirty percent of the concessions take and sales of souvenirs," Alves said.

"Mr. Alves, I'll match whatever the event takes in as a donation," German said.

"That's very generous of you, German. I'll be sure to tell the committee. And by the way, Alpha More's very own Brandon Klovis will represent the committee," said Alves.

Donnie looked very pissed as the entire house cheered Brandon walking to the podium. "Thank you all for this. I know that Ben would have been honored. Thank you," he said, and everyone applauded him.

German, Donnie, Justin, and I went up to German's room.

"G, that was very kind of you to make that donation," said Donnie.

"I need a tax write-off," said German.

"Oh, that's smart," said Donnie.

"What was that about Ben Klovis being hearing impared? I don't remember that," said Justin.

"Maybe you should ask your girlfriend," said Donnie.

"You're an idiot!" said Justin.

"Justin, I hate to agree with Donnie's snarky comment, but that's the only way we could find out," said German.

"You expect me to ask Pip if Ben was deaf?" asked Justin.

"Maybe not ask her like that, but this charity event is going to involve everyone in Pendleton. Since it's in his honor, you can bring it up like that," said German.

Justin looked at us with disgust and left the room.

"Great" said German.

"Hey! You were thinking it too," Donnie said.

"Guys, I gotta go," I said.

"Where you going?" Donnie asked.

"I got a job," I said.

"A job?" German and Donnie asked simultaneously.

"Yep. It's what we normal students have to do to earn some cash. See you guys," I said.

I was a little bothered that they had given me those looks as if they had ever had to work. German was the son of retired pro football player and Donnie was the son of a state senator while I had come from nothing. I hoped I could make enough to cover my tuition payment next month.

I got to Porky's Pizza five minutes late and told Jonesy, the manager, "Hi. I'm Adam Banks. It's my first day."

"Adam, yes, you and the other trainee are five minutes late," Jonesy said as Brody walked in.

"Hey, Adam! You working here too?" Brody asked.

"Glad to see you two know each other, Jonesy said. "I'm short a driver and a front desk clerk. Adam, you'll handle the deliveries. Your tips are all yours. Brody, you'll work with Shannon ringing up our customers. Excuse me a moment, gentlemen."

"Had I known you applied here, we could have carpooled," said Brody.

"I needed my car for deliveries," I said.

We heard a printer whirring and saw it spitting out some paper. Jonesy came out of his office with Porkey's Pizza shirts for us. "Adam, you have a delivery. Come with me. I'll show you how to enter this."

I watched him enter the order and then saw Jessica, the girl I'd met on campus, walk in.

"Hi and welcome to Porky's Pizza," said Jonesy.

"Hi. I'm here to pick up an order for Jessica Caine."

"Sure. One moment, please. Brody, follow me," Jonesy said.

"So we meet again," I said.

"Yes. Had I known you worked here, I would've come here more often."

"It's my first day," I said.

Jonesy and Brody came back. "Here you are, one medium pepperoni pizza extra cheese. That'll be ten ninety-nine," said Jonesy.

Jessica gave me a twenty and told me, "Keep the change. Nice to see you again."

"Adam, your pizza delivery is here," said Jonesy.

He gave me a pizza in an insulated bag, and I took it out to my car. I saw Jessica getting in her car, and we waved at each other. She was hot. I thought I might end up like Justin, a frat boy with a girlfriend.

Justin

Donnie really knew how to push my buttons. I couldn't believe I was about to ask Pip if Ben had been hearing impared. I pulled up to her dorm a bit nervous. I went in and up to her room and knocked.

"Hi, Justin," said Shayna, Pip's roommate.

"Hi. Is Pip around?" I asked.

"Yeah, she's in the shower. Come in."

I walked in and passed the bathroom, and Shayna went back to her computer.

"Doing homework?" I asked as I sat on Pip's bed.

"Sort of. I'm writing this essay on advanced psychology on hypochondria."

"It's funny you bring that up. Would you say someone pretending to be deaf could be considered a hypochondriac?" I asked.

"I supposed so, but I think a better word would be a psychopath."

Pip walked out of the bathroom. "Hey! I thought we were going to meet on campus."

"I had a little extra time, so I figured I'd come by and talk," I said.

"Shayna, can you give us a minute?" asked Pip.

"Sure. I'll be at the library."

Pip sat next to me. She looked concerned. "What's going on?"

"I wanted to talk to you about yesterday. It was awkward when you saw Brandon, and I wanted to know why," I said.

"I hadn't known Ben had a twin, so when he walked in, I thought I was seeing Ben."

I wanted to believe that her seeing Brandon for the first time would have prompted that reaction, but I couldn't. I still felt she was hiding something. I kissed her, but I didn't ask her about Ben because it wasn't the time even though the guys were expecting me to do so.

Back at the house, I went to German's room and saw Donnie on German's bed. "Where's G?" I asked.

"What's wrong?"

"I couldn't ask her," I said.

"Of course you couldn't."

Right then, German walked in and asked, "What's going on?"

"Nothing, man. He didn't ask her," said Donnie.

"Why not??" asked German.

"I couldnt. It just wasn't the right time," I said.

G's computer rang. He went over to it, and Donnie and I looked over his shoulder.

"What the hell …" said German.

"G, what's wrong?" asked Donnie.

"Someone opened the FBI confidential file that the state had sealed."

I didn't know what he meant, but Donnie didn't seem confused; he and G made eye contact, and G was smiling.

"Wow. So he plans to go there," said German.

"I'm confused," I said as the door opened and Adam walked in.

"I'm so tired," Adam said as he laid down on German's bed.

We all smelled the strong aroma coming from Adam.

"Adam, why do you smell like garlic and marinara sauce?" asked Donnie.

"It's because he works at Porky's Pizza," I said.

"Is that where you've been?" asked German.

"I need all the shifts I can get," said Adam.

"Why?" asked Donnie.

Adam looked at German, which caught Donnie's and my attention.

"Adam, stop being ridiculous," German said. He went to his desk for his checkbook.

"G, stop," said Adam.

"Adam, really, there's no reason to kill yourself in a minimum wage job," said German.

"Are you working for your tuition?" asked Donnie.

"I can't reach my mom, and I have no other choice," said Adam.

"Where's your mom?" I asked.

"Don't know. I haven't seen or talked to her since we got back," he said. I knew Adam was worried.

"Look, after the carnival, we'll go with you to see her," said Donnie.

"You guys don't have to."

"We want to. G, write the check," said Donnie.

Having friends like German and Donnie really meant a lot especially because they never let me go without anything I needed. I knew they would help Adam get over his financial hurdle.

Drake

After reviewing the FBI sealed case I didn't have the clearance to review other details on the case. I had information on German Rigen but needed more. I walked to Deele's office. He was the lead commander of my unit. I knocked.

"It's open." I went in. "Detective Drake, what can I do for you?"

I closed the door. "I want to talk to you about a case I have," I said.

"How can I help?"

"Do you remember the Boston Museum robbery led by Jo-Sally Levinsque about two years ago?" I asked.

"Yes, what about it?".

"A case I've been assigned may have someone connected to it," I said. "German Rigen."

"Let it go," Deele said.

"Captain, what do you mean?" I asked.

"The case was sealed by the courts. There'd be no way to connect Rigen to that robbery."

"Sir, surely there's a way for me to connect something to my case. Do I have permission to speak to the FBI about maybe a character evaluation?" I asked.

"Character evaluation?"

His look concerned me. It almost felt like he was telling me not to pursue that case.

"I'll make the call to Boston. Give me forty-eight hours," he said.

"Thank you, sir," I said.

I walked to Bradshaw, who was at her desk. "Meet me in room six in ten minutes," I said.

I walked into the room followed by Bradshaw, who closed the door and asked, "What's up?"

"I think I might have found a way to prove it was murder and indict those four. I convinced Deele to call the FBI in Boston to complete a character evaluation on German Rigen," I said.

"You told him we looked at the file?"

"Of course not. Deele doesn't know we've seen it," I said.

"What happens now?"

"Pendleton's throwing a carnival on the town square this weekend. I'll alert Klovis to stage another attack on them, which would bring them here, and that's where it'll begin. By that time, I'll have what I need to begin," I said.

Bradshaw was silent, but I knew she felt comfortable with that. She nodded and left the room, but my plan was in effect. I knew that once I got this to Klovis, she'd be on board.

Donnie

I woke up and looked at my phone. It was six in the morning the day of the ticket sales for the carnival, and we'd have a tent to sell them along with Theta Monroe. I got out of bed.

"Wake up, buddy. We have to get to school," I told Justin.

I left the room and went downstairs, where I saw freshmen and sophomores getting the tent and tickets ready.

"Hey, Donnie, can you give us a hand?" asked Otto.

"Yeah," I said.

I helped the crew carry the tent to the pickup and called the men to line up. "All right, gents, shirts off. Let's see those muscles," I said.

They took off their shirts. I thought that about five had bodies almost as good as mine, that some needed to do some crunches or push-ups, and that the rest needed to keep their shirts on.

"This is sad, truly, truly sad. What the hell is going on with the dad bods, bros? That's it. No more beer," I said.

"Donnie, come on, these are ticket sellers, not Chippendales," said Brandon.

I chuckled. Everyone looked at him knowing I was going to let him have it.

"Look, bro, I know you're new at this, so let me fill you in. I'm the hottest ticket in the Greek system here. Sex sells my friend, literally and figuratively. You either fall in or fall out," I said.

"You're so full of yourself," he said.

"Yes I am. Let me show what a real body looks like," I said as I pulled of my shirt. I posed and looked at him. "See?"

I called out the guys with the better bodies. "All right, Kenny, Otto, Chester, Len, and Keith will be the attraction. Petey, Chris, Anthony, Bryan, Aubs, and Brandon, you'll run the sales. The rest will run the rotations to get the tickets. We all got our assignments?" I asked, and they nodded. "Let's Ride!" I said.

We arrived at school and began to set up. I saw Theta Monroe setting up as well. Ginger was yelling orders to the Theta woman as I was to the Alpha men. She and I were two of a kind. I walked over to Ginger, who said, "Well, well, well, the enemy."

"Enemy?" I asked with a smile.

"Oh yeah. You see these lovely ladies? We're about to outsell you poor, pitiful souls."

I smiled again trying to come off as flirtatious because I knew she couldn't resist me. I leaned in so close that she thought I was going to kiss her. "We'll see about that," I said.

Students were beginning to crowd around. I grabbed the bullhorn and said, "Ladies and gents of Pendleton! It's my pleasure to present to you the eleventh annual Pendleton Carnival. Tickets are on sale for ten dollars at the Alpha More house and at the Theta Monroe house booths here and beginning now!" Students started lining up. "All right, gents, shirts off!" I said.

Once we got in position, the ladies started yelling and pulling out their phones to take pictures. I was loving the attention, which was pissing Ginger off. Our ticket lines were very long and filled mostly with women.

"Hey, Donnie, can we have a group picture?" a young woman asked.

"You sure can as long as you buy your ticket from us," I said, and she gave me a hundred. I held it up to see if it was real, and it was. "Otto, can you give me ten tickets please?" I asked as I gave him the hundred.

"Yeah!" said Otto. The girls each took a picture with me as German walked up and asked, "What the hell's going on? Why are your shirts off?"

"Sex sells, my friend," I said.

"Oh God. Where do you want me?" he asked.

"Ticket sales. Aubs and Petey have class in fifteen minutes," I said.

"OK, cool," he said.

Ginger stormed over at me with a vengeance. I smiled and asked, "What's wrong, babe?"

"You think you're so clever, don't you?"

"I have my moments. Brains, sexiness—It's all in one," I said.

"Two can play that game!"

Ginger took off her shirt to reveal her bikini top and walked back to the Theta Monroe table. "All right ladies, let's get to work!" The ten members of Theta Monroe took off their shirts to reveal their bikini tops. "Buy your tickets from Theta Monroe!" Ginger yelled as the Theta Monroes did there jingle, "*Woooooahhhh!*"

Alves approached me. "Donnie, I didn't expect a half-naked event for charity."

"Mr. Alves, sex sells at times, and this is as good a time as any," I said.

"You have thirty minutes before the competition is over. Good luck," he said.

"Thanks, sir," I said. I looked over at Ginger, who looked at me and blew me a kiss.

The final minute was arriving. We were in a close race with Theta Monroe. Alves and Mack sounded the siren to make us stop.

"Alpha More and Theta Monroe, may we have your attention please. The competition is over. We've collected the money from both groups. I thank you for all your hard work," Mack said.

We all stood there waiting for the results. German and Justin came over. I was getting nervous. I put my hand on G's shoulders and rubbed them like I was giving him a massage.

"All right, Alpha More. Your total for the event was three thousand four hundred and eighty dollars. Outstanding job!" said Mack.

We clapped and did our jingle, "*Woot woot woot woot woot!*"

"Theta Monroe, your total is three thousand, four hundred and ninety dollars. Congratulations, Theta Monroe! You are the challenge winners, which means you get to host the eleventh annual Pendleton Carnival!" said Mack.

I was in disbelief. I was also always a sore loser.

The Theta Monroes did their jingle, "*Wooooooahhh!*" and Ginger walked up to me. "Now you have to eat crow."

"Congratulations," I said and extended my hand. Ginger shook it and walked off.

German and Justin walked up. Justin said, "Well, the first time we lose in ten years."

"Yeah. Let's get breakfast," said Donnie.

We headed to the cafeteria. I was pretty mad, but we had given it the old college try.

German

I took my fajita omelet to the table where Justin and Donnie were. Donnie was stuffing his face with a huge stack of pancakes. "Damn, Donnie, you must be hungry," I said.

"He always eats when he's mad," said Justin.

Adam came up. "What's up, guys?" He looked at Donnie. "Damn, Donnie, wipe your mouth."

"We missed you today," said Justin.

"Yeah. How'd we do?" asked Adam.

"We lost by ten bucks," I said as Donnie cut off a piece of my omelet and put on his plate. The look on my face was one of shock, but Justin and Adam laughed.

"That makes sense now," said Adam.

"Did you pay your tuition?" I asked.

"Yes, and G, thank you. I'll pay you back I promise."

"Don't worry about it," I said.

"Thanks again," said Adam.

"I won't be able to go with you to see your mom. Something came up," I said.

"Don't worry. I appreciate your offer to go with, but I can go alone," said Adam.

"No, man. Donnie and I'll go with you," said Justin.

I had a few things to do, so I excused myself and went to my car. I called my lawyer, Larry Farnsworth, for some more information on the case Drake had reopened. Larry was one of the best lawyers in New England.

"Mr. Rigen, good morning," he said.

"Mr. Farnsworth, I'm following up with you about the FBI file that was supposed to be sealed," I said.

"Yes. I called my connection at the FBI on your behalf. It seems Captain Rodrick Deele called yesterday to get a character analysis report on you. Sounds like they're going the route of seeing if you're capable of murder since the Klovis case was reopened."

"Do you know if they've sent it in?" I asked.

"Not yet. The Boston mayor will have to sign a release, and that could take two days."

"Will you keep me posted?" I asked.

"Certainly. Good day to you, Mr. Rigen."

"Good day," I said.

The best move I could make was to pay Deele a visit to get as much information as I could. I arrived at the precinct station and walked in as if I owned the place.

"Excuse me, sir. You need to sign in," said the desk sergeant.

"I don't need to sign in!" I walked to Deele's office and noticed two officers trying to get my attention. "I need to talk to you," I said as I walked in his office. Deele sent the two officers away.

"Mr. Rigen, to what do I owe this visit?" he asked.

"You can start by explaining to me how a classified file sealed by the government was just opened and why it happened," I said.

"Mr. Rigen, I have no idea what you're talking about."

I threw a file on his desk. He opened it. The file contained the phone conversation he'd had with the FBI. "Captain Deele, I'm not one for games, because better at them than anyone else. That file has your voice asking for a character analysis on me from the case the FBI had sealed. That file was opened in this precinct's conference room five," I said.

"Detective Drake's the lead on the case. It's not uncommon for that kind of request."

"Could that be due to the fact that the autopsy report specified that Benjamin Klovis had drowned?" I asked.

"Look, I understand you're upset Mr. Rigen, but my hands are tied. I'm not sure what you want me to do."

"Pull the plug," I said.

"You know I can't do that."

"Sure you can. Find a way," I said as I stood and walked to the door. "Captain Deele, I'll make one thing clear. The dirt I have on this precinct could shut this place down. Play games and I'll unleash it," I said as I walked out. I was ready for war, but I would hold my fire just in case.

Justin, Adam, and Donnie had left for Hoboken to go to Adam's home. When I arrived at my condo, I saw someone wearing a Greek hooded gown going down the alley. I locked my car and followed him. I stayed far enough back so I wouldn't be seen.

The man turned around quickly, and I ducked down to be sure he didn't see me. I waited a few seconds before I stood and looked in his direction, but he was gone though I had ducked for such a short time. I thought he might have seen me. I walked farther down the alley to a dead end though I counted five doors leading into buildings. I turned around, and there was the Greek god holding his axe. I dropped to the ground. Just then, one of the doors opened and someone exited a building, which caught the Greek god's attention.

"Hey!" the man said as he saw us. I tackled the Greek god. He and I tussled while the man was yelling at us to stop. The Greek god had me pinned, and he grabbed his axe, but the other guy came over and pulled him off me. The Greek god shoved the man and ran off. I got up to check on the guy who'd just saved my life; he was fine. We looked down the alley and saw that the Greek god was gone. The man and I looked at each other. We couldn't believe what had just happened.

CHAPTER 8

GREEK CARNIVAL

Justin

DONNIE, ADAM, AND I were driving back to Pendleton. When we'd gotten to Adam's home, it was in foreclosure. The police were of no help and not concerned that Adam's mom was missing. I felt bad for Adam. "I'm sure they'll find her, Adam," I said.

"Thanks, man."

"Guys, G isn't answering his phone," said Donnie.

"Did you call the house?" asked Adam.

"Yeah. I called to let Alves know we'd left town. He said he hasn't seen G," said Donnie.

"That's strange. He was at the house before we left," I said. We started to get concerned because it was unlike German not to answer his phone or call us back to say he was good.

"Adam, let's go to his condo," said Donnie.

When we got there, we saw German's car. Adam parked behind it, and we got out and looked in it. We rushed upstairs to the condo. The door was locked, but Donnie found the spare key hidden on the ledge above the door. He opened the door, and the alarm went off. "I got it," Donnie said as he punched in the code to turn the alarm off.

"G!" yelled Donnie.

We looked all around the place, but no G. Adam and I noticed Donnie

71

looking at the monitor, and we see Klovis and the Greek god waving his axe.

"Why can't we hear anything?" asked Adam.

Donnie unmuted the volume, and we heard Klovis say, "That was stupid of you! He could have seen who you were!"

The Greek god simply hung his head and started waving his hands. We realized he was signing.

"Followed you from where?" Klovis asked. The Greek god continued to sign. We heard the door slam. We jumped and turned around to see that it was German.

"G, where the hell were you?" asked Donnie.

"Greek god attacked me," he said.

We turned to the monitor to see the Greek god signing. "I wonder what he's saying," I said as German stared at the monitor.

"He's saying that he would've had me if the guy who'd come out of the door hadn't seen us," German said, and we all stared at him.

A few minutes later, the Greek god and Klovis left the building.

"None of this makes sense. You follow the Greek god and he attacks you?" Donnie asked.

"He attacked Justin. What would make me any different?" German asked.

"You're a target for Drake, not for him," said Donnie.

"Drake, Klovis, the Greek god—What's the difference? They're intertwined," said Adam.

"Yeah, but if the Greek god gets G, their whole plan is destroyed and then they move in on me because I'm the other millionaire in the group," Donnie said.

"Thanks, Donnie. That makes me feel so much better," said German.

None of us knew what was going on, but we thought that since German and I had been attacked, we thought Adam and Donnie would be next. It seemed the plan was to make us fearful.

"The best thing we can do is to put this on the back burner until after the carnival," G said.

We left the condo. Adam and Donnie drove off, and German and I got in his car. Right before we drove off, German looked at Klovis's building.

"G, you OK?" I asked.

"Yeah, sorry," German said as he drove off.

I knew that whatever had happened to him was still affecting him.

"How's Adam's mom?" he asked.

"She wasn't home. The house was in foreclosure, and her car was gone," I said.

"Did he go to the police?"

"Yes, but they were no help," I said.

We pulled up to Alpha More and saw that the house was covered with pink toilet paper.

"What the hell is this?" Adam asked, whom we met in the lot.

"Theta Monroe throwing the first punch," said German.

Pip was in front of the building. She smiled, ran up, and kissed me. "Hey! I missed you!"

"I missed you too, babe. One sec," I said. I turned. "Hey, guys, I'll catch up with you later."

Pip and I held hands as we walked down the block.

"How was the drive?" she asked.

"I feel bad for Adam. His mom's missing," I said.

"Oh no. Sorry to hear that."

"He needs my support right now," I said.

"I understand."

I smiled at her as we kissed again. "Get home safe," I said.

"Bye," said Pip.

I watched her walk down the block and then went into the house. Donnie, German, Adam, and everyone else were coming outside. "What's going on?" I asked.

"Mr. Alves said we have thirty minutes to clean this up," said Adam.

We began pulling the toilet paper down.

"So Donnie, what's the plan to get Theta Monroe back? I know you have something up your sleeve," said German.

"Oh you have no idea. Those girls are going to remember the Greek house that rules this community," said Donnie.

"Hey, Justin, can you help get the ladder?" asked Adam.

"Yeah, sure," I said.

Adam and headed to the shed for the ladder. I could tell he was still deep in thought. "You sure you're OK?" I asked.

"I'm just really worried. My mom and I never go this long without talking."

"I'm sure she's fine. Maybe she's staying with a friend and trying to figure out her next move," I said.

Adam and I grabbed the ladder, and we saw something fall off it.

"What's that?" Adam asked.

I picked up what looked like a roll of film.

"Why would that be here?" asked Adam.

"Don't know. I'll just put it in my pocket for now," I said.

He and I carried the ladder to the front yard, where we heard loud music and saw a red convertible drive up to the house.

"Theta territory!" yelled Ginger.

We saw Ginger and three other members of Theta Monroe pull out the banner saying Theta Territory. They drove off. Donnie smiled. "It is *so* on," he said.

Drake

I got a call from Captain Deele to come to the precinct right away. I was hoping he'd gotten the information I needed. I went to his office and knocked.

"Come in," I heard.

I did. I closed the door. "Captain, you wanted to see me?" I asked.

The look on his face concerned me. I wasn't sure how the conversation would go.

"The case of Ben Klovis versus Alpha More is to be withdrawn immediately," he said.

"What? Captain?" I asked.

He put his hand up. "Detective Drake, there's no room for negotiation. This case is closed."

"I don't understand, Captain. Just forty-eight hours ago, you said you'd call the FBI in Boston and now you're saying the case is closed?" I asked.

"Getting the information to move this case forward has complicated itself. I read the toxicologist's report that was just submitted, and it also implied that Klovis drowned. We don't need to waste any more resources on this case."

"I just reassured Katheryn Klovis that we had some solid evidence. I can't go back and tell her the case is closed," I said.

"As a detective, you know that giving someone that kind of false hope is unethical. Anything can happen, as it did."

I knew that something had happened for the captain to have dismissed this case. I left his office and asked Bradshaw to meet me in a conference room.

"What's going on?" she asked when she came in.

"Deele's closing the case," I said.

"Did he say why?"

"More or less. Something happened, something big for him to dismiss this case without any further review of what I have," I said.

"Do you want me to go with you to talk to Mrs. Klovis?"

"No, I can tell her on my own," I said. "What you can do is ask around the office if Deele had any run-ins with anyone."

Bradshaw left. I was completely frustrated. My plan was in ruins. I pulled myself together and went to my car.

I pulled up in front of Katheryn's building and saw that she was setting up shop. I walked in the side entrance and saw a room full of flowers—roses, orchids, and bouquets.

"Detective, what brings you by?" she asked.

"I didn't know you were a florist," I said.

"Yeah. I had my own shop in Providence that I just closed. I'm relocating here."

"I need to talk to you about the case," I said as we walked to her office in the back.

"What about it?"

"My captain just closed the case," I said.

Katheryn looked disgusted. "So what do we do now?"

"I don't know, but I'll figure something out," I said.

"You better. The four of them are going down. Find a way to make that happen."

"Mom?" asked Brandon as he unexpectedly walked in.

"Hi, honey. What are you doing here?" asked Katheryn.

"I wanted to see you before I went to school."

"You remember Detective Drake?"

"Yes. Hello, sir."

I got a better look at Brandon. I knew he and Ben were twins, but I realized now that they were a hundred percent identical.

"Would you excuse me, Detective?" Katheryn asked.

"Sure," I said.

She walked Brandon to the front of the shop, and I went around her desk and picked up a photo of Ben and Brandon. I couldn't tell them apart. I looked at pictures of her husband and other children. She came back in. "I didn't realize you had a big family. Are your husband and children moving to Pendleton?" I asked.

"My husband and I are separating. My youngest is thirteen, so I'm sure we'll have a custody agreement."

My phone rang. "Excuse me," I said. Bradshaw was calling. "I got word that German Rigen had talked to Deele yesterday, so there's your case dismissed," she said.

"Thanks," I said and hung up. "I have to go, Katheryn. The plan's still on," I said.

Donnie

I was throwing the last bag of toilet paper in the trash when I heard a giggle. I turned around and saw Ginger, who asked, "Well isn't this is sight to see?"

"Yeah. This was a good one, but it means war," I said.

Ginger put her arms around my neck, we kissed, and she asked, "What is it about you that drives me crazy?"

I smiled. "I have that effect on people. It's one of my many charms," I said.

I began kissing her neck. Out of the corner of my eye, I saw G walking to the trash area. I kept kissing Ginger's neck as she was really into that. I winked at G, who smiled and shook his head.

Ginger kissed me and asked, "So are we taking this to my place or yours?"

"Mine's closer," I said as I led her to the house and up to my room, where I put a black sock on the doorknob, the signal that sex was going on inside. She began to take her clothes off, as did I. We engaged in some intense kissing, and I grabbed a condom from my top dresser drawer; we made our way to my bed. She and I had had this ongoing sex habit since freshman orientation. Although she was one of many for me, something was different about her though I couldn't figure out what.

Forty-five minutes later, I removed myself from her. We began kissing side by side. After I pulled my condom of and wiped myself, we cuddled.

"I gotta get back to the house," she said.

"I'm not ready for you to go," I said.

"I know, sweetie, but I have class in the morning and the carnival this weekend. There's a lot on my plate."

I was disappointed, but I understood, and I was sure Justin needed to get to bed. I got out of bed and I began to put on my sweatpants as I kissed Ginger again. I walked her to the door and removed the sock from the doorknob. I got into bed and sent Justin a text saying the coast was clear. I lay down and started to fall asleep. I saw a shadow walking in and figured it was Justin, so I rolled over and closed my eyes. Goodnight, world.

My alarm sounded, and as I pulled my phone out to turn it off, I looked at Justin's bed and saw it was made up. I looked at my phone and read a text from Justin; he said he was spending the night with Pip. I got out of bed and saw that there was a red lipstick kiss on my stomach. I texted Ginger: "Did you kiss my stomach after we had sex?"

Ginger responded, "Not that I can recall. You better ask the other woman."

That was strange. I grabbed my towel and went to take a shower, but all the eight stalls were occupied. "Seriously, I'm running late!" I said. I grabbed my bag and went upstairs to German's room. He was on his computer.

"Morning," I said.

"Morning," he said.

"Sorry, G, but the showers are crowded downstairs and I have to get to class," I said.

"No worries, man. I'm just finishing my term paper," he said.

"Cool," I said and went into his bathroom.

German walked in and sat on the toilet seat. "How was Ginger?"

"Amazing as always," I said.

"I need to talk to you about something."

"What's up?" I asked.

"You ever think about being in a relationship with Ginger?"

I thought it was odd of German to ask me that considering he knew better than anyone. "Why do you ask?" I asked.

"It seems like you always go back to her. You two have that chemistry."

"Ginger and I just have an understanding," I said as I turned off the shower and poked my head out. "G, we need to get you a girlfriend. It's been two years. You've been single long enough."

"I don't want a girlfriend."

I stepped out the shower and wrapped my towel around my waist. "Fair enough, but what about sex? It's been a while, right?" I asked.

"Gotta go. I'll see you at school," he said.

I paused for a bit. German hadn't had a girlfriend since Jo-Sally. I knew it was none of my business, but I was getting vibes that German might not have been into women, but that was OK; I loved the LGBTSQ community. But then I wondered what I was thinking. G wasn't gay. I didn't know why I'd even thought that. I left German's room and went back to mine. Justin was there, and he asked, "Where did you take a shower? I didn't see you in the bathroom."

"G's room," I said as I began to get dressed.

Justin started to walk out of the room. "I'll be downstairs," he said.

I nodded, but I was still suspicious. I'd seen someone come into our room, and it hadn't been Justin.

I went to campus and saw Adam in the lounge.

"What's up?" he asked.

"Can I ask you something?" I asked.

"Sure."

"Do you think G's gay?" I asked.

"I don't know. Does it matter?"

"No, it doesn't, but he was acting strange last night. I saw him peeking in on me and Ginger last night when I was taking out the trash. This morning, I woke up and I had this kiss print on my stomach," I said.

"So you think G kissed you on your stomach?"

"I don't know … Maybe," I said.

Adam chuckled. "I think you're being ridiculous. If G's gay, who cares? Let him come out in his own time, and we can be the hugs he needs."

Adam made me realize that I was reading way too much into this. "Have you heard from your mom?" I asked.

"No. I'm going to call her again after my psych class."

"All right, man. See you at lunch," I said. I felt better about G, but I needed to figure out who had come into my room the previous night.

Adam

While I was in the lounge, Jessica came up and said, "Good morning!"

"Good morning to you," I said.

"How was your weekend?"

"It was good. I took a little road trip to see my mom and handled some frat stuff," I said.

"That explains why I didn't see you at the pizza place."

"You bought another pizza?" I asked.

"A salad."

"Walk you to class?" I asked.

"Sure."

As we were walking to her class, we ran into Justin and Pip. "Come meet my friends," I said.

"Yo Adam," said Justin.

"Hey, guys, this is Jessica. Jessica, this is my frat brother Justin and his girlfriend, Pip," I said as Jessica shook their hands.

"Nice to meet you, Jessica," said Justin.

"We should have a date night. What do you say, Jessica? Would you join me on a date night with my friends?" I asked.

"Sure. That sounds like fun," she said.

"Sweet," I said. I told Justin and Pip, "We'll catch up with you later."

"I appreciate your saying yes to that, Jessica. I know it's a little unethical because we haven't had our first date, but I wanted you to see that being in a fraternity means a lot to me," I said.

"I understand, and I like that aspect of you."

"I'll call you," I said.

"OK."

I walked to my class feeling proud of myself mainly because I hadn't scored a date at all the previous year being wrapped up in the fraternity. I thought this would be exciting.

After class, I headed to the cafeteria to meet up with the guys. I grabbed a ham sandwich, an apple, a bottle of water, and some mints and walked to Donnie's, Justin's, and German's table. "Justin, I owe you big time," I said.

"No you don't. Pip and I were just talking about doing a couples date night."

"A couples date night?" Donnie asked.

"Yeah. I met this girl, Jessica," I said.

"Is she hot?" asked Donnie.

"Oh yeah," I said.

"Yeah. She's pretty cute. Great catch," said Justin.

"Man, I want to see her. G, be my date so we can go," said Donnie.

I put my head down because I knew what Donnie was alluding to.

"Why don't you ask Ginger?" asked German.

"I don't want to give her the wrong impression," said Donnie.

"It's a date, Donnie, not a marriage proposal," said Justin.

"All right, I'll bring Ginger," said Donnie.

"G, Pip has a roommate, Shayna. She's single," said Justin.

Donnie's smile was giving away that he was onto something, but I didn't want to pay any attention to whatever he was implying.

"Sure. Why not?" G asked.

"Cool. The four of us have a date night," I said.

"Adam, what do you want me to do with this?" Justin asked as he pulled out the film.

"What's that?" asked Donnie.

"Don't know. We found it when we were getting the ladder," said Justin.

"Can I see it?" asked German.

Justin gave German the film. He started holding frames up to the light.

"Can you see what it is?" asked Donnie.

"It looks like it's from that party," said German.

"What party?" asked Justin.

"The graduation party," said German.

We all went to the film department to get a print room. We walked in, and German said, "Hi Professor Kraft."

"Mr. Rigen, What can do for you?"

"I need to make prints of these negatives. I was hoping the lab was open."

"Absolutely. It'll be a dollar per print. Do you know how many sheets you'll need?" asked Kraft as he pulled out a pack of photo paper.

"How many come to the pack?" asked German.

"A hundred."

"I'll take that entire pack," German said, and he handed Kraft a hundred dollar bill.

Kraft gave us the pack of paper, and we went to the lab. Donnie closed and locked the door while German logged into the computer and inserted the negatives to get prints of them. The first ones were shots of our party.

"This is definitely the graduation party. I see Paris in the back right corner," I said.

The next picture showed another crowd of students. "There's Ben. I remember what he was wearing," said Donnie.

The next picture showed Ben and Brandon. "Oh wow," said German.

"Wait. Brandon was at that party too?" I asked.

"Justin, I thought you said that Pip didn't know Ben had had a twin," German said.

"That's what she told me," I said.

"Either she didn't see him or she lied," said German.

"Which one's more likely?" Donnie asked sarcastically.

"Shut up, Donnie," I said.

The next print showed the four of us leaving the house with Ben, which stunned us. "Whoever took this knows we left with Ben," said German.

German

On carnival day, Adam walked into my room. "Getting ready?" I asked.

"What are you going to do with those pictures?"

"I locked them up for now," I said.

Donnie walked in. "Guys, have you heard? Theta Monroe has assigned us booths, and you'll never guess where the four of us are." He gave me the list.

"Custodial counter!" I exclaimed. "Excuse me."

I charged downstairs to Mr. Alves's office and knocked.

"Come in," said Alves, and I did very abruptly. "German, what can I do for you?"

"The assignments came from Theta Monroe, and mine is a little cruel," I said and handed him the list.

"Well, that is a tough one considering this carnival is open to the public, German."

"I want to be reassigned. I'm donating to the organization's charity," I said.

"German, you can't buy your way out of everything. The rule is that Theta Monroe gets to assign carnival duties to Alpha More, which lost the challenge."

"Yes sir," I said. I left his office dejected.

Donnie and Adam were waiting for me at the stairs. Donnie asked, "What did he say?"

"He said no, but I have an idea," I said.

I went to my computer and googled Moore's Custodial Services. Donnie and Adam gathered around me, and Donnie smiled and said, "G, you're a freakin' genius!"

"Can you hand me my wallet on my dresser?" I asked, and Adam did.

"So you're hiring a cleanup crew for the event?" Adam asked.

"Yep. Mr. Alves didn't say I couldn't," I said as I booked the crew. "Done. Guys, this will give a chance to be a tad more social. Where's Justin?" I asked.

"He'll meet us at the carnival. He's bringing Shayna too so you can meet her," said Donnie.

"I can't believe you guys talked me into going to this," I said.

"Why not? You need to meet someone and get yourself some," Donnie said.

"Donnie!" Adam said.

"What?" I asked.

"Nothing, G. Are we ready to go?" asked Adam.

"Yeah," I said.

We left the room. Donnie and Adam were acting very strangely. We went to my car and drove to town, and I parked my car on Second and Main, close to the carnival, which was starting at five. We had time to meet up with the others.

We walked to the entrance and saw Justin, Pip, and Shayna. I'd decided to be a part of this couples date night thing to be a team player.

"Hey, guys," said Justin.

We greeted Justin and nodded at the ladies.

"Guys, this is Shayna Moloke. Shayna, these are my frat brothers, Adam Banks, Donnie Diamante, and your date tomorrow night, German Rigen," said Justin.

"Nice to meet you all," said Shayna as we shook her hand.

Just then, Ginger walked over. "Well, well, well. You boys should be in the park for your assignments. Hi Pip," Ginger said, and she and Pip hugged. "Come on, gentlemen. Your picks and trash bags await."

Pip and Shayna walked away.

"Are you serious? We got trash duty?" Justin asked.

"So she thinks," said Donnie.

"What do you mean?" asked Justin.

"Wait and see," said German.

We walked to where the rest of our brothers were and saw the ladies of Theta Monroe standing united and Ginger grabbing a megaphone. She announced, "Thank you, Alpha More, for your cooperation in this meaningful charity event. Since we have an hour until the carnival starts, please go to your designated areas for your assignments."

I spotted the Moore's Custodial Services van and its team of nine. I walked over to meet the crew manager. "Hi. Are you Andrew?" I asked.

"Yes."

"I'm German Rigen. Thanks for coming. The cleaning station's on your left," I said.

I made my way back to Donnie, Adam, and Justin and filled them in. "Well, guys, that takes care of that," I said as Ginger came over.

"What the hell's going on? And who the hell's that?" she asked.

"That my dear is your cleaning crew free of charge. If you squint, four of them look like us, especially the one with the big head, who looks just like Donnie, don't he?" I asked as Donnie laughed and put an arm around me. We walked away as the doors opened.

"What do you guys want to do first?" asked Justin.

"Food, man. I'm starving!" said Donnie.

We got in line, and we saw Mrs. Klovis walking into the carnival.

"What the hell is she doing here?" asked Donnie.

"Enjoying the carnival," Brandon said.

We all turned and saw that Brandon was working at the food concession stand.

"Damn. Where's the customer service?" Donnie asked sarcastically.

"Shouldn't you guys be working?" asked Brandon.

"We are. Look to your right. We're supervising that cleaning crew," I said.

"I'll take the chicken kabob meal," said Donnie.

"I'm going to take the fajita shrimp kabob," said Adam.

"I'll have Tuscan chicken," I said.

"I'm going to take the pulled pork sandwich," said Justin.

Brandon took our order to the grill.

Just then, Drake walked up to us and asked, "Fellas, how you doing tonight?"

"The night's still young," said Donnie.

"Mr. Rigen, may I have a word with you?" asked Drake.

Drake began to walk off, and I followed him not knowing what this was all about but hoping it would be entertaining. He went to the gazebo in the middle of the town square. He turned to me and saw me smirking. "It was bought to my attention that you went to the precinct to talk to Captain Deele. May I ask why?"

"I was told that he made a call to the FBI to get a character analysis on someone involved in a case that had been sealed by the courts," I said.

"You know, you just might be too smart for your own good. You're going to go down for this. I assure you this isn't over."

"Detective Drake, whatever you're planning will fail. Going after me will be career suicide," I said.

"Is that what you told the FBI when you got away with the Boston Museum burglary?"

"I didn't have to. I wasn't involved in that," I said.

"Yet you got seventy-five million in reward money for finding the stolen paintings."

"Someone had to find them," I said.

"I think that you knew exactly where they were and that you set up Jo-Sally Levinsque."

"The world may never know," I said.

"We'll see about that," Drake said. He walked away.

I walked back to where Donnie, Justin, and Adam were eating.

"What did he want?" asked Donnie.

"He's mad I beat him at his own game," I said.

"G, I really don't think you should antagonize a detective," said Justin.

"Oh I'm scared. I think Drake shouldn't antagonize me," I said.

As we were finishing our food, Alves made an announcement. "Good evening, people of Pendleton. I'm Marvin Alves, the den father of Alpha More. This carnival, represented by Pendleton University, will donate fourteen thousand seven hundred and sixty-five dollars to the Maine School for the Hearing Impaired I'm proud to say."

The crowd was clapping as I made my way to my banker, who handed me a big fake check I had asked him for.

Alves finished his speech. "One member of my fraternity house is matching that donation. Please help me welcome German Rigen."

The crowd clapped as I make my way to the stage. Alves gave me the microphone. "It's my honor and privilege to present a check in the amount of fifteen thousand to the Maine School for the Hearing Impaired. Thank you," I said, and I drew more applause. I saw Drake and Klovis giving me the death stare. It felt good to know that I was always a step ahead of them.

CHAPTER 9

DATE OPPRESSED

Drake

FOUND IT AMAZING how well connected German Rigen was to be able to pull strings and get this case closed. I walked Katheryn to her car as we discussed the next move.

"I can't believe this is happening. I had this case, and now it's been thrown out," I said.

"There's nothing else?" she asked.

"I'm sure there is, but if he can get this case thrown out, I'm sure he's capable of throwing out anything else. You're better off suing them," I said.

"It's not about the money. I want revenge, Detective Drake."

She got in her car and left.

I saw Alves walking to his car. "Mr. Alves!" I yelled.

"Detective Drake, did you enjoy the carnival?" he asked.

"Yes, and it was very nice. I have a question for you," I said. "Katheryn Klovis requested a second autopsy for the body. My question is that out of the four guys, do you feel that any of them has been behaving strangely?" I asked.

"Detective, it's a fraternity house. Everything imaginable happens there. Sometimes it's a wonder that all of them are still alive."

"I'd like to observe the house a little more just to help with my investigation. Would that be OK?" I asked.

"That would be fine, Detective, but realize that this is a fraternity house, so be cautious."

I smiled knowing that this was what I needed to get more insight into those guys. I called Bradshaw.

"Hello?" she answered.

"I know it's your day off, but I found a new plan that might work," I said.

"Do I want to know it?"

"Let's just say I might be able to get what I need to further this investigation and get the money. I'll keep you posted," I said.

The next day, I showed up at Alpha More and knocked. The person who answered asked, "Can I help you?"

"Yes. I'm Detective Drake. I'm here to see Mr. Alves," I said.

"Come in."

He walked me to Mr. Alves's office, and I knocked on the door.

"Come in," said Alves. "Detective Drake, welcome. Please take a seat. May I offer you something to drink?"

"No sir, I'm fine," I said. "My goal is to be here for only a few hours a day to observe the environment and put together a cohesive analysis for the DA."

"Understood."

"So to get started, would you take me on a tour of the house?" I asked.

"Sure."

We started on the main floor. "This house has four levels. This is the kitchen. Remember that these are young men, so the majority of the time they'll be in here."

We then went to the media room, the guest bathroom, and the conference room, which Alves said could hold seventy. We then went upstairs.

"On the second level are freshmen and sophomores, and on the third floor are juniors and seniors plus German Rigen."

"German Rigen is a …"

"A sophomore."

"Why isn't he with the other sophomores?" I asked.

"After the incident with Ben Klovis, German wasn't sure he would rejoin the fraternity, and the room that he was assigned was his father's and brother's room."

A fraternity member ran upstairs. "Mr. Alves, Dean Himbrey is on the line for you."

"Thank you, Phil," Alves said. "Detective Drake, would you excuse me for a moment?"

"Sure," I said.

I walked up the next staircase and saw hallways on either side each with twelve doors. I went down one hallway as it was really quiet, so I imagined no one was there. I opened the first door to the right and saw no one there. The room had two beds and two desks. I closed the door and continued down the hallway to the next door, which opened into a bathroom. I closed the door and bumped in to a fraternity member, which startled me.

"Hello, sir. Can I help you?" he asked.

"Yes. I'm Detective Drake, and I'm looking for German Rigen's room," I said.

"The other hallway, first door on the left."

He walked down the hallway as I made my way to the other. I opened the door to German's room, which was very nice and spacious. On the wall was a picture of Chance Rigen and another of German's biological brother. I looked throughout the room and began looking through drawers not finding anything I could use. I opened his laptop on the one desk there. It was locked, so I put in a drive to hack into it. I began searching as the computer went red. I immediately removed the drive and I heard other members of the fraternity. I closed the laptop and walked to the door. I cracked the door open to see if the hallway was clear. I didn't see anyone in the hallway, so I walked out of the room and closed the door. I walked downstairs and saw Alves coming up.

"Sorry about that, Detective. I see you got your tour of the upper level."

"Yes, very nice fraternity house," I said.

"We're you ever in a fraternity, Detective?"

"No, I wasn't that fortunate," I said.

"Ahh well, let me treat you to lunch in the lounge," said Alves as we walked downstairs.

German

The day had been rough. I'd forgotten my laptop, and Adam had gotten a flat tire, so I was giving him a ride home. Adam was looking out the window. I could tell he was down. "You OK, bro?" I asked.

"It's just one thing after another," he said.

"Look man, life happens. It's just a flat tire. We'll get that fixed," I said.

"Yeah, thanks, man."

I got a notification on my phone from my security app that protected my computer. I pulled the car over.

"What's wrong?" asked Adam.

"Someone's hacking my computer," I said.

I connected my iPad to my car's Wi-Fi so I could see what had happened. I opened the app to see what the laptop had recorded. I clicked on view and saw Detective Drake. Adam was shocked, but I wasn't. It was exactly what I had suspected would happen.

"Is that real?" asked Adam.

I pressed on my Bluetooth. "Call Donnie Diamante."

"Hey," Donnie answered.

"Get Justin and meet me at my condo. We need to talk," I said.

"All right," Donnie said. I turned my car around.

When I got to the condo, I saw Donnie's car. Adam and I went into my condo, and I went to my double monitors and pulled up my account.

"What's going on?" Donnie asked.

I pulled up the footage of Drake, and we watched him trying to get into my computer and using a device to enter it. I had an extra layer of security that would block out the device.

"What do we do?" asked Adam.

"I don't know. At this point, Drake is going after me with whatever he can. I need to confront him," I said.

"Confront him? A detective?" asked Donnie.

"He doesn't have probable cause or a warrant to hack into my laptop," I said.

"I get it, but I have a bad feeling about this," said Donnie.

"I'll go alone. You guys go back to Alpha More and wait for my call," I said.

They left, and I called the precinct telling Drake to meet me at the gazebo.

I showed up there and saw Drake get out of his car. He walked over to me.

"Mr. Rigen, to what do I owe this meeting?"

I showed him the video of him hacking my computer.

Drake looked really disappointed as he shook his head. "Some security system you have."

"Drake, I know you're working with Klovis. I want this to stop," I said.

"I wish it were that easy."

"You're a smart man, Drake. I'm sure you can convince her one way or another," I said.

"She wants revenge, Mr. Rigen."

"Revenge for what? Her son's death was an accident due to a stupid prank that fraternity houses pull. We all put our lives at risk to make it in," I said.

"That's not how she sees it."

"So her plan is to potentially harm us so I would pay to make it all go away?" I asked.

"That amongst other things."

"And you, a detective, are going to allow that to happen? The payoff must be amazing to risk your career for it," I said.

Drake gave me a strange look, which made me smile. "Oh come on! You really think I wasn't going to announce that you were involved in this scheme?" I asked.

"It's your word against mine, and I'm a respected detective here."

"That may be so, but I have evidence of the plan you set up and also witnesses. I know I'm just prelaw, but what I do know is that the stronger the evidence, the better the case. You either put a stop to Mrs. Klovis or go down with her," I said.

"What about the person in the Greek costume?"

"What do you mean?" I asked.

"He's apparently after you for a completely different reason."

"You sure it's not Brody?" I asked.

"I'm a hundred percent sure. I hired him to keep an eye on your every move. That's all he was involved in."

"You're going to do something for me Detective Drake. I want you to find out who's under that costume," I said.

"How exactly am I supposed to do that?"

"I don't give a damn how you do it, but you're going to do it or this evidence of you hacking my computer without a warrant goes to IA," I said as I walked away.

I got in my car and left hoping Drake had taken me seriously. Having him tell me that that Greek god was after us for a different reason put some fear in me that this was more personal than a mother seeking revenge.

Adam

I was getting ready for our couples date night. This was the first time that I had done something like this, and I was excited.

Brody walked in. "Hey, Adam, thanks for giving me your shift tonight. I need the cash."

"Anytime, man," I said.

"Where you heading?" he asked.

"I have a date tonight," I said.

"That hot girl who came to the restaurant?"

I nodded.

"Nice! All right, man. Have a good time," Brody said.

I wanted to ask him about Drake, but I knew it was not the right time. I got dressed, put a little gel in my hair, and sprayed myself with my favorite cologne, Calvin Klein. When I left my room, I saw Justin.

"Hey sexy," Justin said, and we chuckled.

"Where's G and Donnie?" I asked.

"Getting ready. Pip texted me that she, Shayna, and Ginger were on the way."

"That reminds me. I have to pick up Jessica. Can I use your car?" I asked.

"Yeah, man," Justin said and gave me the keys.

"Cool. I'll meet you there," I said.

"I'll walk down with you."

We went downstairs and saw Pip, Ginger, and Shayna walk in giggling.

"Hey, ladies," said Justin.

"Hey! Where's my date?" Ginger asked.

"He and G are still getting ready," said Justin.

"I swear, Shayna, we have the most high-maintenance men in this house," Ginger said, and we all laughed.

"Adam, where's Jessica?" asked Pip.

"I have to pick her up. I'll meet you guys there," I said as Donnie and German were coming downstairs.

"Ladies, ladies, ladies! You want me. I know it," said Donnie.

"They may want you, but I have you," said Ginger, who kissed Donnie.

"See you there," I said as I walked out to Justin's car.

I arrived at Jessica's apartment and knocked. She answered. She looked gorgeous.

"Hi," she said smiling.

"Wow … You look amazing," I said.

"You look nice as well!"

"Shall we?" I asked, and she came out and closed her door.

We walked to Justin's car, and I opened the door for her.

"What a gentleman," she said.

We drove off, and she asked, "So what are we doing for date night?"

"We're doing the escape room," I said.

Jessica smiled when I grabbed her hand. We arrived at the place, and we walked in holding hands.

"Hey, guys," I said as I spotted the others.

"Everyone, this is Jessica. Jessica, you already know Justin and Pip. We have German, Shayna, Donnie, and Ginger here too," I said.

"We have two rooms in the escape room, so how are we doing this?" asked Donnie.

"The obvious—guys versus girls," Ginger said.

"You know we're going to win," Donnie said. "G's a genius. He'll have it figured out in a minute."

"My girl Shayna is pretty smart as well, and Jessica looks extremely bright, so kick it dudes," said Ginger.

"What happens if we win?" I asked.

"Winner gets to pick the restaurant we go to after," G said.

"I like, I like, I like!" said Donnie.

We headed in and split up. The girls waved at us, and we went to our respective rooms. Ours looked like a sauna and a Jenga game mixed up.

"The game will start when I close the door," the attendant said.

"We're ready," said German.

The door closed, and Justin read our assignment. "We're CSI agents investigating the murder of Harold Lawry, who was murdered in a sauna after a two-hour workout. In the room are five clues that may help the murder investigation. Here's our first clue. A half-full glass may or may not be water, so please examine it for any toxins."

We looked around for the glass of water.

"Why would a glass be in a sauna?" asked German.

"Maybe there's something more to it than that," I said.

"Is it me, or did it just get stuffy in here?" Donnie asked.

We looked around. "Found it," said German.

"Look. It's green. Maybe it's poison," said Justin.

German looked under the glass and saw three numbers underneath. "Four, six, and nine, guys."

"What's that?" I asked.

"Look for something with a padlock on it," he said.

We all looked around.

"Y'all, it's getting really warm in here," said Donnie.

"It *is* hot. Ring the doorbell so we can let them know to turn the heat down," I said.

Donnie did, but the doorbell didn't sound that time or the next time he tried it. "What the hell?" He tried to open the door, but it was locked from the outside. "Should we bust it down?"

"Guys, I see a gym bag," said German. We went over to it and saw a padlock on it. German punched in the numbers, and the lock opened. A note inside read, "Congratulations! You have reached clue number 2. Pranks are always on the horizon with dealing with a fraternity. I'll give you a big hint this time. Think back to a time a horn was used to the beat of a drum."

"Wait. What?" Donnie asked.

"Why did that sound personal?" asked Justin.

"Yeah, like this room is addressing us," I said.

93

We looked around to see if we could find an image of the clue. I stumbled upon a cabinet; inside it was a spray horn. "No way!" I said.

We all looked at the spray horn, and it made us remember something.

Adam

One day when Donnie, German, Justin, and I were freshmen, we were in German's room. Donnie walked in and gave German a bag, "What's that?" I asked.

"Let's just say this prank will be funny," said German.

"Grab the board," said Donnie.

We put the board on the ground and then put the names of four freshmen on it. We spun the arrow on the board; we would prank whomever the arrow pointed to, and that ended up being Steven Schmidt.

"Here's the plan," Donnie said. "We'll hide in his room and turn off the lights. When he comes in, before he can turn on the lights, we blow the horn."

Donnie grabbed the horn, and we went to Steven's room. German and I hid in the closet, Justin was keeping lookout outside, and Donnie was behind the door. We got a text from Justin saying Steven was on his way in. When he entered, Donnie blew the horn right in his ear. We laughed and raced out. But Steven's ears started to bleed. He was rushed to the hospital, where he found out that he had lost 90 percent of his hearing in both ears.

Justin

We pound on the door of our escape room but got no response.

"Man, this can't be happening," said Donnie.

German picked up the horn and saw our clue number three. "Guys, check this out. Clue number three, blast from the past, at least the blast from my ear. Go to the side you struck for the next clue."

"So this room was based on the prank we played on Steven Schmidt," said German.

German went to the mannequin, and Donnie tried to stop him. "G, come on."

"I want out of this room. It's getting hotter," said German.

German went to the manikin's ear and pulled out the final clue, which he read. "Final clue. If where you lack is how you succeed, go to my studies, which will set you free. What was Steven's major?" he asked.

"How the hell am I supposed to know?" asked Donnie.

"I don't remember either, G," said Adam.

It had to be at least eighty-seven degrees in this room, and it was getting warmer.

"Wait, guys. We're in a sauna," German said. "This had nothing to do with the prank. Steven was studying business because he wanted to open a fitness center. What year was he supposed to graduate?"

German went to the door and punched in 2023 on the lock. The door unlocked, and we left the room. The hallway was cooler. I felt relieved. We walked to the lobby of the escape room place and saw the girls waiting for us.

"Well, well, it looks like someone lost," said Ginger.

German asked the clerk at the front desk, "Excuse me, but how did you come up with that plotline for our room?"

"It was sent in to us."

"By whom?" I asked.

"I'm sorry, but I can't give out that information."

The four of us gathered. Donnie said, "Guys, that was strange. It was almost like …"

"Steven Schmidt was looking for revenge as well," I said finishing Donnie's thought.

"No one's seen him since he left on medical leave," said Adam.

"I think we need to talk to Mr. Alves about what's going on," said Donnie.

"Are you crazy? He wouldn't believe us," said German.

"Why not?" asked Donnie.

Ginger walked over. "Hate to break up your all-boys' meeting, but I'm hungry. Shall we?"

We went to the Blue Abbot, a popular restaurant that was way out of my budget.

"Babe, can we afford this place?" Pip whispered.

"It'll be fine," I whispered.

"Has anyone been here before?" asked Jessica.

"All the time," said German.

"That makes sense," said Shayna.

"Why do you say that?" asked German.

"It's no secret who your father is. I'm sure he's taken you to all these fancy restaurants before," she said.

That stunned most of us, but Donnie almost laughed.

"In all fairness, love, he can't help who his father is. I'm the mayor's daughter," said Ginger.

"I'm the son of a state senator, so I also eat at fancy restaurants," said Donnie.

"I'm the daughter of a minister. I've never eaten at a place this fancy," said Pip.

"Really?" Donnie asked sarcastically.

"Yeah."

I knew where Donnie was going, and I gave him a look.

The waiter came over. "Good evening. I'm Walter, your waiter. It's my pleasure to welcome you to the Blue Abbot. May we start with refreshments?"

"I'll have a mocktail," said Ginger.

"Make that two," said Jessica.

Shayna wanted just water, and Jessica ordered a Coke.

"How about for you, gentlemen?"

We all ordered mists.

"Are you ready to order?" Walter asked.

German ordered the surf and turf combo, Donnie ordered linguini with scallops, Adam ordered the stuffed chicken with wild rice, and I ordered buffalo chicken sliders.

"And for the ladies?"

"Though it was rude for these handsome gentlemen to not let us order first, I'll take the cobb salad with grilled chicken," said Ginger.

Pip, Jessica, and Shayna ordered the same.

"You ladies come to a fancy restaurant and order salads?" asked Donnie.

"Considering you four ordered first, be thankful we're still here. Ladies, let's go to the restroom," said Ginger.

The women went to the restroom as we guys wondered what had just happened.

"Way to go, G," said Donnie.

"Me?" asked German.

"You did order first," I said.

"If I don't get laid tonight, I'm slapping you," said Donnie.

"Don't blame me. How the hell was I supposed to know that? I don't date women," German said as Donnie looked at Adam and smiled. Adam shook his head, and I was really confused. When the girls came back, we guys were awkwardly silent.

"You guys are really quiet. What happened?" asked Pip.

"Nothing," I said, and we kissed.

Donnie

After dinner, Ginger and I walked out behind the others.

"I've been thinking," said Ginger.

"Uh oh," I said.

"You ever think about being in a serious relationship with me?"

"Not really," I said.

She looked shocked. Ginger and I had had the understanding that we would have only a sexual relationship, friends with benefits.

"I'm starting to get feelings for you," she said.

"What kind of feelings?" I asked.

"I want more from you."

"Look, Ginger, I'm in a fraternity, remember?" I asked.

"So is Justin, but look at him and Pip. They're together."

"Justin is different from me," I said.

"Yeah, I know. He isn't an asshole."

We rejoined the other couples, and Ginger grabbed Shayna and walked off.

I walked up to German and asked, "What's up?"

"Ginger took Shayna away. What did you do?" German asked me.

Justin walked over. "Donnie? What the hell?"

"Ginger wants our relationship to be more than just sex, but I don't want that. Are you guys serious right now?" I asked.

"You're the one with commitment issues," said Adam.

Shayna, Jessica, and Pip walked over to us, but Ginger stayed away.

"Ginger's really upset," Pip said. "We called a car service. We're going to Jessica's."

"I can take you home," said Adam.

"It's OK," said Jessica.

Pip and Justin kissed, and Jessica gave Adam a hug.

"It was nice meeting you, and thanks for dinner," Shayna said as she hugged German.

The girls walk over to a minivan that had just pulled up.

"There goes sex," said Justin.

"I'm going to my condo to see if the video caught anything," said German.

"We'll go too. I don't want to be an Alpha More right now," said Adam.

At the condo, German reviewed the day's surveillance tapes.

"I'll be lucky if Jessica ever goes out with me again," said Adam.

"There's plenty of girls out there, Adam. You can find another," I said.

"You just can't help yourself," said Adam.

"I'm just saying," I said.

"There's nothing here," G said. "Just people installing her equipment."

We all got text messages about a house meeting.

"I'm not in the mood. I'm not going," I said.

"Donnie, you have to," said German.

"Not since I ruined your nights, all of you. Well, maybe not you, G," I said.

"What's that mean?" asked German.

"Nothing. Donnie's just being stupid," said Adam.

"Look. I'm not an idiot, Donnie. You've been coming at me for a while now. What's wrong?" asked German.

"Are you gay?" I asked. German's reaction confirmed for me that he was.

"No! Why would you ask me that?" asked German.

"Yeah, Donnie," Justin asked. "Why would you ask that, and why would that matter?"

"It doesn't," I said.

"Then why ask?" German asked.

I looked at Adam, which made German and Justin look at him as well.

"Don't put me in this. I told you it was stupid," said Adam.

German's highly disappointed look made me feel guilty. He went into his room.

"Was that really the best way to out your friend?" asked Adam.

"You know I didn't mean it that way," I said.

"You never do," said Adam.

Adam shook his head and left. I was really upset and started pacing the condo. I looked at the monitor and saw the Greek god removing his hood. I tried to zoom in to see if I could see his face. He put his hood back on, and I saw a fancy watch on his wrist. I rewound the footage and zoomed in on his watch, which I took a still shot of. I couldn't tell what kind it was, but it was a clue. I printed the picture and left the condo.

Back at Alpha More, we were sitting in the front row of the podium room, and Alves walked up to the stage. "Good evening, Alpha More. Because homecoming is in a few days, we need to focus on our float and talent show piece for the homecoming football game. I've been informed that our very own legacy, Chance Rigen, will be in attendance!"

"*Woot woot woot!*" and foot stomping was our response to that.

"Theta Monroe will be throwing the homecoming Greek affair, which means it will be black tie," said Alves.

I was disappointed that we had lost to Theta Monroe, but worse, I felt that Ginger was right. I had no intentions of making our relationship serious, but I needed to stop making it seem like how we were acting was OK.

"Any questions?" None of us had any, so Alves said, "All right, you're dismissed. Thanks."

I looked at German, Justin, and Adam as we walked out. "Let's go to G's room. I want to show you something," I said.

We got to G's room, and Justin closed the door.

"What's up? Adam asked.

"Look at this picture," I said.

"I've seen that watch before," said German.

"Yeah, me too," I said.

"I'll be back," I said.

"Where're you going?" asked Justin.

"I have to make things right. G, I'm sorry, man. What I did was really shady. I love you just the way you are," I said and then left and headed to Theta Monroe.

There, I walked around the back and saw Ginger and her sorority sisters in the kitchen. I knocked on the window, they saw me, and Ginger went over to open the door.

"What do you want?" she asked.

"Can we talk?" I asked.

She came out onto the deck.

"I know we've had this sexual relationship from since we were freshmen, but I had no idea you wanted more," I said.

"You had to have known, Donnie."

"How would I have?" I asked. She was silent. I grabbed her hand. "If you weren't going to tell me, how would I have known what you really wanted?"

"I thought that one day you'd see me differently, beyond sex, but you haven't. Part of that is my fault for not making my boundaries clear. Starting today, we'll no longer have sex. I don't want anything if I can't have it all."

She just went back into the house, but I was glad I'd gotten that off my chest.

CHAPTER 10

HOMECOMING PART I

Justin

HEARD MY ALARM clock go off and then Donnie yelling, "Bro! Shut it off!"

I turned it off and stretched. Donnie had his back to me. He seemed irritated.

"You all right?" I asked.

"I'm good, man. Just tired."

We heard a knock. German came in. "I got a call from my dad. He and my stepmom are coming for homecoming."

"Are you surprised? I remember Paris lived for homecoming. Remember our float from last year?" Donnie asked.

"I remember," said German.

"What was it again?" I asked.

"It was the Wiz," said German.

We all chuckled; Donnie seemed to be in better spirits.

"What's up with you? You seem down," German said to Donnie.

"Ginger's mad at me. She said she was done having sex with me unless I got more serious with her," he said.

"What's wrong with that?" asked German.

"You really have to ask?" I asked, and German laughed.

"In all seriousness, Donnie, you always find your way back to her even when you have other ladies. Maybe she's the one," said German.

"G, get out of here. You're scaring me," said Donnie.

Adam walked in. "Hey, G, Mr. Alves is looking for you."

"Saved by Mr. Alves," said Donnie.

"I'll be right back," said German.

Adam sat on the bed. "what's wrong?"

"Don't ask," I said.

"Can I catch a ride with one of you? My car's still in the shop," Adam asked.

"I thought it was just a tire," I said.

"There's a gas leak as well."

"I'll give you a ride. Give me twenty minutes," said Donnie.

"Cool. Thanks, bro," said Adam.

"I have to meet Pip for breakfast. I'll see you at lunch," I said.

I walked out of the room and saw Drake coming down the hall. "Good morning, Justin."

"Good morning, Detective," I said.

"I'm looking for German Rigen."

Just then, German came out and saw Drake. "Just the person I was looking for," said Drake.

"How can I help you?" asked German.

"I have a search warrant here and also a signed consent form to review your transactions at the seven banks listed in the warrant," Drake said smirking.

I was really nervous, but German seemed calm and poised. He signed the form and said, "I have nothing to hide."

"You both have a good day," Drake said. He left.

"I got a bad feeling about this," I said.

"He'll come to dead ends on each account. The one he's looking for isn't in my name."

"OK," I said, but I was confused.

I drove to Pendleton and saw Pip next to her car. "Morning," I said.

"Good morning," Pip said, and we kissed.

"So about last ni—" I started saying.

"Don't worry about it. It wasn't you. It was your roommate."

"Donnie's a real good guy. It's because of him that I'm in Alpha More," I said.

"Ginger was really upset last night. If he could do that to her, how good could he be?"

I was quiet about that because I didn't feel Donnie was wrong for not wanting more.

"So homecoming is here and I'm not going to be available as much," I said.

"I understand," Pip said, and we kissed; she headed for her class.

Brandon walked up; I wasn't expecting to see him at school. "Hey, Justin."

"What's up?" I asked.

"My mom's delivering a big flower order to Theta Monroe for the homecoming party, and we could use an extra hand. Do you think you and the other guys could help? You'd be doing me a huge favor."

"Sure. I'll talk to the guys about it," I said.

"Thanks, man. See you later," Brandon said as he attempted to walk away.

"Hey, Brandon." I pulled out the picture of him and Ben at the party. "I didn't know you were at the same party the night you brother died," I said.

"Yeah. He begged me to dress in the same clothes and act like I was him. We did that a lot. Even our parents couldn't tell us apart at times, so we figured no one else would either."

"And your brother was deaf?"

"More like hard of hearing. He'd been diagnosed with Meniere's disease, constant ringing in the ear. The doctors said that he'd likely lose the majority of his hearing as it progressed."

"Sorry to hear that," I said.

"Thanks, man. I'm late for class. Thanks again for helping us out."

I couldn't believe that I agreed to help. I knew that Donnie, Adam, and German would kill me once I told them. I ate a lot when I was nervous, and I was nervous about helping Brandon and his mother. At lunch, I sat with Donnie, Adam, and German. "Hey, guys, I need to talk to you," I said.

"I was just filling them in on something I need to talk to you about," said German, who pulled out a picture. "I got a match on the watch. It's a Rolex GMT Master 1675. It's vintage, and only a few stores sell them. The last store to sell this particular watch was a place in Manhattan; it sold it in 1988. I'm not going to have access to my money for seventy-two hours, so I need you guys to go there in my place."

"G, what's going on?" asked Donnie.

German looked at me as I knew what Drake had found. I nodded at him, and he said, "Jo-Sally transferred a hundred million to an alias account I have. The FBI wasn't able to find the account, so they sent that case to Drake, who's investigating my bank accounts."

"Are any of them the big one?" asked Adam.

"No," said German.

"Then why are you worried?" asked Donnie.

"My dad has no idea that I inherited three hundred million from Jo-Sally's estate along with her possessions. He also doesn't know I received seventy-five million as the reward for finding the paintings or that I have investments grossing over fifty million a year."

"You're afraid that your father will find out if you leave town?" I asked.

"Exactly."

We all looked at each other and agreed to go to the jewelry store.

"Before I forget," I said, "I talked to Brandon about that party. He told me that Ben and he were there to strengthen his chances of getting into Alpha More."

"Then how do we know that was really Ben?" asked Adam. We all looked at him in confusion. "C'mon! I can't be the only person who thought of that possibility!"

"I think it would be odd that his family would bury him knowing that he was living in our house," said German.

"G kind of has a point," said Donnie.

"Please don't kill me, but I agreed to help Brandon and his mother deliver flowers to Theta Monroe. Uh, I also volunteered you guys as well."

The three of them look at each other. "Justin, you're a freaking genius!" said German.

"He is?" asked Donnie.

"Guys, if we have access to the inside, we can snoop around and maybe find more details about who that Greek god is," said German.

"That is indeed genius," said Donnie.

"Meet me at my condo tonight," German said.

Drake

I walked into the forensics lab. "Boyd, how's it going?" I asked our tech analyst.

"This is one smart investor. He has over fifty million in investments," he said.

"Anything on that hundred-million-dollar transfer for Bangladesh?"

"Nothing that I can see. All four hundred and twenty-five million are legal funds."

"Impossible," I said.

"I ran through all the funds in the last eighteen hours. Every transaction, transfer, and deposit is legitimate, Detective."

"How's it possible that a twenty-year-old is worth that much?" I asked.

"He hasn't made one bad investment from what I can see."

"So there's nothing suspicious?" I asked.

"There's one thing," Boyd said as he brought up a specific transaction on screen. "There's a security company that he owns that deals with military intelligence software. When I pulled the LLC, I found out that it was under an alias. It's in an old warehouse in Hartford, Connecticut."

"How's it profitable if it's an alias and has military intelligence software?" I asked.

"How about selling this software back to the military?" Boyd asked.

"You think Rigen gained access to military intelligence and sold it back to our government under an alias?" I asked.

"It's a theory, but I can't prove it."

"What if I were to get you his laptop? I tried hacking into it, but he caught me," I said. "When I plugged a flash drive into it, it sent him a signal and took my picture."

"You have proof it took a picture of you?"

"Why do you ask?" I asked.

"That might be able to prove my theory."

Boyd's theory was the move I needed to make. I knew I could find what I needed to frame German Rigen.

German

I pulled up to Alpha More, parked, and went in, where I saw Brandon.

"Hey, G, did Justin tell you about the favor I needed?" he asked.

"Yes. We're all down," I said.

"Cool! Thanks, man. I appreciate it. Later." He walked off.

I went to my room. I opened the door and heard my dad and Mr. Alves laughing.

"Dad!" I said.

"Hey, son," he said.

My father was a famous NFL player as well as an Alpha More legacy.

"German, your dad wanted to see this room. Hope you don't mind," said Alves.

"Don't be silly! This was my room before it was his," my dad said.

"I'll leave you two alone," Alves said as he walked out.

I didn't want Alves to leave as sometimes I got nervous around my dad.

"I like what you've done with the room, son. Very nice."

"Thanks," I said.

"Is there something you want to tell me, son?"

"No," I said with confidence.

"So you come into this room to lie to me?" Chance asked as he came up to me.

"Lie about what?" I asked in a sharp tone that my dad caught right away.

"Watch your tone before you lose your tongue," he said. "Tell me why the police are investigating your trust fund."

"I don't know," I said.

"Boy, if you lie to me again," he said as he raised his hand.

"The detective reopened Ben Klovis's case, and he's checking every angle," I said.

"What would your bank account have to do with the death of this young man?"

The door opened. Paris came in. "Yo! I'm here!"

I hadn't known he was coming, but I was glad he had. I was about to get my ass whipped.

"Dad, why are you looking so serious?" asked Paris.

"Your brother's actions. Do you need a room at the hotel, son?"

"No. I'm going to bunk here with G and help out with the float."

"Oh good. I'll let you get settled in. Don't forget we're having dinner with Senator Diamante and the first lady tonight. German, make sure you bring Donnie as well."

"Yes sir," I said as my dad left.

"Haven't seen Dad this mad since you took his Ferrari to Gwendolyn Nelson's party," Paris said.

"Shut up. I thought you had your internship this weekend," I said.

"Uhh, about that. I never got that internship. I told Dad that just so he wouldn't check my trust fund."

"Where have you been?" I asked.

"Indonesia. I met this girl, and I really like her, G." I looked at him and folded my arms. He said, "Don't hate!"

"I'm going to the store. You need anything?" I asked.

"No. I'm going to take a shower and get dressed for dinner."

"All right," I said as I walked out of the room thinking that this was going to be a long weekend.

I started my car, and I got a call on Bluetooth. It was Donnie. "Hey," I said.

"Hey, bro, we're on our way back."

"Any luck on the watch?" I asked.

"None. The place wasn't open today, G."

"Figures," I said.

"Any word on Drake and your bank accounts?"

"No," I said. "I'm about to call my lawyer and see what my options are. Also, your dad is on the way. We're having dinner with our parents. My dad wanted me to extend the invite," I said.

"Oh that's just great!" Donnie said sarcastically.

"I'll see you at my condo," I said.

"Later," said Donnie.

I called my lawyer and asked him to meet me in front of the restaurant below my condo. I didn't know what Drake was going to find going through my bank accounts. Farnsworth said he'd meet me in ten minutes, which relieved me. When I got there, Farnsworth was getting out of his Mercedes-Benz briefcase in hand. "Mr. Rigen, nice to see you," he said.

"Thanks for coming," I said.

"My pleasure. I took the liberty of looking into the case the FBI sent to Drake." He pulled out a folder and handed it to me, and I started reading it. The FBI was investigating the money laundering that Jo-Sally had been doing before we'd met. "I'm confused," I said.

"You and I were both confused when I found out that after reading this case, the detective was successful in getting a warrant considering this case had nothing to do with you."

"What do we do now?" I asked.

"We wait to see the outcome. Trust me, if you're arrested, I'll bail you out in a minute."

"Thanks for that," I said.

"Sure. I'll be in touch."

Farnsworth went back to his car. I went up to my condo, sat on my couch, and was deep in thought. I didn't know what to expect, but I knew I had to be ready.

The three of them walked in. "G, that was a waste of time," said Donnie.

"I know, but I appreciate your going down there," I said.

"Any updates on Drake?" asked Justin.

"Not yet, but the warrant was only for seventy-two hours, so I'm sure he hasn't found anything," I said.

"What time's dinner?" asked Donnie.

"In an hour. I got tuxedos for all of you," I said as I handed each a wardrobe bag.

"G, I can't accept this," said Adam.

"They're paid for. As much as I want to go in jeans and kicks, we have to dress up," I said. "Try them on. I have to go to Alpha More to pick up Paris. I'll meet you guys at the restaurant," I said as I walked out abruptly. I was running late; my dad would give me a hard time about that.

Paris and I arrived at Kendall's, a popular steakhouse. My dad and stepmom were waiting in the lobby. "You two are late," said Chance.

"Oh stop it," said Verna.

Verna Rigen was Paris's mom. Our dad had an affair with my mom twenty years ago, and she had died in the process of giving birth to me.

Verna never treated us any differently when we were growing up, and she referred to me as her son. Paris gave Verna a hug and a kiss on the cheek.

She looked at me with a huge smile. "Come give your mom a hug."

I hugged Verna and saw my dad giving me an evil look.

"Why were you late, German?" he asked.

"Oh Chance, stop it. The senator and the first lady aren't even here yet," said Verna.

"I'm sorry. I had an errand to run," I said.

"Where's Donnie?" asked Chance.

"He, Justin, and Adam are on the way," I said.

"I thought I told you to bring him with you," said Chance.

Before I could answer, Senator Diamante and his wife arrived. My father and the senator hugged, and my dad gave his wife a light kiss on the cheek.

Senator Diamante looked at Paris and me. "Hello, boys."

"Senator Diamante," I said.

"Good to see you two. Where's Donnie?" he asked.

"Right here," said Donnie, who had just walked up.

"Hey, son," the senator said and hugged Donnie.

"Hey, Mom," said Donnie as he hugged his mom.

Adam and Justin hugged my and Donnie's parents, and the waiter let us know our table was ready. We all followed him, but Donnie and I stayed a bit behind. "I want to be anywhere but here," I told him. I sat with my friends and far from my father. Paris sat next to us in case our parents started talking about something boring; he could then sneak into our conversation. I looked at Donnie. I was beginning to get annoyed with being there. I kept making faces at him, which made him laugh.

Donnie

Sitting across from German was hilarious, but I spotted his father giving him the serious parent look, which made him stop. I chuckled quietly.

"Everyone, order whatever you want. Dinner's on me," said Chance.

"Don't have to ask me twice," I said as I looked at the menu.

"Do you recommend anything here, G?" asked Adam.

"Ribeye is the best here," he said.

"I couldn't even afford the mac and cheese side," said Justin.

"So what's the theme for the Alpha More after-party?" asked Paris.

"You'll have to check with Theta Monroe," German said.

"Wait. Why would it be at Theta Monroe?" asked Paris.

"Because of the yearly charity event we lost to them with the ticket sales," said German.

"Are you serious? How could you have lost to Theta Monroe?" asked Paris.

We were silent. Paris shook his head and laughed as if he were disgusted with us. "You know what you have to do, right? You have to win the homecoming float. Once we win, they'll have no choice but to forfeit."

"Yeah, but how will we prepare for the party?" asked Justin.

"Don't tell me you four all got lazy on me," said Paris.

"Look, just because you had all that booze while you were in the house doesn't mean we all live by the same guidelines," said German.

"I can't even tell you the last time I was at a Theta Monroe party," said Paris.

We ate and talked as our parents talked politics. I saw German look at his phone and look up in frustration. "What's wrong?" I mouthed to him. German slid his phone to me. One of our brothers had texted him, "Detective Drake is looking for you." I looked at German as I gave him his phone back. "Excuse me," I said as I stood. German, Adam, and Justin followed me to the lobby.

"What's going on?" asked Justin.

"Do you think he's found something?" I asked.

"I don't know. Let's just go to my condo after we see the float at Alpha More," German said.

Chance walked up. "What are you guys doing out here?"

"We were talking about the float, Dad. Did you pick a theme?" asked German.

"I did. The float will be 'Thriller,' by Michael Jackson."

I saw that German wasn't too thrilled, and neither was I.

"I'll see you fellas at the table," said Chance as he walked back to the table.

"Thriller?" asked Adam.

"We'll fill you in," I said as we returned to the table.

After dinner, we drove back to Alpha More. In front was a tow hitch with a graveyard. We were confused. We saw Paris and Chance smiling.

"What the hell is this?" I whispered to German.

"Haven't you ever seen Michael Jackson's music video?" he whispered.

"Gentlemen, here we are," said Chance.

The rest of Alpha More was coming out to see the float.

"Let's go to the backyard to learn the dance routine," said Paris.

"Dance routine?" I asked.

I felt that Chance and Paris were crazy for even having had this idea, but Adam and Justin didn't seem to have an issue with it.

"Yes! We're Alpha More!" said Paris.

I looked at German; we were both annoyed with the idea his brother and father were throwing at us.

All fifty of us headed to the backyard. My father and Chance met up with Alves on the porch as we began to line up. Paris started giving us the routine's steps. "OK, guys, one two three four five six seven eight, bop, bop, bop, bop!"

I was trying my hardest not to laugh. Only German and I weren't taking Paris seriously.

"G, why aren't you moving?" asked Paris.

"Because I know this routine better than you do."

"Oh well then, show your big bro," said Paris.

German walked up and did the same steps a lot sharper than Paris had. I had to admit my boy German could do anything. I was very proud. The whole house and even Paris clapped; he was amazed to see his little brother shine. I looked to the right and saw Drake walking into the backyard, which surprised me. German, Adam, Justin, and I looked at each other as Drake walked over to my dad, Chance, and Alves. The four of us walked over as the guys were learning the dance routine. We weren't sure what to expect, but we knew it wouldn't be good.

"Senator Diamante, Mr. Rigen, it was a pleasure to meet you," said Drake as we walked up to the porch. "German Rigen! Just who I was looking for."

"German, what's this about?" asked Chance.

"I just came to say that your bank accounts have been released and that I have a warrant to confiscate your laptop," said Drake.

"German, answer me!" said Chance.

Drake looked at German and smiled.

"May I see the warrant please?" asked German.

Drake gave German the warrant as Chance began to get angry. "German, you know I only ask once. What's going on?"

"Aren't you going to answer your father?" asked Drake.

"Dad, can you come upstairs with me please?" asked German.

The two walked into the house. Drake looked very pleased with himself. "Senator Diamante, I have a question for you," asked Drake.

"Yes, Detective?" the senator asked.

"Are you up for reelection next year?" asked Drake.

"Yes sir, and hope to be governor soon," said the senator.

Chance and German came back out. "Here it is, all unlocked and open," said German.

"Thank you, sir. Well, gentleman, it's been nice. I'll be in touch, German," said Drake.

Drake walked away, and German signaled us to come inside.

"German, we're not finished talking, son," said Chance.

"I know, Dad. We'll come back to this conversation," said German.

We went to G's room, and he said, "OK, listen. I gave Drake my new laptop. He won't find anything but a bunch of math problems and poems."

"What about your dad? He seemed pissed," Justin said.

"I'm not worried about him right now. Drake's trying to tie me to Jo-Sally's money- laundering scheme. I'm not tied to those accounts, but the information he has could take down her family. If they find out that I took all her investments, they'll come after me," said German.

"What do you want to do?" I asked.

"We need to get that FBI file from Drake," said German.

"How are we supposed to do that?" asked Adam.

"I'm going to look in the precinct. I need you guys to search his house," said German.

"Are you asking us to break into a detective's house?" asked Justin.

We all looked at German as if he'd gone crazy.

"I don't have a choice. Either you're with me or you're not," he said.

That made us feel guilty. We agreed to help him.

Adam

On homecoming day, my alarm went off. I looked over and didn't see Brody in his bed, but I saw a notebook under it. I went and picked it up. I knew I shouldn't open it, but since Brody was acting strangely and was working with Drake, I figured why not. I opened it and read dates and times involving the four of us. Brody had been keeping a good eye on us. I went to Justin's and Donnie's room. "Guys, look what I found," I said. "I found this under Brody's bed."

"What were you doing under Brody's bed?" asked Donnie.

"That's not the point. Look at this," I said as I opened the notebook. Donnie and Justin looked at the notebook and gave me confused looks. "We know he was working with Drake. This is what he was doing; he was piecing all our schedules together so that when we were alone, we could be attacked," I said.

"We have to tell G," said Donnie.

"Paris is up there. We can't right now," said Justin.

"Let's show him at lunch. We have to get the file for him," I said.

"I don't know, Adam. G wants us to commit breaking and entering on a detective's place. What happens if he shoots us?" asked Justin.

"He won't," said Donnie. "He's not going to be home when we do it."

We looked at each other in agreement.

When I got to school, I saw Jessica, who said, "Hey, Adam! I tried calling you."

"Sorry. I've been busy. It's homecoming week, and to a fraternity, that's almost as bad as finals," I said.

"I just wondered if you wanted to go get coffee."

"Yeah, but after homecoming," I said.

"Great. I'll see you around."

I walked into the cafeteria anxious to tell German about the notebook. I saw him, Donnie, and Justin at a table, and I sat. German said, "They told me you have something to show me."

"I do. Take a look at this," I said as I gave it to him.

German started turning the pages. "This is how Drake got into my room and got on my computer. He knew I wasn't going to be there. Does Brody have anything else?"

"Like what?" I asked.

"I don't know ... emails, books, anything," said German.

"G, I don't think we need anything else. I mean, c'mon. This proves that Drake's working off the badge," I said.

"It's not enough. I need something more concrete. This proves only that Brody has some crazy obsession with us, and though it's odd, it doesn't make him Greek god," said German.

He had a point. This information wasn't enough to prove that Brody was the Greek god, but it did prove that he was playing a role in this. I was willing to look for more information.

German, Donnie, and I drove to Klovis's flower shop. When we walked in, Brandon, Justin, and Pip greeted us.

"Hey, guys, I appreciate you coming on such short notice. Thanks," Brandon said.

"Guys, Mrs. Klovis and Brandon gave us a little education about the flowers," said Justin.

"Nice. So what exactly are we doing?" German asked.

Mrs. Klovis entered the room. "The arrangements are in the sunroom in back," she said.

We went there and saw the arrangements Theta Monroe had ordered. "How many arrangements are there?" asked German.

"Mrs. Mack ordered fifty," she said.

"We're celebrating fifty years of Pendleton homecomings in conjunction with the Greek system," German said.

"Oh, I didn't realize that fifty had a meaning," said Klovis. "I'll have five vans out there. Each can hold ten arrangements. I'll need one of you to stay back and lock up after we leave."

"I'll do it," I said.

"Thank you, Adam. Brandon will direct the rest of the crew to the vans and show them how to properly place the arrangements."

"You got it, Mom," said Brandon as Klovis and I walked to her office.

"The keys are always left in this green box," she said as she opened the box and pulled out a ring of keys. "I really appreciate you four coming to help me despite what's happened between us. I'm happy we're moving forward, Adam."

I didn't know what to say or even how to acknowledge her. In the hallway, we passed a door that was cracked open. "The delivery door has a padlock. I won't be getting any deliveries today, so I'll lock it," she said. "Before you lock the front door, set the alarm. The alarm code is zero five two three. I'll write that down for you. Any questions, Adam?"

"No ma'am," I said.

The others were almost finished loading the vans. German said, "Good call on staying, Adam. Scope the place out. See what else you can find."

"I'll take one van," Klovis said. "Brandon, you, Donnie, German, and Justin take the others. Thanks again, Adam."

They left, and I closed the door and started looking around. I walked back to that door in the hallway and looked in; I saw a cot in the room. I turned on the light and tripped a breaker. "Damn!" I yelled as the door closed. It wouldn't open, which meant the lock was broken or someone had locked me in.

"Hello?" I asked. "*Hello!*" No answer. I knew that the Greek god was there.

CHAPTER 11

HOMECOMING PART II

Adam

ELLO!" I YELLED a third time with still no response. I pulled out my phone to call someone and saw that I had just 2 percent power remaining. I called German.

"Hello?"

"G, I need you to come back. I'm locked in a room," I said as my phone cut off. "Damn!" I heard a scraping sound. I saw a shadowy figure I just knew was the Greek god. I ducked as he swung his axe, which went through the door, letting some light in. I tackled him and hit him in the face. The hole he had made in the door was big enough for me to fit my hand through, and I was able to reach out and turn the doorknob. I tried to close it, but the Greek god was pushing on it. I let him push it a bit, and when he stopped, I slammed it closed, and I heard him fall. I closed the door and locked it, and I pushed a table against it. I ran out of the shop, closed the door, and ran to G's car. I got in, but he had taken the keys. "Damn!"

The Greek god ran out, jumped on the hood, and slammed his axe through the windshield, which made me jump into the back seat. He was pulling his axe out of the shattered window when the car was struck from behind. It was German in a rental van. The Greek god slid off the hood and took off. I got out of the car, and German got out of the van.

116

"You OK, Adam?"

"Yeah. What about you?" I asked.

"I'm fine, but it looks like we lost him."

We hopped in the van, but it wouldn't start. "Damn!"

"You did crash into your own car with this," I said.

"I did that to make sure he didn't get to you!"

A police car pulled up. "Gentlemen, are you OK?" an officer asked.

"We're fine," I said.

We waited as the officer called in the accident. I was sorry I was letting Klovis down.

About thirty minutes later, Drake pulled up, much to German's annoyance. "Well, well, Adam Banks and my friend German Rigen. I'd ask what happened, but it's clear one of you crashed into this parked car, which looks like German's. How'd this happen?"

"I was helping Mrs. Klovis deliver flowers. I'd forgotten my wallet. I turned around and lost control of the van," said German.

"Not believable," said Drake.

"I don't care what you believe. That's what happened, Detective."

"Mr. Banks, do you attest to this?"

"Yes sir," I said.

Drake smirked at that. "What happened to the windshield?"

"Must have happened in the accident," said German.

G and I saw that Drake wasn't convinced.

We saw Donnie, Justin, and Pip. "G? Adam? You guys OK?" Donnie asked.

"We're fine," said German.

Klovis and Brandon arrived. "Oh my goodness! Are you OK?" she asked.

"Peachy," G said.

"You're all good to go," said Drake.

"I'll handle the van situation," said Klovis. "Get home safe, everyone."

Donnie looked at Pip and shook his head in disbelief.

"I'm going to help my mom," Brandon said. "Any of you need a ride?"

"No, we're good," I said.

We walked across the street to German's condo carefully to make sure we were not seen. When we got in, Donnie asked, "What happened?"

"Greek god attacked me," I said.

"She did that on purpose," said Donnie.

"Look. We don't know anything right now," said German.

"G, what about your car?" I asked.

"I'm getting one of my SUVs sent to me. It'll be here in a couple of hours."

German's phone rang. He looked at it. "It's Paris." He put the call on speaker. "What up?"

"Where are you guys? We need your help with the float."

"We Got into an accident. We're waiting on my other car to get here. We'll be over soon, P."

"Are you OK?" Paris asked.

"I'm fine. Just don't tell Dad."

"See you when you get here. Bye," said Paris.

German turned to us. "Guys, let's regroup. We need to stick to the same story. Giving Drake a story about that Greek god in front of other people will just take him out of the equation and make us look guilty of something."

"Yeah, but don't you think sooner or later everyone will find out?" asked Justin

"We'll cross that bridge later. Less is always best." He got a text. "My car's outside."

Drake

Things were getting odd. Rigen and Banks had lied about what had happened. I felt German had purposely crashed that van to cover something up. I went back to Klovis's shop and asked, "What the hell happened?"

"I don't know," she said.

"Do you have any idea how risky this behavior is?" I asked.

"You're talking to the wrong person, Detective."

"Where is he?" I asked. I heard a knock on the wall behind me. I turned and saw the man in the Greek hooded gown. "Who the hell are you?" I asked.

The person started signing.

"Can he not hear me?" I asked.

"He can hear you. He just chooses not to speak. He signed that not knowing me is a part of the process."

"What does that mean?" I asked.

The person signed again, and Klovis explained, "He said that he has his own issues with those four and not to worry. He's not going to kill them. He just wants to scare them."

"I don't know what kind of games you two are playing, but I'm not leaving until he reveals who he is," I said.

The person signed some more. "He said that you know who he is, that we both know."

"Is he your son?" I asked.

"Brandon?" asked Katheryn.

Something about that didn't feel right. I walked out to my car and called Bradshaw. My call went to voice mail. "Meet me at the coroner's office immediately."

I drove to the hospital coroner's office and found Doug Lucey. "Hey, Doug," I said.

"Detective, how can I help you?"

"I need to review Klovis's autopsy again. If I told you why, you'd think I was crazy," I said.

"There's nothing I haven't heard before."

"How was Klovis identified?" I asked.

"His mother identified the body," said Doug.

"Was there any affirmative action to fingerprint him?" I asked.

"Are you going to tell me the crazy story?"

"I believe Ben's alive and the person buried is not him," I said.

Bradshaw walked in. "Not only is that crazy, it's impossible."

"Regardless, I want Ben Klovis to be reexamined and identified," I said.

"Right away," said Doug.

Bradshaw and I walked out of the room. "I don't think Ben Klovis is dead. I'm going to prove it," I said.

Justin

We pulled up to Alpha More and saw our brothers dressed up as zombies. Instead of looking like those in Jackson's "Thriller" video, they looked like the cast of *Dawn of the Dead*.

"Guys, are you OK?" asked Paris.

"We're fine," said German.

"I'm glad. Your costumes are in G's room. I need you guys down here in ten," said Paris.

We went up to German's room. "I'm glad Paris bought the right costumes," said German.

"Did you guys see the others?" asked Adam.

"Yeah. Did Paris hire a mortician?" asked Donnie.

We chuckled as we put on our costumes. We went downstairs, where the makeup artist turned us into zombies.

Paris came in. "OK, guys, ten minutes until we leave."

We heard a noise and saw the Theta Monroe float coming. The Thetas were dressed in lingerie; their float was full-tilt burlesque. The Thetas break into a dance routine and yelled, "Theta, Theta, burn. We are Theta Monroe! Sign out!"

They drove off, and Paris shook his head. "They don't know who they're messing with."

We began walking with our float to campus, a quarter-mile down the road. We lined up with the other Greek houses; our campus had five fraternities and five sororities. To see the entire Greek system rally with different floats was awesome. We lined up with Theta Monroe leading Alpha Core, Beta Tin, Sigma Ly, and Omega Pa Zeta.

Brandon walked up to Adam and me. "Hey, Adam, I didn't get a chance to say something earlier. How are you?"

"Fine, thanks."

"What happened?" asked Brandon.

"Right now's not the time, Brandon," said Adam.

Adam and I walked away. "That felt really awkward," I said.

"I feel he knows something, so let's keep quiet about it for now."

We entered the football field at halftime. We'd all get four minutes to perform. Other houses were up before us, so we had some time to practice.

"Justin!" Pip yelled. I ran over to her, and she said, "Hi! You look so cute!"

"I need to talk to you," I said.

"What's wrong?"

"Is there something you want to tell me?" I asked.

"What are you talking about?" she asked.

"I can see that Brandon spooks you. You said you'd never met him before, but I feel you're lying," I said.

Pip gave me an upset look. "When I saw him in your room, I thought he was Ben. They look so identical. I never really got closure when Ben died."

Though something about the situation still seemed off, she was my girlfriend, so I had no choice but to trust what she was saying.

"Give it up for Theta Monroe!" the announcer said.

"I have to go," I told Pip and walked over to our float.

"Pendleton University, give it up for Alpha More!" said the MC. Our float sprayed steam, and the crowd cheered. We did the dance routine as the song played. I was a little stiff, but no one noticed that. I'd have to admit that Paris had called this one just right; it was super cool.

After our dance routine, Chance, German's dad, appeared on the float, and the MC said, "Pendleton, give it up for six-time Super Bowl winner Chance Rigen!" The crowd cheered, and he took a bow. The performances ended, and the crowd dispersed. Many wanted Chance's autograph. German, Adam, Donnie, and I went off to the side.

"You all right, Justin?" asked German.

"Not quite. I've been watching Pip behaving weirdly around Brandon almost as if he knew something she's not telling me."

Donnie had that look in his eye, and he smiled. "You think he slept with her?"

"What? No!" I said.

"It makes perfect sense. You couldn't tell those two apart," said Donnie.

"C'mon, Donnie. Brandon wouldn't have done that to his own brother," said Adam.

The announcer called us back to the field; the judges had called a winner for the float competition, and it was Alpha More. The crowd cheered, and Ginger's look was priceless. She looked very disappointed, and I knew Donnie wasn't going to let that slide.

German

After the game, we went back to get our makeup off. When I got out the shower and into my room, my dad was sitting on my bed. "Dad!" I said.

"Come here, son. Sit down."

I put on my robe and sat next to him.

"Son, I don't know what kind of trouble you're in, but you're a grown man now."

"I'm not in trouble, Dad. They're just trying to tie up loose ends in the Klovis case," I said.

"OK. We're going," he said as he stood and kissed my forehead. "You might not believe me, but I do love you, son."

He walked out leaving me in shock; he'd just told me he loved me, but I never felt he had.

My phone rang. It was Drake. "Hello," I said.

"I need you to meet me in one hour."

"What's this about?" I asked.

"I know this will be hard for you to do, but I need you to trust me."

"OK, fine," I said.

"I'll text you the address. German, come alone."

I hung up and was getting dressed when Donnie and Justin came in.

"Yo, G, I'm starving. Where are we eating?" Donnie asked.

"I have to run an errand. Get Adam and meet me at my condo, I'll order pizza from the car," I said as I rushed out.

I got in my car. The text from Drake told me to go to a diner in Rochester, New Hampshire, an hour away. The place was empty except for Drake, who was at a table.

"You can't tell anyone what I'm about to tell you," he said. "I don't think Ben Klovis is dead."

"What?" I asked.

"The body was never identified by fingerprints or dental records."

"But Mrs. Klovis identified the body. She told you it was her son," I said.

"Correct."

"So because they're twins they would share the same DNA so running that wouldn't make a difference?" I asked.

"Exactly."

"Why are you telling me this?" I asked.

"I feel that Ben is the one attacking you and your friends," said Drake. "I want to set a trap. I talked to Mr. Alves, and he said that you'd be at a sorority house party tonight. I want you to stray from the party and get back to Alpha More so we can catch him," Drake said. He left.

I drove back to my condo; Adam, Donnie, and Justin were watching TV and eating pizza.

"Have some pizza, G. You know Theta Monroe party food sucks," said Donnie.

"Where you been?" asked Adam.

"I met with Drake," I said.

"You what?" asked Adam.

"You crazy?" asked Justin.

"Why? asked Donnie.

"He reached out to me. He told me that he believed Ben wasn't dead. He said that the body had not been scientifically proven to be his, Twins share the same DNA," I said.

"Yeah, but we pulled him out of the water. We knew he was dead!" said Justin.

"The night of the party, he said he was Ben Klovis," said Adam.

"I know how it sounds, but I believe in the possibility that it could be true," I said.

"How?" asked Justin.

"I'm going to help him prove it," I said.

"G, what about the FBI file he has on you? This could be a trap," said Donnie.

"I know. That's why you three are going to get the file back. My leak in the precinct searched his desk. The file wasn't there, so it has to be at his home," I said.

"G, I have a bad feeling about this," said Justin.

"You guys will be fine," I said. "Drake's going to be at Theta Monroe's party tonight, which means you three can go to his house, find the file, and get back to the party before anybody realizes you're not there." I go to the closet to get the gear—three black suits, rubber shoes, and ski masks.

"G, you really are crazy," said Donnie.

"When you get the file, put in my room in my safe. The code is Donnie's birthday," I said.

"Twelve twenty-four," said Justin.

"Wait for my signal," I said as I walked out of the condo.

I walked up to Theta Monroe in my black-tie wardrobe as Young Hollywood was the theme. The ladies were in the hallway serving drinks. A hired butler took my jacket.

Ginger walked over to me wearing a purple, velvet, fishtail dress and said, "G? Wow. You look very handsome."

"And you look beautiful. That dress is everything!" I said.

"You like?" asked Ginger.

"I love," I said.

"Where's you entourage?"

"They'll be here shortly," I said.

"Yeah, sure. What's Donnie up to?"

"I'm not sure what you mean," I said.

"Don't play dumb with me, German Rigen. I know you four are up to something."

"I showed up solo. If there's a plan, I don't know about it," I said as I walked out to the patio. A live band was playing, and people in fancy attire were dancing. I saw Drake, and I went over to him. He and I faced the crowd.

"You came alone. That's unusual," he said.

"You're not the first to notice that," I said.

"Are you still keeping our secret, Mr. Rigen?"

"Secrets are always safe with me," I said.

"I'm going to confront Katheryn Klovis tonight."

That threw me off. "How're you going to prove Ben's not dead?" I asked.

"I'm not going to confront her about the antics of that. I have feeling that she and her son are behind all of this—the attacks, the blackmail."

"You're going to turn on her just like that? Don't you think you're in too deep?" I asked.

"Nothing she has points to me. It's all on her and whoever that is."

"I want to know everything she has on us. I want to know her entire plan," I said.

"I'll give you everything I find out from her. What are you going to do once I give you the information?"

"I'm going to take her down," I said.

"You know I can't let you," said Drake.

The moment Drake said that, I felt that he would double-cross me, but I was five steps ahead of him. "Drake, you should have learned by now that I'm more than formidable. I'm more dangerous than anything you've ever laid eyes on. If you cross me, I'll bury your ass in that ugly suit," I said and walked off. I texted Donnie, "Now." It was showtime.

Donnie

I got the text from G. We got out of Adam's truck and took the backpack full of items we needed to break into Drake's house, the upper unit in a two-unit duplex. We circled to the backyard, and I said, "Guys, look." I pointed to a window that was cracked open. "Lift me up."

Justin and Adam joined hands, and I put a foot on them just like a cheerleader lift. I removed the screen, pushed the window up, and climbed in. I looked around to make sure no one was there and then stuck my head out the window. "It's clear. Come on." Justin lifted Adam, and I grabbed his hands and pulled him up and in. Justin had backed up. He ran across the yard and jumped up. Adam and I grabbed his hands and pulled him up and through the window.

"That was awesome!" I said.

"Focus," said Adam.

"Right," I said.

"Where do you think this file could be?" asked Justin.

"I don't know. Office, desk maybe. Let's look in there," I said.

We walked into the very clean and well-organized living room.

"There's a bookcase over there," Adam said and went to it.

I looked in Drake's bedroom and saw a dresser and two nightstands. I looked in the drawers and saw just neatly folded clothes. I saw just a gun in the drawer of one nightstand and nothing in the drawer of the other.

"It's not out there," said Justin coming into the room.

"It's not in here either," I said.

"There's a room at the end of the hall," said Adam.

We went there and entered the room, which contained a desk and files hanging in a rack. I picked up a red one and opened it. The title read, "FBI/German Rigen."

"This is it," I said. I looked up and saw Adam and Justin looking behind me. I turned and saw a Doberman growling at us. "Uh oh," I said.

"Uh oh is right. What the hell are we supposed to do now?" asked Adam.

"Not move," said Justin.

We went from nervous to terrified.

"We can't break eye contact," said Justin.

"No worries about that," said Adam.

"Justin, I swear if I get bit in the ass, I'm kicking you in yours!" I said.

"On three, let's jump out of this room," said Justin.

"You have lost your mind," said Adam.

"One," said Justin.

"Oh damn," I said.

"Two."

I took a deep breath.

"Three!" Justin said, and we jumped out of the room.

Justin tried to close the door, but the dog was in attack mode and was trying to fight his way out of the room.

"Go!" Justin yelled. He pushed on the door harder, and the dog retreated into the room. He closed the door, and we raced to leave the place the same way we had gotten in. Adam and I lowered Justin to the ground with the backpack holding the file. I then lowered Adam, and Justin grabbed him. I lowered myself, and they grabbed my feet. Adam gave me the screen, which I put in place. We got back to the car and drove off.

"We made it, thank God!" I said.

"Promise me we'll never do that again," said Adam.

"Why when we're so good at it?" I asked, and we all laughed.

We got back to Alpha More and parked in the lot. "Should we text G?" asked Justin.

"I'm on it," I said. I texted G with the good news. We went in and up to his room. I opened the safe and put the file in while Justin and Adam stood lookout. "Let's go," I said.

We went to our rooms to change clothes and then headed back to Theta Monroe. We snuck through the side entrance and went straight to the backyard, where German was waiting for us. "Is Drake still here?" asked Adam.

"He's right over there," German said as we all looked over at Drake, who smiled at us.

"He has a pretty dog," I said.

"A pretty dog?" asked German.

"Don't ask," said Justin.

"Drake said that he plans to confront Klovis," said German.

"When?" asked Justin.

"Tonight," said German.

"He has some balls," I said.

"I think he's being a tad bit irrational," said German.

"I agree," said Adam.

Ginger walked over to us. "Well, well, well, the four of you. Where is it?"

"Where's what?" asked Adam.

"I know you guys are up to something."

"I think you're paranoid," I said.

Ginger smirked at me, but then she asked, "Can I talk to you?"

"Sure," I said.

We walked off a bit, and I asked, "What's up?" with a smile.

"I miss you, Donnie. I overreacted that night. Once I thought about it, I knew that I was asking for something you couldn't give me."

"It's not that I don't want to give you that. It's that I'm having fun," I said.

"Don't I know that!"

I smiled at her knowing that she couldn't resist my smile. She smiled back, kissed me, and walked off leaving me all excited. I knew I'd get laid. I walked back to the guys, who were laughing.

"I guess you and Ginger are back on," said Adam.

"Oh yes. She wants me," I said as I grabbed German from behind.

"Get the hell off me!" he yelled.

Pip came over. I wasn't excited to see her.

"Hi guys," she said, but we all gave her the silent treatment, and that included Justin.

"Can I talk to you?" Pip asked Justin.

"I'll be back, guys," said Justin as he and Pip walked off.

"Bye!" I said.

"Donnie! You're such a jerk," said German.

I was still laughing. "Tell me something I don't know," I said.

All of this excitement, but all I could do was watch Justin to see what was going to happen.

Justin

Pip and I walked to the Theta Monroe gazebo. "I don't know what's going on between us. You seem different," she said.

"The only thing that's different is the new member of my fraternity house, your late boyfriend's twin brother, and your ghost response to his presence," I said.

"What do you want me to say?"

"The truth," I said.

Pip took a deep breath. "I'm not over Ben. I was using you to fill that void."

That crushed me. "We're done," I said, and I walked away.

I walked back to the guys, who could tell something was off.

"Everything OK?" asked Adam.

"We just broke up," I said. Donnie and German came over to comfort me. "I need to leave."

"Damn, man. I'm sorry, but we can't leave the party," said German.

"I have to get out of here before I lose it," I said.

I walked out of the house, and German, Donnie, and Adam followed me. When we got to Alpha More, we looked to our right and saw the Greek god with axe in hand.

When G started signing, Donnie asked, "What are you asking him?"

"Whether he's Ben or Brandon."

The Greek god shook his head, charged German, and swung his axe at him. German sidestepped him, and Donnie tackled him from the side;

Adam and I jumped on the guy, but he somehow was able to swing his axe, hit the three of us, and break free. He ran off.

"Donnie? You OK?" asked German.

"Yeah," said Donnie.

"C'mon! Let's get him!" said Adam.

We all ran to see where he had gone.

"Are you guys OK?" Mr. Alves asked as he appeared to our right.

"We were just attacked," said Adam.

"By whom?" Mr. Alves asked.

"We don't know," said Donnie.

Mr. Alves called the police, and Drake showed up shortly. "What happened?" he asked.

"My boys were attacked, Detective. This is the fourth time. I want answers," Alves said.

"Mr. Alves, I completely understand your concern. Please rest assured that we're doing everything we can to find whoever this is."

Drake looked at German as the police squad car arrived; he walked away. We all looked at each other as we knew he was going to confront Klovis.

After the police took our statements, we looked at each other. "What now?" asked Donnie.

"We know what he's up to," German said. "Let's go to the condo to see what happens."

We went there in German's car and immediately looked at the video. We saw Klovis and the Greek god.

"Drake hasn't made it in there yet," said German.

"Turn up the sound," Donnie said.

The Greek god signed something, and she asked him, "He wants to talk with us?"

"Katheryn!" Drake yelled as he approached Katheryn and the Greek god. "Everyone's getting suspicious. I need to know who you are," said Drake.

The Greek god signed something.

"What did he say?" Drake asked.

"He said that the four of them know who he is," said Klovis.

"Whoever this is is attacking them left and right. It's only a matter of time before the FBI joins in, and the trail will lead to me. I'm not having it!" said Drake.

"We're really close, Detective. We have them right where we want them," she said.

"Are you hearing yourself, Katheryn? His attacks are raising suspicion. I can't be involved in this. It's gone too far," said Drake.

"What are you saying?" Klovis asked.

"I'm out," said Drake. He turned around to leave, but the Greek god pulled out a gun and shot him.

"That did not just happen!" I said.

"He did not just shoot him!" said Donnie.

"Oh my God!" said Adam.

We saw the Greek god signing. "G, what's he saying?" asked Donnie.

"I need to rewind it," said German.

I rewound the footage and stopped it right when he began signing.

"He said, 'We're being watched and have been since we moved here,'" German said as the Greek god pointed at the camera. That made us gasp.

"There goes that plan," said Donnie.

The Greek god put his face in the camera, and the screen went blank.

"What do you we do?" I asked.

"I'm pulling the flash drive. This was all recorded, so I'll figure out what to do with it. Let's get back to Alpha More," German said.

On the way back, Donnie said, "G, we can't sit here with live footage and not say anything."

"We won't be silent. I just need to figure out a way to not go to prison," said German.

"No news has picked up the story yet, which means she hasn't called the police," said Adam.

"It's been only thirty minutes, but I really believe the police will be the last people she'll call," said German.

"Why do you think the Greek god shot Drake?" I asked.

"You heard what he said. His attacks on us will raise suspicion at some point, but Klovis still wants to proceed with this plan. Drake had no choice but to cross her," said German.

"So Drake never proved that Ben was still alive? What do we do with that?" asked Adam.

"We need to lay low for a while. There's a lot unanswered … Klovis's plan, who the Greek god is, and if Ben's really dead. We'll get to the bottom of this," German said.

We got back to Alpha More and saw Brody and Brandon standing at the entrance. "Guys, Mr. Alves is looking for you," said Brody.

The four of us got to Alves's office just as Steven Schmidt was leaving it. I could have sworn that Steven had resigned from the house. He made eye contact with each of us as he walked past us.

German

Steven Schmidt walking past us was like the walking dead coming back to life. We didn't know how to react to seeing him or what Alves wanted to see us about, but I was nervous.

"Fellas, please come in and have a seat," said Alves. "I'm working with Detective Drake to make sure whoever is committing these attacks on you is caught."

"Has Detective Drake shared any new information on the attacks?" asked German.

"As of now, no, but I'm hopeful that will change soon, boys. There's also something else I wanted to share. You saw Steven Schmidt leaving my office. I've decided to reinstate his contract with Alpha More, so I want you to tread lightly—No pranking him or any others, understood?"

We all agreed to that, and he dismissed us. We went to my room. I turned on the TV to see if there was any news about Drake, but there was none.

"So I guess we can now add Steven to the list of problems," said Donnie.

"Why hasn't she called the police by now?" asked Adam.

"I'd be shocked if she did call them," I said. "This is murder we're talking about."

I pulled my safe out from under my bed and opened it. The file was gone. "Guys! I thought you said you got the file," I said.

"We did! I put it in the safe," said Donnie.

I looked around. I was thinking my room was bugged.

"G? What are you looking for?" asked Donnie.

I put my finger to my mouth to shush them. They began helping look around, and I saw Justin holding up a bug. I flushed it down the toilet. "That's how they got the file," I said.

"Who? asked Justin.

"Who do you think?" I asked.

"What do you want to do?" asked Donnie.

"I need to see my lawyer. I'll keep you posted." I grabbed my laptop and left.

I asked Farnsworth to meet me at a private conference room that I booked at the Fillmore Hotel. When he got there, I said, "Mr. Farnsworth, thanks for coming. My friends were able to obtain the folder from Detective Drake, but it's been stolen, and Drake might be dead."

"Why do you think he's dead?"

I turned my laptop to Farnsworth. He watched the video of Drake being shot. He closed the laptop. "How did you get that?" asked Farnsworth.

"I planted surveillance cameras in her store."

Farnsworth nodded and pulled his laptop out of his briefcase.

"What should I do?" I asked.

"You have to get ahead of this story. We need to be prepared for your arrest. Transfer a hundred thousand to my business account. Your bond will be a million easy."

I opened my laptop and made the transfer. "What next?" I asked.

"You have to leak the video to the police."

"If I go down, you can get me out?" I asked.

"Without a doubt. Who shot him?"

"That's the question of the century. No one knows who's under that hood. All I know is that it's someone who's in proximity to me and has something to do with Alpha More," I said.

"If you're not arrested, cooperate with the police. You might be able to walk."

I nodded, thanked him, and left.

I got back to Alpha More to fill the guys in on what just happened and my new plan. When I walked into the house, I saw Detective Bradshaw and Alves talking.

"German, come over here please," said Alves.

"Hi, German," said Bradshaw.

"Detective Bradshaw," I said.

"I'll give you two a moment," said Alves; he walked away.

"What can I do for you, Detective?" I asked.

"I wanted to find out if you've seen Detective Drake. He hasn't shown up to the office this morning. I went by his apartment. Nothing. The last I checked in with him, he had just left here and from my understanding, you were attacked?"

"We were. There was a police report filed. It was the fourth attack in a month," I said.

"Please be assured that we'll solve this and justice will be served."

"I've heard that before," I said. "I overheard him saying that he was going to visit Mrs. Klovis at her flower shop."

"Did you overhear why?"

"No," I said.

"Well, have a great day," she said, and she left.

The others were in my room. "About time you got back. What's going on?" asked Donnie.

"Guys, I have to leak the video," I said.

"Are you crazy?" asked Donnie.

"You'll go to jail!" said Adam.

"I'm prepared for that. My lawyer said I had to get a few steps ahead," I said.

"Who are you going to leak it to?" asked Justin.

"The police. I'm guessing they don't want this to go public. It could be my get out of jail free card," I said.

"When are you going to do it?" asked Donnie.

"Soon. Bradshaw was downstairs, and I pointed her in Klovis's direction. I'm sure the timing will be just about right," I said.

They all looked at each other; I could tell they were nervous. But there was one thing I could get myself out of a crime.

Katheryn Klovis

I went to the spot to clean the blood with hydrogen peroxide. "I can use some help," I said.

The Greek god signed, "You bought this on yourself."

"How exactly?" I asked.

"You really think that this plan is going to work?"

"I know that it will," I said. A bell rang. I went up front and saw Detective Bradshaw.

"Mrs. Klovis, good morning."

"Good morning, Detective. How can I help you?" I asked.

"Is now a good time?"

"Good as any," I said.

"I'll keep it short. Detective Drake hasn't shown up at the office this morning, and he isn't home. Have you seen him?"

"No, I haven't," I said.

"May I ask when the last time you saw him was?"

"Last night. He was at the sorority I delivered flowers to," I said.

"OK. If you hear from him, would you ask him to call me?"

"Sure thing," I said.

Bradshaw walked out, and a man walked in. "I'm sorry, but we're closed. I should have locked up," I said.

"Hey, Kathy."

"Cyrus?" I was shocked to see my estranged husband. "What are you doing here?"

"I hired a lawyer. I'm filing a lawsuit against the university."

"I went to a lawyer, Cyrus. They told me I didn't have a case since it was reckless endangerment," I said.

"Obviously that lawyer wasn't equipped to handle this," Cyrus said. He looked around. "This place is a lot bigger than your shop back home."

"I got a really good deal on the lease," I said.

"This is where you want to be, Kathy?"

"I wanted to be close to Brandon," I said.

"What about your other children? Are you just going to neglect them too?"

"I haven't neglected my children. When I have some stability, I'll send for them," I said.

"What about me?" he asked.

I took a deep breath. He was talking about our marriage. "I told you I haven't been happy with us in a long time," I said.

"So you're done is what you're saying?"

I remained quiet because it was hard for me to put it in words that I could believe. I'd been with him for twenty-five years.

"Fine. I'll be in touch through the lawyers. Have a nice day."

He left, and I locked the front door and started crying. It wasn't like my husband to not fight, but I guessed he was done with me.

Bradshaw

I felt that something was off but didn't know what. I needed to do more investigation. Back at the station, I asked the assistant, "Has Detective Drake checked in?"

"No, Detective, he hasn't shown up."

"Thanks." I went to Captain Deele's office and said, "Knock knock."

"Come in."

"Sir, I've been over every inch of Drake's cases. There's no sign of him anywhere," I said.

"Have you called his family?"

"Yes. I called his mother. She said he hadn't spoken with her. I called his ex-fiancée. She hasn't heard from him since they split," I said.

"That's strange. And something else is odd. His transmitter says his squad car is in the precinct."

"Have you checked his car footage?" I asked.

"Not yet, but you have permission to do that. If he doesn't check in in the next twenty-four hours, we'll have to make this a missing person's case, Detective."

"Yes sir," I said. I went out to the parking lot, opened Drake's car, pulled up the footage, and began to review his whereabouts. The last time Drake's car had stopped was nine the previous night. I ran the footage at that time and saw that he'd parked in front of Klovis's shop.

Adam

Homecoming had been nothing but a circus. I was glad it was over. I needed a moment away. I went to Jessica's place with dinner. I knocked on the door, and she answered with a "Hi!"

"I've come bearing dinner," I said with a smile that matched hers.

"Come in," she said, and I did.

"Wow! That's some kitchen," I said looking at her big island and big chef's stove.

"Yeah. This loft is really expensive, but I manage by booking extra jobs to pay the rent."

"I'm going to enjoy myself," I said pulling out what I'd brought from the bag.

"Wow! You went all out. I see lobster, pasta, heavy cream, cheese …"

"Lobster Alfredo is my specialty," I said.

"I'm excited! I'm going to freshen up a bit. I'll be right back."

I started making dinner, and I set the table. I saw some candles, and I lit them. I turned and saw her coming out of her room in a very short black dress. "Whoa!" I said.

She smiled as she walked up to me. "You like?"

"I love," I said with a smile.

I pulled out her chair, and she sat. I brought my dish to the table and served her first.

"It looks very good."

"Thank you," I said.

"How are Pip and Justin?"

"They aren't together anymore," I said.

"Why not? I thought they were so cute together."

"It's a long story. How's your dinner?" I asked.

"Amazing! This Alfredo sauce is so good."

"It's my own recipe," I said.

"I'm impressed."

I smiled as she came over to kiss me. I kissed her back, picked her up, and carried her to the bed. I took off my shirt, and she took off her dress. We made out knowing it was leading to sex. I got a condom out of my wallet …

After sex, I woke up. Jessica's head was on my chest. I ran my fingers through her hair and kissed her forehead. I got out of bed, and Jessica pulled the covers over herself. I smiled at her and got dressed. I left her place feeling good.

Back at Alpha More, I saw brothers throwing a football around. I went up to my room, where Brody was playing video games. "Hey, man, sorry if I'm being too loud," he said.

"It's cool. I'm just grabbing a change of clothes," I said, and I did. I went up to German's room, where he was on his laptop and Donnie was lying on the bed.

"Whoa! You're glowing," said Donnie.

"G, can I shower in here?" I asked.

"You don't have ask man," he said.

"Cool. Thanks, bro," I said.

"I want details," said Donnie as I headed to the bathroom, but then we heard the news on TV. "Pendleton detective Darren Drake has been reported missing for two days. City officials and the Pendleton PD are asking citizens with any information on him to please come forward."

German turned off the TV. We were looking at him as Justin came in.

"Well, guys, here's my way in," said German.

We looked at each other. We knew this was going only downhill from there.

CHAPTER 12

HURRICANE RIGEN

German

I DROVE TO ALPHA More. Inside, the majority of the house was watching the news.

"This is an extreme precaution. In about three days, a hurricane will hit all the New England states and in particular Maine, New Hampshire, Rhode Island, and New Jersey. We're asking citizens to report to their local shelters for cover."

"G, there's a meeting in thirty minutes," said Petey.

"Thanks," I said. I went to my room and got on my computer. I looked to see where my parents were, and I saw they were in California and Paris was in New York. That meant that the Rigen estate would be empty.

Adam walked in. "Did you hear about the hurricane?"

"Yeah," I said. "The family home is empty, and that's where we're going. I'll tell Alves that the four of us are leaving. Can you round up Donnie and Justin? Tell them we're leaving to my parents' place after the meeting."

"Sure," Adam said as I walked out of the room and down to Alves's office. His door was open. He was on the phone. He waved me in and ended his call. "German, we're going to have a house meeting in about twenty minutes."

"I heard, Mr. Alves," I said. "I wanted to tell you that Donnie, Justin,

138

Adam, and I are going to the Rigen estate for shelter. That area won't be badly hit, and the house is hurricane-proof."

"That's four of you off my plate, so I have to worry about only forty-six. Our shelter in place for a hurricane is the gym. The university's making all students register for cots. We and Theta Monroe have not been listed, so Mrs. Mack and I are letting you know so you can register as soon as possible."

"Mr. Alves, I know that this might be a bit of a reach, but our house and Theta Monroe can come to my house for shelter," I said.

"Are you parents OK with that?"

"My dad wouldn't have it any other way," I said.

"Thank you, German. That's amazing."

"We're going to go there and set up the house. We'll see you all there," I said.

The house was walking to the podium room as I walked up to my room, where Donnie, Justin, and Adam were along with their bags. "We're skipping the meeting and heading to my parents' estate. Our house and Theta Monroe are coming to the Rigen estate, so we need a head starts. Let's ride," I said, and we headed out.

Katheryn Klovis

It was getting windy as I was trying to prepare for the hurricane.

"Hey, Mom," said Brandon.

"Hi, honey," I said and gave him a kiss.

"We're all going to German's parents' estate in Boston for shelter. Mom, come with me."

"I'll be fine," I said.

"You should listen to him," said Cyrus, who had just walked in.

"Dad?" asked Brandon.

"Hi, Brandon," Cyrus said.

Brandon and Cyrus hugged. They hadn't had a tender moment since Ben's death.

"Where's Burt, Barbara, and Braxton?" asked Brandon.

"There at Grandma's house in Connecticut. I'm driving up there now. I was going to suggest that you two come up there with me."

"I'll be fine, Cyrus. After the hurricane, I'll pick up the kids. They can spend the weekend with me," I said.

"Don't be ridiculous, Kathy. My mom and our kids want to see you."

"Mom, you really should go. It won't be safe here when this thing hits," said Brandon.

"Boys, I'll be fine. Honey, you should be with your fraternity in Boston," I said.

Brandon hugged me, and I gave him a kiss on the cheek. "Be safe," I said.

Brandon hugged his father. "Don't worry, Brandon. I'll make sure she's safe," said Cyrus.

Just then, ten CSI agents walked in with Detective Bradshaw.

"What the hell's going on?" I asked.

"Katheryn Klovis, I have a search warrant to search your shop, and I have a warrant for your participation in questioning," said Bradshaw.

"What the hell is this, Kathy?" asked Cyrus.

"I'm sorry, sir. You are …?" asked Bradshaw.

"Cyrus Klovis, her husband. What's this all about?"

Bradshaw handed us the warrants. "We have evidence that suggests Detective Drake may have been murdered. Mrs. Klovis could be a suspect."

"My wife isn't capable of murder!"

"Mr. Klovis, as long as Mrs. Klovis cooperates, I'm sure everything will be fine."

"Mom?" asked Brandon.

"It's OK, Brandon. Leave so you can get to shelter," I said.

"I'll be at the precinct waiting for you," said Cyrus.

Bradshaw escorted me to her car, and we drove off.

Donnie

We arrived at the Rigen estate, and German said, "We'll have company coming in soon."

We went in, and the place was super clean. German turned on the lights.

"So what's the plan?" I asked.

"The four of us are going to take my father's man cave in the lower level," said German.

We go to the elevator, and German puts a key in it. "My father doesn't like anyone in his man cave, so he built a whole other floor dedicated to him. It's sound proof and has fifteen hundred square feet."

The door opened, and we descended. When we exited it, the lights came on in an amazing man cave complete with a pool table, Jacuzzi, theater room, wine bar, and kitchen.

"Whoa, G, this is a whole other house down here," said Justin.

"I know," he said.

We walked to a bedroom that had a California king bed and sleeper sofas.

"Damn, G. I'm really impressed," I said.

"The best part about this is that no one can come down here without a key. Which reminds me ..." said German. He went to a safe, entered a code, and pulled out three keys. "If I'm not around, use these," he said as he handed one to each of us. "We need to find out how much food we have and what we can make for the others."

We went back up and followed German to the kitchen.

"Adam, you can get to the walk-in deep freezer through the door in the butler's pantry over there. It's downstairs against the wall. Justin, give him a hand. Donnie, we'll go the pantry to see what we have. Can you grab that cart?" asked German.

I grabbed the cart, and we rolled it through the pantry. "Pasta," I said.

"Grab it," German said.

He pulled out his phone to read a text as Adam and Justin walked in. "G, there's six pounds of ground turkey and ten pounds of chicken breasts. I can make spaghetti, burritos, whatever," said Adam.

"Let's have pasta tonight and figure out what to make after that," said German.

"What did you see on your phone?" I asked.

"Katheryn Klovis was taken in for questioning," German said.

"You think she's going to jail?" asked Justin.

"Don't know, but she was there, and I think she knows who the Greek god is."

"Maybe this is her karma. She was after us from the start and wanted revenge," I said.

We all looked at each other. They were thinking the same thing.

We started cooking, and German turned on the TV.

"We have an update on Hurricane Judy as she's coming in. We go to Robert for an update," we heard. "Thank you, Joe. I'm out here in Portland, Maine. The hurricane is expected to make landfall in twenty-four hours. Those in counties including Pertwilla, Poho, and Pendleton will need to evacuate immediately. Back to you, Joe."

"Alves texted that everyone's on the way but stuck in some traffic," German said.

The doorbell rang. German answered it, and Brandon walked in. "Hey, guys," he said, and we all greeted him.

"Did you come alone?" asked Adam.

"Yeah. I went to see my mom before I drove up."

"Is she going to find shelter? Pendleton's supposed to be hit," Justin said.

"My Dad's with her and I'm sure they'll go to my grandparents house," Brandon said.

"That's good as long as she's safe." said German.

We all looked at German as the pleasantry was unfamiliar to all of us.

"Do you guys need help?" asked Brandon.

"Sure. You can help Justin cut up the salad," Adam said.

"I'll get you an apron," said German.

I followed German out of the kitchen. "Are you out of your mind?" I asked.

"I know, but it's his mom. What was I supposed to say?"

"No. Matter of fact, *hell* no," I said.

"Look, I agree with you, but she'd be on my turf with over a hundred witnesses. She wouldn't cause a scene here."

We heard knocking. It turned out to be Petey, Otto, Bryan, Adore and Brody.

"Yo, G! This place is awesome!" said Petey.

"How big is this place, G?" asked Brody.

"Over a hundred thousand square feet on forty acres."

"I wish my father was a pro football player. This is insane!" Otto said.

Mr. Alves and Mrs. Mack showed up. "German, we appreciate your taking us in as well," she said.

"My pleasure," said German.

Alves asked, "What's the room situation so we can get everyone settled in?"

"The property has over thirty bedrooms. I'm not counting Donnie, Adam, Justin, and me in that count. So we can have about four people per room," said German.

"Has everyone shown?" I asked.

"No. We're missing about five, and Mrs. Mack is missing about ten girls," Alves said.

"We're working on dinner. How about if you get everyone to the living room so you can make an announcement about that," German said.

G and I went to the kitchen, where Adam, Justin, Otto, Petey, Brandon, and Brody were working. "How's dinner going?" G asked.

"We're just about done," said Adam.

"Good. We're waiting on about fifteen Greek members. We can organize a line for the food," I said.

I saw Steven looking at me. I couldn't say I was nervous, but he gave me the creeps.

Pip

Ginger showed up in her '69 red Mustang convertible and said, "Hey!"

"You really have the top down?" I asked as I got in and we drove off.

"I'll put it up later. It's not going to rain for about an hour. Pip, did you know that the Rigen estate has over a hundred thousand square feet?"

"I can't believe you convinced me to come. I should've gone with Shayna to her parents' house in Philly," I said.

"You said you missed Justin. This is your chance to be with him in a different setting."

"It's really hard to let him go," I said.

"Which is why going up there is the best thing you can do. You'll have a chance to get him alone and express how you feel."

"Fat chance of that happening with his crew in the way," I said.

"Don't worry. Donnie will be distracted," said Ginger.

The thunderstorm erupted, and we screamed.

"I need to pull over so we can put the top up," Ginger said.

Bradshaw

I walked into the interrogation room where Katheryn Klovis was.

"Bradshaw, we're evacuating the building in an hour," said the officer.

"That's plenty of time," I said. I turned to Klovis. "Mrs. Klovis, I appreciate your patience. I'll keep my questions to the point. You're here because Drake's disappearance is very odd. His car was last parked in front of your flower shop before the car cam was disconnected, and I have a source that said he was meeting you last night," I said.

"He never came to see me, Detective."

"Did you notice his car parked in front of your shop?" I asked.

"No."

"Mrs. Klovis, I have to be honest with you, Detective Drake logs everytime he stops at a location. Your business was the last log."

"I don't know why Detective."

Her behavior was very odd. I couldn't tell if she was clueless or being honest. It was time to evacuate the building. "OK, due to weather conditions, I'm going to stop this interrogation, but I'll be in touch," I said.

I stood, and she did too. We walked to the lobby, where Mr. Klovis was waiting.

"Kathy," he said.

"Cyrus, what are you doing here?"

"We need to go to safety, My parents house is only two hours away."

"I can drive you," I said.

"That won't be necessary," Mr. Klovis said as thunder erupted.

"I insist. It'll be my civic duty," I said. They looked at each other.

Justin

The last guests arrived. "Food's ready," said Adam.

"Thank you guys for stepping up and cooking. I really appreciate it," said German.

"The weather's getting worse," I said.

I look over as I see Ginger walking in with Pip as Donnie approaches me, "Oh wonderful," said German.

"What the hell is she doing here?" asked Donnie.

I was dreading this. We all walked over, and Ginger said, "Hey, guys!"

"Ginger, can I talk to you?" asked German.

"Sure."

She, Donnie, G, and I went over to a corner. "Why did you bring her here?" asked German.

"She didn't have any other place to go," said Ginger.

"That's sweet and all, but you know that she and Justin just broke up. Now we have to be held up with her for a couple of days," said Donnie.

"Oh my God, you act like it's the end of the world," said Ginger.

"Have you even asked how Justin felt?" asked Donnie.

"No. Let's ask him. Justin, how do you feel about Pip being here?"

"It's fine," I said.

"Perfect!" Ginger said.

"Thanks, German, for taking me in," said Pip.

"You're welcome. Make yourself at home," he said.

"This has become awkward," said Donnie as he patted me on the back. He walked away, and I made eye contact with Pip again.

We all gathered when Alves started speaking.

"Ladies and gentleman and guests of the Greek system, let's thank the Rigens for taking us in. We need to remain calm as the hurricane passes through. It seems that that will take about forty-eight hours. Let's entertain ourselves, but that's after you do your homework. Mrs. Mack, do you want to add anything?"

Mrs. Mack stood. "Ladies and gentleman, we're all adults. Let's be respectful of this beautiful home and not engage in any fornication. Thank you." Everyone laughed at that.

Pip approached me. "Hi."

"Hey," I said.

"I sorry for how things turned out between us. I hate that it's awkward now, Justin."

I didn't know what to say. Pip ended up walking away and catching up with Ginger. I walked over to German and Donnie, who were getting food ready.

"Mrs. Mack is crazy if she thinks I'm not getting laid tonight," said Donnie.

"She seemed serious to me," said German.

"G, come on. There has to be another floor your dad built that your parents got it on in," Donnie said.

"That's disgusting," said German.

Donnie looked at me and saw I was upset. "What's wrong, Just?"

"Pip apologized to me," I said.

"Why do you look so sad then?" asked German.

"I don't know," I said.

"Here, take a plate of food," said Donnie.

"Thanks, but I'm not hungry. I'll see you guys back in the room," I said.

"You sure, man?" asked Donnie.

"Yeah," I said.

I didn't want to tell them that I missed her and wanted to forgive her because that would just start a big argument I didn't want to have.

Adam

I made my way to the kitchen and saw German, who said, "Hey. I was going to text you, but we lost reception about an hour ago."

"My bad, bro. I was talking to Justin," I said.

"I know he seemed really upset. He didn't eat anything, which is unlike him."

"He's upset about Pip. I think he didn't want to break up with her despite what she said," I said. "Can I ask you something, G?"

"Anything."

"Why don't you have a girlfriend? I mean, you have a lot to offer," I said.

"I don't even think about it half the time, Adam."

"Is there any truth to what Donnie was saying about you?" I asked.

German put his head down. "Donnie and I went to the same high school, and the kids were always bullying me because I was short and had a high-pitched voice compared to Paris's. He was popular and athletic, and I was the outsider. One day, I wrote a story about I thought my brother was handsome and it was taken out of context. The others started calling me every gay slur in the book."

He began to cry. I went to comfort him. "Kids used to bully me as well. My mom had a reputation that has stuck to this day," I said.

"I'm sorry, man," said German.

"You have nothing to be apologize for. I want you to be whoever German Rigen is. Never be afraid to be who you are," I said.

German dried his tears. "Thanks, man. Love you."

We hugged, and I said, "Go to bed. Love you, man," I said.

He left the kitchen. I heard a noise in the broom closet. I opened the door and saw Donnie and Ginger. "You two were in this closet the whole time?" I asked.

"Yeah, we heard everything. Thanks for ruining our make-out spot," Donnie said.

"We need to be there for our brother."

Donnie kissed Ginger, and we left the kitchen.

We arrived in the man cave, where German was watching TV.

"Hey, G," said Donnie.

"What's up?" German asked as Justin walked into the room.

"Ginger and I were in the broom closet making out before Adam busted us, but I heard what you said, and I want to apologize to you. There's something I need to tell you about the high school rumors. I started them. I was being a prick, but I never meant to hurt you. I swear to you I didn't mean to," said Donnie.

I wanted to rewind time or wake up from this nightmare.

"You son of a bitch!" German said as he punched Donnie in the face knocking him down. Justin grabbed German, and I helped Donnie up.

"Do you have any idea what I went through? I trusted you, but the whole time, you were behind the very thing that destroyed me! Do you really want me to admit it, Donnie?" German said and began to cry. Donnie kept quiet. "Fine. I'm gay, Donnie. The rumors you started were true all along. It never occurred to you that I struggled with this, and you know who my father is. How could Chance Rigen have a gay son? He's the

alpha male. My dad told me I was a disgrace when those rumors began."
German walked away.

"G, come back!" I said as he got in the elevator.

"Damn. He hit me hard," said Donnie.

"You deserved a whole ass beating, but I'll settle for that punch," I said.

"Should we go see if G's OK?" asked Justin.

"No. Give G some time. He'll come around," said Donnie.

I put some ice in a plastic bag and gave it to Donnie, who said, "I'm going to bed. Good night, y'all."

"What do we do?" asked Justin.

"Give it time," I said.

We all went to the room and Hope that a good night sleep was on the horizon.

CHAPTER 13

AFTER THE STORM

Donnie

I FELT BAD ABOUT German. I wanted to apologize, but he wasn't in his bed, so I went to the bathroom and saw the shiner on my face. He'd hit me hard. I took the elevator up to see if he was there. The kitchen was empty. People were sleeping on couches and floors. I went to Ginger's room, where she and Pip were asleep. I tapped Ginger's shoulder, and she woke up, but she rolled over; she was giving me the silent treatment. I tapped her again, she turned around, and I gave her the side nod to come into the other room. She got out of bed, and we went out to a small porch in the middle of the house. "I can't believe you" said Ginger.

"Look. I feel bad for what I did to G. I was an idiot, and I was popular in high school. It just happened," I said.

"That's the worst excuse I've ever heard. You don't bully somebody and out them with something as serious as his sexuality!"

"I know, but I just don't need another person mad at me," I said.

"I'm not mad at you, Donnie, but I can't say I'm surprised at you. I'm really disappointed that something that cold exists in you." She walked away.

I went back in to the kitchen for more ice for my eye, and I saw Alves making coffee.

"Good morning, Donnie."

"Good morning, Mr. Alves," I said.

"Oh my goodness! What happened to your eye?"

"It was an accident," I said.

"What's going on?"

I took a deep breath. I didn't want to tell Mr. Alves, but I knew it was the right thing to do.

"When I was in high school, German wrote a story about living in his brother's shadow. He talked about how handsome his brother was, how he could never compare to Paris, and it was confusing for everyone, but I wanted to be what I was known for, so I started a rumor about him being gay, and it got around school and then to his home. His father was angry with him," I said.

"So that black eye was German's revenge?"

"I guess so," I said.

Alves grabbed a steak from the fridge and put it over my eye. "Keep this on for a while."

I sat on the bar stool. Adam walked into the kitchen and asked, "Hey! You all right?"

"I feel like shit. Have you seen G?" I asked.

"No. He didn't sleep in the room last night."

"I need to find him. See you later," I said.

I walked out of the kitchen and went upstairs to the room that led to the attic. I walked up to the attic and saw German looking at this poster board with pictures of the four of us in all the moments. German looked at me as I stood next to him. "I remember this photo like it was yesterday. It was taken at Snyder's Creek. You were scared to jump, so I pushed you. OK, so maybe that wasn't the best memory to bring up. Sorry," I said.

"I think that if you hadn't pushed me, I wouldn't have found the courage to climb up there and jump." He turned to me. "I'm sorry I hit you. There's no excuse for what I did. I didn't know those feelings still bothered me."

"No man, don't apologize. I deserved this," I said.

"This is my favorite memory. When we joined Alpha More, the four of us made a pact to always have each other's back. Some things will never change," said German.

I gave him a hug. But of course I had to make a joke out of this. "You always did have a crush on me, didn't you?" I asked.

"I hate you! Let's get some breakfast."

We went downstairs to the kitchen, where Ginger, Pip, Adam, Justin, and other Greeks were making breakfast for the house. "I see you two've made up," said Adam.

"He can't stay mad at me," said Donnie.

"Tell that to your friend on your face," said Justin, and everyone laughed.

"Hey! German has a good right hook. This still hurts."

Ginger came over to me and said, "I have something for the pain."

We kissed, and she dragged me out of the room. "Later, guys," I said.

Justin

Donnie and I finished the dishes and listened to the news about the aftermath of the hurricane: "The roads have opened, and it's safe to travel," we heard.

"All right, ladies and gentlemen, let's pack up and head out," Alves said.

"G, do you need help cleaning up?" Adam asked.

"No. I ordered a cleaning crew, but you're welcome to hang around until they leave."

"For sure," Donnie said, and Adam and I nodded.

Pip came up to me and asked, "Can you help me with my bag?"

"Sure, Pip. I'll catch up with you guys in a minute," I said.

She and I went to her room for her bag. "Ginger, you need help with your bag?" I asked.

"Sure," she said.

I grabbed their bags and took them out to Ginger's car. She opened her trunk, I put the bags in, they got in, and they took off.

"Let's help G," said Donnie. We walked into the house. "G?" I yelled.

He came up from the basement; he looked shocked. "You guys have to see this."

We went downstairs, and he led us to the walk-in deep freezer. In it was a body bag.

"What the hell is that?" asked Donnie.

"That's a body bag," said German.

"I hope that's not who I think it is," I said, and we all looked at each other.

"Maybe there's nothing in it. It could be a joke. Let's open it," said Donnie.

"Who the hell would be playing with us like this?" asked Adam.

"I don't know. G, why don't you open it?" asked Donnie.

"I'm not opening it," said German.

"Justin?" asked Donnie.

"No way, man," I said.

"I'll do it," said Adam.

"Wait a sec," German said. He walked out of the freezer and came back with gloves.

"Good idea, G," I said.

Adam donned the gloves and unzipped the bag. "Oh, that's bad!" he said.

We all covered our noses due to the smell.

"Is it Drake?" I asked.

"I can't tell. His face looks distorted," said Adam.

"Zip it up," said Donnie.

"What does this mean?" I asked.

"It means that the Greek god was in the house with us," said German.

"Let's get out of here," said Donnie.

We went upstairs to the kitchen and faced each other.

"How would the Greek god get in here without us noticing?" asked Adam.

"We monitored every part of this house when everyone arrived. There's no way he could have gotten in," said German.

"Do you think it's Mr. and Mrs. Klovis? I mean, we know that the Greek god couldn't have been Brandon or Ben," Donnie said.

"That makes sense. Mr. Klovis hasn't been around, so why would he show up out of the blue?" I asked.

"That's too easy. If Mr. Klovis is the Greek god, that would mean Detective Bradshaw would be involved," said German.

"There's Pip," said Donnie.

"Really?" I asked.

"I'm kidding, bro. Calm down," said Donnie.

"Who else could it be?" asked Adam.

"Steven," said Donnie.

"It makes sense. He was here," I said.

"We need to get rid of that body," said German.

"How? And where are we supposed to take it?" asked Adam.

"I don't know, but I know that that body is a plant and we need to get it out of here," said German.

I knew he was right about that.

Adam

"We need to make sure no one in the cleaning crew sees it," said German.

"How?" I asked.

"Follow me," said German. He led us to the garage, where we saw an Aston Martin. "It's my dad's. We can move the body in it and drive it back without being noticed."

"Where are we going to hide the body?" asked Justin.

"I have the perfect place," Donnie said.

German opened a safe on the wall and retrieved some keys that he gave to Donnie. "Donnie goes alone. You guys will follow him in this car." German pulled a sheet off a Jaguar F type and handed me the keys to it. "Make sure you're not followed," said German.

We got in the cars after putting the body in the trunk of the Aston Martin and drove off leaving German at the house.

We arrived at Klovis's flower shop. I couldn't believe Donnie wanted to dump the body there of all places. Donnie convinced me to break in through a broken window on the second level of the building. I walked downstairs to the front door and punched in the code, 0, 5, 2, 3. The light went green, and I opened it.

"Damn! What took you so long?" Donnie asked.

"Let's get this over with," I said.

We carried the body into the back of the shop and put it under a bed of flowers.

"Let's go," said Donnie.

I let Donnie and Justin out, set the alarm, and left the same way I'd gotten in. We drove off. I felt horrible about what we'd just done, but I understood why Donnie had put it there. We drove back to the Rigen estate and parked our cars in the garage.

German walked into the garage with cleaning products in hand. "Did you guys hide it?"

"Yeah. It's all good," said Donnie.

German started wiping down the cars. "The house is clean, and everything is back in its place. So we're going back to Alpha More and going back to our normal."

He looked at me and Justin as we looked really guilty. "What's wrong?" he asked.

"Nothing," I said.

"You sure?" asked German.

"Yeah man. We're good," said Justin.

We got in German's car and drove off. "All of you look like you've seen a ghost," G said. "Well, except Donnie. What happened?"

I figured I'd throw Donnie under the bus since it had been his plan. "Donnie, is there something you want to tell German?"

"We hid the body in Klovis's flower shop," he said.

German smiled. "Perfect, my source tells me they have to return everything back to her shop tomorrow before she can enter the place."

"They'll find the body," said Justin.

"Exactly," said German.

We got to Alpha More and saw Alves and Dean Wilkinson walking out.

"Hello, gentleman," said Wilkinson.

"Good evening, Dean. What brings you by?" German asked.

"Just a little chat with Mr. Alves. I should be going. Goodnight."

"Adam, your mom called," Alves said.

"She did?" I asked.

"Yeah. She left this number for you," he said and handed me a piece of paper.

"Thanks, Mr. Alves," I said. I went to the backyard and pulled out my phone. I didn't recognize the number, but I dialed it.

"Smith's Health and Rehabilitation. This is Eileen."

"Hi. I'm looking for my mom, Lana Banks, I'm assuming she works there," I said.

"May I ask who's calling?"

"Adam Banks," I said.

"One moment please."

As I waited, I saw Alves in the kitchen putting his hand to his head. He seemed frustrated.

"Mr. Banks, your mother is a patient here. She has phone privileges between four and five p.m."

"I'm sorry … Patient? I don't understand," I said.

"Yes. I can have Dr. Hamilton, your mother's physician here, give you a call. He can tell you more about your mother's condition."

"My mother doesn't have a condition," I said.

"I apologize as I understand this may be a complete shock to you. Dr. Hamilton will be sure to call."

I wondered what my mom was doing in a rehab center. I hoped she was OK. I couldn't wait to hear from her.

CHAPTER 14

CHOOSING FACTOR

German

I WENT DOWNSTAIRS AND knocked on Alves's door.

"Come in and close the door please," he said.

I closed the door and sat across from him.

"I wanted to share this with you, but I need you to keep this an absolute secret, agreed?"

"Sure," I said.

He put a folder in front of me. "Mr. Cyrus Klovis has filed a fifty-million-dollar lawsuit against the university for reckless endangerment. Dean Wilkinson said that if the lawsuit is successful, the university will close Alpha More."

"That can't happen," I said.

"It doesn't look good on our part, German."

"I'll write the check. This house cannot close down," I said.

"I can't ask you to do that. However, I need you to talk to your dad about this."

"I will," I told him.

I learned that Mr. Klovis had checked into the Fillmore Hotel. I went there and saw the manager. "Mr. Manley," I said.

"Mr. Rigen, here for another staycation?"

"Actually, I'm looking for Cyrus Klovis," I said.

Manley typed in the name. "He's in room fifteen oh five."

"Thank you," I said. I took the elevator up to his floor and knocked on his door.

He opened it and looked confused for a second or two, but then he said, "German, right?"

"That's right," I said.

"What can I do for you?"

"May I come in?" I asked.

He waved me in, and I sat on a couch.

"You filed a lawsuit against Pendleton. I came here to ask you to withdraw it," I said.

"Not a chance."

I pulled out my checkbook and my pen and began writing. "You're suing for fifty million. I'm willing to write you a check for sixty million to drop the case," I said.

"You're trying to make this go away by writing a check for ten million more than what I'm suing for?"

"Correct," I said.

"Not to insult you intentionally but I don't believe you have that kind of money and I would hate for your father to find out about this."

"Mr. Klovis, quite frankly I don't care about what you believe, I have money that's way longer than my fathers and I'm offering you a chance to take this money free and clear." I said.

"No deal, I know that if I win the lawsuit, the university has to close the fraternities down and that's the objective besides the money." Said Cyrus.

"Seventy-five million." I said.

Mr. Klovis went to the door and opened it as I walked past him. I didn't have the words in that moment to fight so I left and after he closed the door, I knew this wasn't going to be easy.

I went back to the house not knowing what my next move was. The guys were in my room.

"G, where'd you go?" asked Donnie.

"I had to run a few errands," I said, and they looked at me suspiciously. "Any news on Drake?" I asked.

"Not yet," said Justin.

"What do you think will happen?" asked Adam.

"Mrs. Klovis is going to do life in prison," said Donnie.

We all looked at Donnie, who was smiling. "What?" he asked.

"That's not funny," said Adam.

"They know that she didn't kill him," I said. I went to my computer.

Donnie followed me. "What are you looking for?"

"Maine's missing-persons list. I want to see if there's a reward for Drake," I said.

"For what? It's not like you need the money," said Donnie.

"There are other reasons. I'll tell you once I find his profile," I said.

As I scrolled through the pictures, Donnie grabbed my shoulder and said, "Go back up."

I scrolled up and saw someone named Matthew Richards.

"He looks like Drake," said Donnie.

I agreed with Donnie. "It says he went missing the same day Drake was killed," I said.

"What are the odds of that?" asked Donnie.

I wrote the address down and said, "We're going for a ride."

We drove to Marable. The address turned out to be a farm that looked deserted.

"It smells," said Donnie when we got out.

"It's a farm, Donnie. What do you expect?" asked Adam.

"Don't these animals ever bathe?" asked Donnie.

We all laughed. Being the son of a state senator was really kicking in for Donnie.

We see a man with a wheelbarrow and go over to him.

"Excuse me?" I asked.

The guy turned around. He seemed very down. "Can I help you?"

"We're from the university. We came to see Matthew Richards about an experiment," I said.

"I'm sorry, but Mr. Richards is not here today."

"When will he be back?" asked Donnie.

"I'm not sure, but I'll be sure to tell him you stopped by."

We went back to the car. Donnie said, "Something about him isn't right."

"I thought I was the only person who thought that," said Adam.

"Do you think he knows Richards is missing?" asked Justin.

"He has to. It's public record, and I have a feeling he was the one who reported it," I said.

We saw the man get in his truck and leave the farm. He stopped at the gate to lock it and then drove off. We ducked down so he wouldn't see us. I didn't see the lights anymore, but that didn't mean he wasn't there. "Donnie, check it out," I said.

"Why me?"

"Because you're the farthest from the window. He won't see you," I said.

Donnie popped his head up and looked. "He's gone."

"OK, let's go," I said.

We got out of the car and went back to the farm.

"OK, so what are we looking for?" asked Justin.

"Something that would connect this guy to Drake," I said.

"I don't know about this, guys," said Justin.

"Look, I get it. I'll go in," I said.

"I'm going with you," said Donnie.

"Good. Adam, Justin, take a corner of the house. Text us if the farmer comes back."

"OK," said Adam. We split up just as the lights came on. We thought we had been spotted.

Adam

The lights coming on all over the property scared us. I wasn't sure what was going on, but we looked around and saw nobody. German pointed to one light and said, "They're on sensors." He found the box with a power switch and flipped it off. "That didn't turn them all off, but this is a lot better."

German and Donnie found an open window and climbed in. Justin and I headed to opposite ends of the property but still within eyesight of each other. I looked to my right as I thought I'd seen someone. I walked in that direction to be sure of what I'd seen and came across this ditch with a wallet. I grabbed the wallet as I fell into the ditch about seven feet deep. My head hurt. It was extremely dark. I looked up when I saw a dark shadow.

"Justin!" I yelled. He didn't respond. I pulled out my phone, but I had no reception down there even when I held it way up. "Justin!" I yelled again. I began to panic. I knew they wouldn't leave without me, but I wasn't confident that they would find me down where I was.

"Adam!" yelled Justin from a distance.

"Justin! I'm down here!" I said.

"Adam!" yelled Donnie.

"Donnie!" I yelled.

"Where are you?"

"Down here!" I yelled.

I saw a dark figure overhead. "Adam?" Justin asked.

"Yeah, man. It's me," I said.

"Guys, he's over here!" he yelled.

"Don't worry, man. We'll get you out of there," said Justin.

G and Donnie approached the hole. "Adam, how'd you get down there?" Donnie asked.

"This isn't the time, Donnie!" I said.

"How are we supposed to get him out of there?" asked Justin.

"I have a rope in my car. Justin. Come with me," said German.

"For real, bro. How'd you get in there?" asked Donnie.

"Donnie, if you don't shut up!" I said.

I heard a car pulling up. "What's going on?" I asked.

"It's G," said Donnie. I saw German holding a rope.

"It's secure," said Justin.

"All right, Adam, grab really tight to this rope. Don't let go until you're up here," G said.

I grabbed the rope. "What are you going to do?" I asked.

"Trust me. You have a tight grip on it?"

"Yeah," I said.

"He's good. Hit it," said German.

I heard the car accelerating, and I was pulled up quickly. Donnie and G grabbed me, and Justin stopped the car. "That really hurts," I said.

"I know, man. Sorry about that," said German.

We headed back to Alpha More. "What did you guys get?" asked Justin.

"His Social Security number from a lease document," said German.

"What are you going to do with that?"

"I'm going to order a full background check. I think this will lead to something. Adam, how're you doing?" asked German.

"My arms are sore," I said.

"You're going to feel that in the morning too," said Donnie.

"Which sucks because I have class tomorrow," I said.

We got back to the house, and we stopped and saw everyone watching the big screen TV. The anchor said, "The body found in the Roses Are Red flower shop was identified as Detective Darren Drake. The Pendleton PD has issued a statement by chief commander Rodrick Deele."

"At this time, we have no suspects. Despite where the body was found, we'll continue to investigate every inch of this case," said Deele.

When we got to German's room, Donnie said, "That body reeked. I'm not surprised they found it."

My phone rang. "Hello?"

"Good evening. My name is Dr. Garret Hamilton. I'm looking for Adam Banks."

"I'm Adam Banks," I said as I walked out of the room.

"Mr. Banks, I understand you're Lana Banks's son."

"Yes. I was informed that my mother was a patient at your facility," I said.

"That's correct. A month ago, your mother overdosed on methoxphenidine. Were you aware that your mother had a drug addiction?"

"No. I don't live with her. She was fine the last time I saw her. Is she OK?" I asked.

"I think she tried to commit suicide, but she's stable now and in treatment. I recommend that you come here and speak with her."

"I'll be there tomorrow," I said.

I was in disbelief. I went to my room and lay down.

I woke up the next morning and went to German's room.

"Morning, Adam. How are you feeling?"

"I'm really sore, but I got bigger problems," I said. "My mom's in a rehab center. Apparently, she's a drug addict, and she tried to kill herself," I said as I began tearing up.

"Sorry, bro," German said as he rubbed my arms.

"Will you come with me to see her?" I asked.

"Of course. Go get dressed."

"Thanks," I said. I was so thankful that German was willing to go with me. I went to my room to get dressed and saw pictures of her and me on my desk. I smiled.

German

On the way to see his mom, I saw that Adam was nervous about it. We got there, and he grabbed the bouquet he had brought. "Ready?" I asked.

"Yeah."

We went in, and the receptionist said, "Welcome to Smith's Health and Rehabilitation. How can I help you?"

"I'm Adam Banks. I'm here to see my mom, Lana Banks."

"One moment please."

She typed on her computer a little and put two visitors' passes on the counter. "Please wear these at all times, and have a seat. Dr. Hamilton will be with you shortly."

Adam and I sat in the lobby. He asked, "How do people end up in places like this, G?"

"Pain. Pain is different in people, but it's game we all have to play," I said.

A doctor walked into the lobby and asked, "Mr. Banks?"

"Yes," Adam said.

"I'm Dr. Hamilton, your mother's physician."

Adam and I stood, and Adam said, "This is my friend, German. I want him to be with me when I see her."

"Certainly," said Hamilton.

We walked into the facility and passed rooms with doors open. We saw patients sitting on their beds or staring out windows looking very down. Hamilton said, "We're hoping to get your mother out of here in a year. She'll have daily counseling, and pretty soon, she'll be exercising."

He led us into her room, and Adam hurried to her bed. "Mom?"

Lana turned her head. "Adam?"

"Yeah, Mom, it's me."

Lana began to cry, which made Adam tear up. "I'm sorry, baby," she said. They hugged. It was a very emotional moment. Adam sat on her bed and looked at me. I handed him the flowers, which I was carrying.

"I bought these flowers for you, Mom."

"Hi, Mrs. Banks," I said.

"Hi, German. It's good to see you."

"You as well," I said. "I'll leave you alone. Take care, Mrs. Banks," I said.

"Bye, German. Thanks for visiting me."

I was in the car when Adam came out an hour later emotionally drained. I felt bad for him.

"Thanks for coming with me. I couldn't imagine doing this alone, G."

"Of course, man. We're brothers. I just got an email that my package is coming in a few hours. I called Donnie and Justin. They'll meet us at the condo," I said.

Justin

We got to German's condo and saw Adam and Donnie at the computer looking over the footage. German came out of the kitchen with a tray of drinks, saying, "Donnie, I have your energy drink on ice. Adam, here's your espresso, and for Justin, hot chocolate with extra whipped cream."

"Thanks, G," we said.

"How's it going?" asked German.

"This is it right here," said Adam.

We looked at the video but didn't see any way it was connected to Matthew Richards.

"Looks like a dead end, guys," said Donnie.

"Yeah, I'm not seeing anything either," said German.

The doorbell rang, and German opened the door.

"Delivery for German Rigen."

"That's me."

"Sign here."

German signed the monitor and took the package, which contained public records on Matthew Richards. "Perfect timing," he said.

We sat in the living room as German pulled out tons of forms that he handed around. We looked over the papers, and Adam said, "This is a dead end. We know he leasing the farm."

"He majored in economics and agriculture and graduated last year with a four point GPA," said Donnie.

"Here's something. He was Detective Drake's half-brother," said German.

"Wait … What?" asked Donnie.

"So that's how he's connected to Drake," said Adam.

"The real question is why would he go missing the same time Drake went missing? Well, when he was killed," German said. "Something's not right."

Our phones rang; we all got texts from Alves about a house meeting in thirty minutes.

"Let's find out what this is about," said German.

We all headed back to the house.

Donnie

We met up with everyone else in the podium room, and Alves began the meeting.

"Good evening, Alpha More. I know we're heading into midterm week, but with everything that happened with the hurricane, I've decided you can throw a party unchaperoned this weekend."

Everyone cheered. Unchaperoned parties occurred usually at the end of the year. Alves pulled out his spinning wheel to determine which class would throw the party. He gave it a spin, and it landed on the sophomores. We jumped up to cheer our class, "*Woot woot woot woot woot!*"

"It's settled. The sophomores will host this party, which will be tomorrow night. Have a good night, gentleman," said Alves.

"This is exactly what we need—a party to take our minds off some of this stress," I said.

"So what's the theme of this party?" asked Brody.

"Dynamic Duos," I said.

"That same party idea from when we pledged?" asked German.

"Yep," I said.

We were all into that.

"Can't wait to see how this is going to play out," said Adam.

"How's this going to work?" asked Justin.

"It goes by roommates," I said.

"That means I have to pair up with Brody?" Adam asked.

"And I don't have a roommate," German said.

"Trust me, G. I have something up my sleeve for you," I said.

My alarm clock woke me on Friday. I didn't want to go to class. I wanted to go to the party.

Brody knocked and came in. "I got the flyers all printed!"

"Brody, Brody, Brody … We have advanced to actual technology. Flyers are so nineties, my friend. I sent an email to the student body last night," I said. "Nice try, though," I added when I saw that Brody seemed disappointed. He left, and Justin got up.

"You're such a douche, Donnie," he said.

"Hey, man, c'mon. He had that coming," I said.

"Did you get our costumes?"

"I have to get them and G's tonight," I said.

"Who's he dressing up with?"

"Paris," I said.

"You got Paris to come down here?"

"Yep. They're going to dress up as Brother Bear," I said, and we burst out laughing.

"You suck, man," said Justin.

Adam walked in just then. "What are you to laughing about?"

"Nothing, man. What's up?" I asked.

"I need a lift to school. My truck won't start," he said.

"I got you, bro. Meet you downstairs," I said and went to take a shower.

The bathroom was empty. I stripped down and took a selfie of my torso, which I sent to Ginger with a text, "You want?"

She replied, "I had. I'm bored."

My ego was a little shot. I hadn't expected that. "Lunch?" I texted her, and she responded with a thumbs-up emoji. I smiled. I showered. I got dressed. I went downstairs and saw Adam. "Ready?" I asked.

"Yep," he said. We walked out of the house and were greeted by Savannah Paxton and Lollie Clang. "Hi Donnie, Hi Adam," said Savannah.

"Ladies, is it the sparkle in my eyes or are you happy to see me?" I asked.

"I don't know about Lollie, but I'm always happy to see you," said Savannah.

"How about later tonight you show me how happy you are?" I asked.

"It'll be my pleasure," said Savannah as they walked away.

"You are unbelievable," said Adam.

"Hey, man, this what college life is all about," I said as we walked to my car.

We got to school and were walking to our classes. Jessica walked up to us and kissed Adam.

"Hey, babe," said Adam.

"Hey," said Jessica. "And hi, Donnie."

"You coming to our party tonight?" I asked.

"I have to work unfortunately, but I hope you have a great time."

"See you later, bro," Adam said as they walked away.

I got a text from Ginger: "Meet you on the quad after lunch." I responded with a thumbs-up and kiss emojis.

At lunch, I saw Adam and German in the cafeteria. "What's up, guys?" I asked.

"Adam was filling me in on Savannah Paxton. Repeat of last year?" asked German.

"I'd forgotten about that. Must not have been memorable," I said; they shook their heads.

"Where's Justin?" I asked.

"His last class got cancelled. He's helping the freshmen set up the place," said Adam.

"Cool. I have to meet up with Ginger and go to town to pick up the costumes. Speaking of which, G, can I use your condo?" I asked.

"Sure. What for?"

"Come on. By now, you should know," I said.

German gave me the keys, and I said, "See you guys tonight!"

I met Ginger on the quad. "About time you showed up," she said.

"My fault. I had to pick up something," I said.

"What?"

I held up G's keys. "Figured we'd add some class to our routine sex session," I said, and she smiled.

We drove to German's condo, where I saw Klovis outside her store. She waved at me and Ginger, so we waited outside for a while; I didn't want her to see me go inside. When she went in her shop, Ginger and I went up to German's condo. We immediately started kissing and went into the master bedroom. She pushed me gently onto the bed, climbed on top of me, and began to undress. "How much time do we have?" she asked.

"Maybe an hour," I said as we kissed and continued the intimate moment. We engaged in thirty-five minutes of passionate sex as I held her from behind.

"When do you think we'll be a couple?" asked Ginger.

"I don't know. I said I was going to try," I said.

"I know what you said, but you haven't made any effort." She looked at me; I was really in the moment of after-sex. "I can't keep doing this," she said.

"Wait! You said—" I started, but she cut me off.

"I know what I said, but I changed my mind."

I got annoyed with that. "You know what? Fine. You need some thinking time, and I need some pamper time."

Ginger got dressed. "See you at the party," she said and left.

It wasn't that I didn't want to be with Ginger. It was that I liked being a single Greek. That was way more fun. I texted German that I was picking up the costumes and that his surprise should be there within the hour. Let the party begin!

CHAPTER 15

PARTY CHAOS

Paris

I WAS EXCITED ABOUT going to an Alpha More party, the first since I'd graduated. Donnie told me not to text German as it was supposed to be a surprise, so I texted Donnie saying I'd arrived.

Donnie responded, "I'm in the parking lot. Come to my car."

I walked over to Donnie's car. He got out and asked, "Yo P. How's it going?"

"Doing well, my brother," I said.

He reached in his car and pulled out some boxes. "These are the costumes. I told G that I'd bring these to his room. He should be up there now."

We walked into Alpha More and saw they were setting up for the party.

Justin came up to us. "Hey, Paris, how's it going, man?"

"Good, bro. Happy to be back for a party," I said.

"Is G upstairs?" Donnie asked.

"Yeah. He and Adam just got in," said Justin.

"Sweet. Let's go to his room," Donnie said, and we went up with the costumes. I stayed in the hallway, and I heard Donnie say, "Hey, G. Got the costumes."

"Cool! Who's the other half of my duo?" he asked.

"He's walking through the door as we speak."

I came in, and German was shocked. "Surprise, little brother!" I said.

"Donnie, you sneaky ass! This was a good one," German said.

"Your costume is even better. It's in the box Paris has," said Donnie.

I put the box on the bed and opened it. "Is this a fur coat?" I asked.

"Not quite. You remember that movie *Brother Bear*?" asked Donnie.

German's face was priceless. He was not feeling the whole costume thing.

"Donnie, I know you didn't pick out bear costumes," German said.

"I think that's cool! Justin and I are coming a Chip 'n' Dale," Donnie said.

"The chipmunks?" I asked.

"No, the male models," said Donnie.

"That's Chippendales," said German.

"What's the difference?" asked Donnie.

German and I shook our heads as Donnie picked up his boxes and left.

"I guess we have to make the best of it," I said.

"Guess so. Have you talked to Mom and Dad?" German asked.

"Yeah. They're in Paris. Dad's selling the condo there and investing in a winery estate," I said.

"Dad's bored again," said German.

"Pretty much," I said.

"How do you feel about me moving back to Pendleton?" I asked.

"Why would you move back?"

"It's strange, but maybe you'll feel like this when you graduate. It feels like home whenever I'm here," I said.

"That's because it is your home. We spent our whole lives here. Every year, Dad would come here, so it would be bad if you decided to pick up and come back."

"True. Well, let's get in these costumes," I said.

Justin

I put on our costumes; we were wearing black jeans with white belts. Donnie was oiling his chest to make his muscles appear better.

"Damn, bro," he said, "You need to do a hundred sit-ups, make your abs look like mine."

"Shut up and give me that oil," I said.

"I wonder what everybody else is wearing," he said.

Adam walked in with an afro and a black tuxedo, and Donnie and I fell over laughing.

"What?" asked Adam.

"Nothing, man. Your costume is awesome," said Donnie.

"What are you two supposed to be?" asked Adam.

"Chip 'n' Dale," said Donnie.

"Those are chipmunks. You mean Chippendales?" Adam asked.

"What's the difference?" asked Donnie.

"Yeah. Next time, I'm in charge of costumes," I said.

"You're just mad because you're not in great shape like me," Donnie said as German and Paris walked in. We looked at them; it wasn't really Brother Bear, more like Goldilocks and the three bears.

"Donnie, I'm going to kill you!" said German.

"G, come on! You look awesome!" said Donnie.

"Awesome compared to what? You and Justin are some strippers and Adam and Brody are from *Pulp Fiction*?" German asked.

"Looking at y'all, we should be entertainers at a five-year-old's birthday party," said Paris.

"The party's already started. Too late for different costumes," said Donnie.

"G, I have a brilliant idea. Let's go back to the room," said Paris.

"I'll see you guys down there," said German as he and Paris left.

"Donnie, those costumes suck," said Adam.

"What? I think their costumes are cool. I'd want to do that with my brother. Let's go down."

"I'm going to get Brody. See you guys down there," said Adam.

"All right," I said. We went downstairs and saw people everywhere dressed up as dynamic duos. Donnie sent a text to Tyler, our house DJ, to play "Pony" by Ginuwine so we could make an entrance. Tyler immediately changed the song, and Donnie and I moved onto the dance floor and began with the Magic Mike dance, and we had the crowd's attention.

After the routine was over, Donnie grabbed the mic. "This is the real Dynamic Duo!"

Tyler started playing "Ain't my type of hype," from the movie *House Party*, and another duo started dancing as Kid and Play doing the same dance. They were grabbing more attention than Donnie and I had. Donnie smiled; he was really impressed.

German and Paris had the crowd cheering as they came over. "These are the right costumes," said German.

Ginger, Jessica, and Pip entered as Charlie's Angels and neared us. "Oh, wow! Sexy," said Ginger.

"I thought I made it clear that this party was dynamic duos, not trios," said Donnie.

"Too bad. We're a trio," said Ginger.

Pip and I kissed, and Adam walked over. "Hey, babe," he said.

Jessica burst into laughter. "Wow! That afro!"

"*Pulp Fiction*," said Adam.

"That movie's a classic," I said.

"Guys, have a good time," Adam said as he and Jessica walked off.

Savannah and Lollie came over. "Hey, everybody!" said Savannah.

"What the hell are you supposed to be?" asked Ginger.

"The Bobbsey Twins, just sexier versions," said Lollie.

"Definitely," said Donnie.

"Let's dance," Savannah said to Donnie.

"I'll be back," he said leaving Ginger, Pip, and me on the sidelines. Ginger got angry and walked off.

"I'll be back, babe," said Pip. She went after Ginger as German and Paris came over. We all looked at Donnie, and Savannah and Lollie were all over him.

"Donnie's dressed exactly as he acts," said German.

"You two just missed Ginger. She stormed off," I said.

"Who could blame her? Donnie's playing the mack," said Paris. We laughed at that.

"I'm going to check out the rest of the party. See you later," said Paris.

"Enjoy," said German.

"It's nice to have a party and not have to think about the craziness," said German.

"I agree," I said.

Donnie came over to us as the girls were dancing with each other. "Bros, they're down for a threesome!"

"What about Ginger?" I asked.

"Hey, man, I'm single. This is what I do. Enjoy the party, my brothers!"

German and I walked to the backyard to check out the rest of the party, and we saw Paris and Pip comforting an upset Ginger.

"You OK?" asked German.

"OK as I can ever be," said Ginger. She walked off, and Paris followed her.

"I'm going to enjoy the party. See you guys later," said German.

I sat next to Pip on a bench, and we cuddled. But then I saw Steven and Brandon both in Sorcerer costumes dressed as the Greek god, and that got me thinking. "Hey, babe, I'm going to the restroom. I'll be right back." I walked over to Adam, who was dancing with Jessica. I went up to him and said, "I need to talk to you."

Adam looked at Jessica, who nodded, and Adam walked off with me. "What is it?"

"Let's find G," I said, and we went to the kitchen, where we saw German eating.

"What's up?" he asked.

"I need to talk to you guys about something. Let's go to your room," I said.

We got to German's room and saw Savannah and Lollie in bed with a handcuffed Donnie, which made us laugh.

"Wow!" said Adam.

"My bed, Donnie? Really?" asked German.

"Hey, don't worry, G. There's room for you too," said Lollie.

"Get your asses out of my room," said German.

Savannah and Lollie walked out leaving Donnie handcuffed.

"I hope you know you're getting my sheets dry cleaned," German said, and we laughed.

"What's up, Justin?" asked Adam.

"He wanted to ruin my threesome," said Donnie.

"I saw Steven and Brandon dressed as the Sorcerer," I said.

"So what? It just means they're unoriginal," said Donnie.

"Hear me out. What if the Greek god didn't kill Drake but Drake killed Matthew Richards?" I asked.

"What you're saying is that Drake dressed as the Greek god to kill Matthew Richards? Why?" asked Adam.

"Maybe to throw us off. I mean, why would he tell G that he was backing out of a plan that was well thought out?" I asked.

"You're losing it, bro," said Donnie.

"It's a good analysis however," G said. "The body *was* identified as Drake's."

"Just like the body was identified as Ben Klovis's body," said Justin.

We all looked at each other.

German

The next morning, I felt someone in my bed. I thought it was Paris, but when I rolled over, I saw it was Donnie. I wanted to wake him up, but I let him sleep. I smiled knowing that he was in my bed. I couldn't believe I was acting on the impulse of homosexuality. Donnie stretched, and I turned around to make sure he didn't catch me staring at him.

"Morning, bro," he said as he rubbed my head.

"Morning," I said.

"Hope you don't mind. There was a sock on my door, and your bed was big enough for us."

"Next time, warn me before you use my bed in any capacity," I said.

"You have aspirin?"

"On my desk," I said.

He got up and walked over there, and Adam walked in. "I have a huge headache."

Donnie gave him some aspirin and a bottle of water.

"Party was a little crazy," I said.

"A little? That had to be the best party we've had all year," said Donnie.

"I bet it was for you," said Adam.

"Why do you say that?" asked Donnie.

"Your threesome."

"Man, I need to set that back up," said Donnie, and he and Adam cracked up.

"Have you guys seen Paris?" I asked.

"Not since last night," said Adam.

"Maybe he met some hot chick and had a nightcap. Did you forget who your brother is?" asked Donnie.

"True. I'm going to get dressed. I have a few stops to make, and then I want to look at that footage again," I said.

"G, c'mon. What Justin said didn't make sense and you know it," said Donnie.

"It's not that it doesn't make sense. It's that it would be hard to prove. The possibility of Drake's being alive are really remote," I said.

"Yeah, well, I guess when this is all over, we'll find out the truth," said Adam.

"What makes you think this will ever be over?" asked Donnie.

"He has a point," I said, and we all laughed.

I looked at my phone but didn't see any messages from Paris. I sent him a text asking him to call me or let me know he was OK. I showered, dressed, and planned my day. I looked at my email and found one from my lawyer; it read, "Double take." *What I think I'm hearing isn't what I actually am hearing?* I asked myself. I went to Donnie's and Justin's room. Justin was still sleeping and Donnie was lying in bed on his phone. "We need to get to my condo," I said. "I have an idea."

"I was sent an email from my lawyer that read, 'Double take,'" I said.

What's that?" asked Adam.

"It's an FBI theory based on a movie made twenty years ago. The FBI uses it as a tactic to confuse someone in the moment," I said.

"How does that apply to this?" asked Donnie.

"The night the homecoming party Drake told me that he felt Ben wasn't dead and that he may be the one after us for revenge He was going to confront Katheryn Klovis about it.

"Why didn't he in the video?" said Adam.

"That's why I don't think he's dead. I think he killed Matthew Richards as a part of his plot." I said.

"Why would he kill a family member and make it seem like he was killed?" asked Adam.

"The plan was to plant Matthew Richards body at my house the night of the hurricane," I said. "Bradshaw was supposed to identify the body there meanwhile framing us for Murder and winning the lawsuit Mr. Klovis filed against the school. It's a win-win for them."

"But they can't do it now. The body was found at Mrs. Klovis's shop. They're not going to believe that we moved the body," said Adam.

"What do we do now?" asked Donnie.

"We beat them at their own game starting with revealing that Drake's alive," I said.

We all looked at each concerned that that would be hard to prove.

I left the guys at my condo and paid a call on Captain Deele. I walked into the precinct as I was let in by the desk manager and headed to his office. Deele looked not too thrilled to see me.

"Mr. Rigen, to what do I owe this unannounced visit?"

"I want to be sure that the body found was indeed Drake's," I said.

"Forensics did a full DNA scan and it matched."

"By fingerprint?" I asked.

"Follicle match."

I smiled and shook my head. Deele's response let me know he was involved in Drake's and Klovis's scheme. "I find it amazing that a detective is murdered and when the body is identified as him, it wasn't fingerprinted as he was when he took the job. The irony's amazing," I said.

"I can assure you the body found is in fact Detective Drake," said Deele.

"You're assurance is not trusted. I'm going to find out the truth. I hope for your sake that you had nothing to do with what you're trying to bury," I said.

"Our time is up here. Have a great day," said Deele.

I left, and I stopped at a post office to mail a file that I had in my bag to Internal Affairs. The dirt I had on this precinct was enough to send a few detectives and Deele to prison.

Adam

We got back to Alpha More and met up in German's room.

"How did it go at the station ?" asked Donnie.

"We need to wait it out. I shook things up at the precinct, and that might put some time on our side," said German.

"Yeah, but what exactly are we trying to prove?" I asked.

"For starters, Drake, finding out who the Greek god was, put a stop to Klovis's plan to sue the university and tried to make things get back to normal," said German.

"Yeah, but are you sure this is going to work?" asked Justin.

"I don't, but I know that the move I'm making will give us a great advantage," said German.

"G's right. The police are playing dirty if Drake is alive, so we have to play the same game," said Donnie.

"What do you think they're going to do?" I asked.

"My guess is that they'll convict Katheryn Klovis for the crime, and as of now, I'm not against that," I said.

"But we know she didn't do anything," said Donnie.

"The key words you said are 'didn't do anything.' She didn't call the police when Drake shot him. Instead, she helped him plant the body and cleaned up any evidence in her shop. I'm not so sure she's innocent. If she goes down for Drake's murder, I wouldn't be as mad," said German.

We couldn't argue about Mrs. Klovis's actions. All we could do was continue forward since time was on our side and Internal Affairs was about to have a field day with that mysterious package.

Donnie

Back at Alpha More, I called Ginger, but it went right to voice mail. That was odd. She always answered my calls. I called Theta Monroe to see if she was home.

"Theta Monroe. This is Mrs. Mack."

"Hi, Mrs. Mack. It's Donnie from Alpha More. Is Ginger home?"

"Hi, Donnie. I'm sorry, but she stepped out. I'm sure she'll be back soon. Would you like to leave a message?"

"No thanks. I'll try her cell phone again. Thanks, Mrs. Mack," I said.

I went to German's room; he was on his computer. "Hey," I said.

"What's up?"

"I was trying to get a hold of Ginger, but I can't reach her. Have you talked to her?" I asked.

"Not since the party. I'm not sure she'd want to talk to you anyway after what you did."

"Ginger and I have an understanding," I said.

"Sure."

"Adam still sleeping?" I asked.

"Yeah, and Justin's with Pip."

"Let's go hang out at the arcade," I said.

"I can dig it. Air hockey. You're going down."

"You wish," I said.

When we got to the arcade, I asked G, "What do you want to do first?"

"Air hockey."

"Loser pays," I said as I put coins in the slot.

German and I knocked the puck back and forth, and he scored and scored. "*Yes!*" he said. "That was too easy."

"Yeah, yeah, let's eat," I said.

When German and I were walking down a street full of restaurants, I saw Ginger in one. She was laughing. Paris was with her. I got angry for a few reasons, the first being that Paris was my fraternity brother, and two, I felt that Ginger was mine.

German asked, "Hey, man. You ready?"

"Yeah, man, let's go," I said. I was happy German hadn't seen Paris and Ginger because I wasn't ready to hear his opinion on the matter.

We got back to the house, and Justin was in the room on his computer. "What's up, bro?" he asked. "Are you all right?"

"I saw Ginger with Paris at a restaurant," I said.

"Whoa. You sure it was Paris?"

"Yep," I said. I started pacing.

"Calm down, man. It's not that serious."

Adam walked in. "What's going on?"

"Hey, close the door," I said. "I saw Ginger at a restaurant with Paris."

Adam and Justin looked at each other, and Adam asked, "So what?"

"Bro, Ginger and I have been a thing since freshman year, and Paris knew that," I said.

"Donnie, you two aren't a couple. She's given you chance after chance after chance, but you didn't make a move for her to be your girlfriend, so she moved on," said Justin.

"You two just don't get it," I said.

"You're right. I don't get it at all," said Adam.

"I came to get your study notes for trig," Adam said to Justin.

"Yeah, I got you," said Justin.

"I need to talk to her," I said as I stood.

"Wait a minute, Donnie," said Adam.

"You can't barge in there and confront her about something that isn't wrong," said Justin.

"Guys, I love you both dearly, but if you don't move out my way, I'm going to start swinging," I said.

They moved out of the way, and I walked out of the room.

German was in the hallway. "What's going on?"

"Later," I said. I stormed out of the house, walked to Theta Monroe, and knocked on the door. Mrs. Mack opened it. "Hey, Mrs. Mack. Is Ginger home?" I asked.

"Sure. Come right in."

I went to Ginger's room and knocked on the door.

She opened it and walked away from it. "What do you want?"

"Why him?" I asked as I walked in.

She looked at me in supposed confusion, but she knew who I meant. "Who told you?"

"I saw you out with him," I said.

"I can't wait forever, Donnie. I give my heart and expectations hoping I get what I want."

"What about what I want?" I asked.

"You're so selfish. You need to leave."

She opened the door. I said, "I'm sorry." I had hoped that my sad look would move her.

When I walked out of Theta Monroe, German, Justin, and Adam were there. We walked back to Alpha More. I knew that this was the end of it for Ginger and me.

Bradshaw

I got a call from Deele and went to his office.

"Please come in and close the door," he said.

"Everything OK?" I asked.

"Everything's very far from OK," he said. He put a folder on his desk. "We're about to be investigated by Internal Affairs."

"For what?" I asked.

"It's all in the file."

I opened the file and started reading documents on an evidence claim, and I saw surveillance photos of Drake carrying items out of the evidence room.

"Someone's making an accusation that Drake staged his murder to cover up his tampering with evidence. We have proof he took a hundred thousand from a bust we did a year ago."

"How did Internal Affairs get this?" I asked.

Special Agent Rochelle Markston open the door. "Good morning, Captain Deele, Detective Bradshaw. You two are being investigated at this time. If we find any evidence of corruption, we'll investigate the entire precinct." Another agent walked in. "Assisting me in the matter is Special Agent Greg Valve. He'll be handling the interrogations."

"May I ask why I'm being investigated?" I asked.

"Certainly, Detective Bradshaw. Last year, you helped Detective Drake on an accidental death case. It was reported that a Rolex GMT Master 1675 was missing from the victim that had not been reported stolen. Six months later, that same watch was found in a pawn shop in New York. The owner provided a photograph of you," Valve said as he showed me the photo.

Captain Deele looked at me in total shock. I was guilty.

"Agent Valve, would you take Detective Bradshaw to interrogation?" Markston asked.

I stood, and Valve walked with me to interrogation. In the room, he turned off the camera, which I thought was strange.

"I have a thousand questions for you, but I'm not going to ask them because I know why you did what you did. You thought you wouldn't get caught," said Valve.

"So you don't want to ask me about the watch?" I asked.

179

"No. Between you and me, I'm taking the bar exam in a month. I want to become an assistant district attorney and take down someone we both know."

I sat back. He knew I was nervous.

"You know who sent this information to us, right?"

"No I don't," I said.

"Think about it. Who else would have this information and not be noticed?"

"German Rigen," I said.

Valve smiled. I knew that was whom he was talking about.

CHAPTER 16

UNEXPECTED TROUBLE

Justin

MY BIOLOGY MIDTERM was the next day, but I couldn't focus on my book. Donnie was listening to music through his headset and dancing by his bed. I get a text from Pip: "How's the studying going?"

"Help!" I responded.

"Meet me at the library in twenty minutes."

I packed up my bag, and Donnie asked, "Where you going?"

"Library. I can't focus," I said.

"Need me to come with?"

"No offense, bro, but you're the reason I can't focus," I said.

"Because I'm so good looking?"

"Whatever you say, bro. See you later," I said.

Downstairs, Brandon approached me. "Hey, Justin. Heading out?"

"I'm meeting my girlfriend at the library," I said.

"I'm heading there as well. Mind if I catch a ride with you?"

"No, I don't mind," I said.

"Sweet. I'll get my backpack. Hang on." He headed upstairs.

I was waiting for Brandon in the main room but close to Alves's office. The door was open, and I overheard his phone conversation.

"Dean, I understand the message is to settle, but there has to be another way. Not to mention I'm not sure how I can break the news to the gentleman here that this house will close."

"Ready?" Brandon asked startling me.

Alves walked to his door. "Justin, did you need something?"

"No sir," I said, and Brandon and I went out to my car.

"You all right, man?" he asked.

"Yeah," I said.

"You sure?" he asked.

"How's your mom?" I asked.

"She's good, but she's still in disbelief that that detective was found in her shop."

"Did she know him?" I asked.

"I remember him being the responding detective when Ben died, but I didn't know she had any other communication with him."

Brandon said that I knew that he couldn't have been the Greek god. I pulled into the library parking lot, and I saw Pip waiting by the entrance as we walked up to her. "Hey," Pip said, and we kissed. "Hi, Brandon," she said.

"Hi, Pip. Thanks for the ride, Justin."

"No prob," I said as Brandon walked away.

"That was nice of you to give him a ride," said Pip.

"I was heading this way, so why not?" I asked.

"Ready to study?"

"Yes," I said.

Pip and I were sitting at a table. I was getting really frustrated; my mind was elsewhere. "I'll be back," I said. I went to a vending machine, and I saw Steven watching me. I gave him a nod. He walked away. I was curious about where he was going, so I followed him. He went to the running track, and I saw the Greek god rise up out of the bleachers. The two started signing to each other. I pulled out my phone and recorded the conversation, which became intense. The Greek god grabbed Steven, who looked very panicked; he nodded. I went back to the library.

"How was your walk?" Pip asked.

"Good. I left my creative thinking book at home. I need to go and get it," I said.

"You can use mine."

"It's OK, babe. I have mine highlighted. See you later," I said and I kissed her.

I drove back to Alpha More and went to German's room. He was at his computer. "Hey, bro," he said.

"You studying?" I asked.

"I am. You all right?"

"Look at this," I said as I gave him my phone.

German watched the video and was studying the signing going on.

"Steven said that he couldn't go through with the plan," said German.

The next part of the video showed the Greek god grabbing him and signing with one hand.

"You will" German said.

"He will what?" asked Donnie. German went back in the video to see if there's more information and I caught the video too late. "It's a dead end at this point, but we need to watch Steven too." German said.

German gave me back my phone as I felt bad it wasn't enough. Things were getting complicated and I felt like Throwing in the towel and turning myself in. We all leave German's room as Donnie wanted to go to the Gym and I had more studying to do.

Paris

Ginger and I were parked in front of the Theta Monroe house and were making out heavily.

"You know, you almost had me, Mr. Rigen," she said.

"Please! I know what I have," I said.

"You have to go back today?"

"Yeah, but the longest I'll be gone is a week. I need to move my stuff out of my apartment and figure out a plan since I'm coming back to Pendleton," I said.

"A plan like what?"

"I guess I'll figure that out in the meantime," I said as I smiled at her.

Ginger smiled back and began to blush. "I can't believe I'm in a car with Paris Rigen."

"Believe it. We're here," I said.

"Where?"

"Here, talking about the future. I'm moving back to be with you if you'll have me," I said.

"Paris Rigen is asking me to be his girlfriend?"

"Will you be my girlfriend?" I asked.

"Are you kidding? Yes!"

We kissed, and she smiled again. "I have a boyfriend!" said an excited Ginger. "Are we meeting for dinner tonight?"

"Of course. I have to go to Alpha More first to talk with G," I said.

"Can you not tell him about us?" asked Ginger.

"Why?" I asked.

"You know I have history with Donnie, and if you tell G, I know he'll tell him."

"He's going to find out eventually," I said.

"I know, but let eventually be a while, please."

I sighed. It wasn't a big deal for me, but I'd respect her wish. "All right, fine," I said.

"Thank you," Ginger said as she kissed me. "See you later."

"All right," I said as she got out of my car.

I drove to Alpha More, where I saw Alves getting out of his car. "Hey, Mr. Alves," I said.

"Paris, what brings you by?"

"I want to talk with my brother," I said as we walked into the house.

"Did you enjoy the party?"

"It was a lot of fun. I miss being in Alpha More."

"Never forget that this is always your home."

"Yes sir," I said.

I went upstairs to German's room; when I walked in, he said, "Well if it isn't my only biological brother. You done kissing Ginger on the streets?"

"Damn. So you know?" I asked.

"Donnie told the guys he saw you out and he confronted her. Why Ginger?"

"Why not? She's sexy as hell and a sorority leader just like I was. Did you forget?" I asked.

"Why would you do that to Donnie? You know those two have a history."

"Look. One thing led to another, and it happened. Now she's my girlfriend," I said.

"Oh geez."

"that's another reason I'm moving back to Pendleton," I said.

German looked shocked. "You're always doing something crazy for some girl"

"I want to be with her. You know I'm not one for long-distance relationships," I said.

"Don't you think you're jumping just a tad bit far in this? What are you going to do here?"

"I'll figure it out," I said.

German shook his head in disbelief, but I didn't care. This was where I wanted to be.

Adam

A lot was going through my mind—my mom, midterms, Mrs. Klovis … I remembered the day I met Ben and wished I'd done things differently.

Brody walked into the room as I was wiping my tears. "Hey, man, you OK?"

"I'm fine," I said.

"How's studying going?"

"It's going. I'm going to take a break for a while, make a sandwich. You want one?" I asked.

"Yeah, thanks, man."

I went down to the kitchen and saw Steven, who gave me a creepy look. "Hey," I said. He raised his cup to me. I pulled items out of the refrigerator and asked, "Would you like a sandwich?" He shook his head, but he continued watching me. "Dude, what's your deal?" I asked.

He chuckled. "My deal?"

That was the first time I'd heard him speak since he'd come back.

"I haven't been the same since you four did what you did."

"Look, man, I'm sorry. I don't know how many more times I can say that to you. There's not a day goes by that I don't regret what we did," I said.

"The problem is that you four think you're untouchable, especially Donnie and German, but you wait. Your day is coming." He left the kitchen.

That exchange ruined my appetite. I went up to German's room; he was on the computer and Paris was sitting on the bed.

"Hey, Adam, how are you?" asked Paris.

"Hey, P. I'm good. How are you?" I asked.

"Good man. Just came to see G. I'll see y'all later," Paris said as he left us.

German asked, "You all right?"

"No I'm not, man. I don't know how much more of this I can take. We're going too far with all of this," I said. I sat on the bed.

German came over to me. "What's going on?"

"I'm just going through a lot. All of this and what's going on with my mom. I feel like I'm going to break," I said.

"It's OK to break, man. You're going to pick up the pieces and pull it back together."

"I don't want to hear that. I'm not like you and Donnie. I don't have money. My mom is all I have, G, and I can't even go to her," I said. I began to cry.

German hugged me. "Look, man, everything's going to be OK. Your mom, the situation we're in … We're all going to make it through and find some way to laugh about this, I promise."

He hugged me again. I needed that.

I went back to my room. Brody was getting dressed. "Hey, man, never mind the sandwich. I got called into work," he said.

"I'm sorry. I got downstairs but never made the sandwiches," I said.

"No worries. Guess it wasn't meant to be," said Brody, and he left.

I get on my computer to video chat Jessica.

"Hey, you," said Jessica.

"Hi," I said.

"You OK?"

"I have a lot on my mind, and then I have my first midterm tomorrow morning," I said.

"You'll do just fine, Adam."

Justin walked into the room. "Justin's here. I gotta go," I said.

"Hey, Jessica," said Justin.

"Hi, Justin. Have a great study session," Jessica said as she blew me a kiss.

I closed my laptop. "Hey, man," I said.

"I came down to talk you and get some advice?"

"I might not be the best person to ask advice from. I'm not in the right head space at all," I said.

"What's wrong?"

"Tell you later, bro. I just had a breakdown and don't want to have another," I said.

"I get it, man, but hey, don't stay in that place too long. Midterms start tomorrow."

"Thanks, man. You ready to study?" I asked.

"Yeah." He pulled out his book. "I need a highlighter."

Justin went to Brody's desk for a highlighter and Brody's computer came on. "Look at this," said Justin. I got up and looked at the monitor. We saw that German's, Justin's and Donnie's, and my room were being monitored.

"What the hell?" I said. I texted German and Donnie to come to my room.

Donnie came in in just a few seconds. "What's going on?" We pointed to Brody's screen.

German walked in next, saw us watching the screen, and looked at it too. He immediately left, and we followed him to his room. He spotted the camera in the vent. He opened the vent, got it out, and walked out of his room. We followed him to Donnie's and Justin's room, where he also found a camera in the vent. German looked angry. "It'll go down when Brody gets home."

Brody walked into the room, which was dark. He went to his computer. The screen turned on, and he saw all the cameras pointed at him. I turned the lights on. We had him cornered. "I know what this looks like," he said.

"You have no idea," said German.

"Why the hell did you plant cameras in our rooms?" asked Donnie.

"Look ... I was hired to do that."

"By whom?" asked Justin.

"Can't tell you that."

"Uh, Brody, you don't have choice," said Donnie.

"Brody, it can only be Steven, Brandon, or Mrs. Klovis. Spill it!" said German.

"It's none of them," said Brody.

"Brody, I'm going to reason with you. What you did violated Greek rules, but we won't tell Alves and get your contract revoked if you tell us," said German.

"Detective Bradshaw gave me the equipment. She's working with someone who's trying to take you down, German."

"Who?" asked German.

"I don't know. All I know is that she wanted me to report to her about certain triggers and when you were not in your room."

"That doesn't make sense," said Donnie.

"It's the truth," said Brody.

"I don't believe him, G," said Donnie.

"I don't either," said Justin.

I kept my opinion to myself because I wasn't sure, but German said, "I believe him."

"What?" Justin asked.

German left the room, and we followed him outside to his car.

"Why'd you believe Brody's story, G?" asked Justin.

"Because I set up Bradshaw with Internal Affairs."

"How the hell did you do that?" asked Donnie.

"Please. I have enough dirt to shut down that entire precinct. I needed to get her off me and have Drake's murder solved by someone without her influence."

"Damn, that's smart," said Donnie.

"So you believe she got Brody to bug our rooms?" I asked.

"It's so like her," said German.

"Who do you think she's working with?" asked Justin.

"Don't know, but I'll pay her a visit to let her know I'm on to her," G said.

German

I called Bradshaw and asked her to meet me at a gas station five miles out of town. She arrived and got out of her vehicle. "You called me here?" she asked.

I handed her the cameras. "When you try to be sneaky, make sure the person you're watching isn't just as sneaky. Who put you up to this?" I asked.

Bradshaw was obviously not thrilled to have been caught. "You put out an accusation that Drake wasn't dead. If that's true, I need to know the source that you're using to confirm it."

"It would be the same source that provided me the information that you stole a rolex GMT Master 1675. From the evidence of a case and pawned it. The same one that Drake purchased to make it seem like it was a legitimate sale."

"How do you know that?" asked Bradshaw.

"The same way I knew that you and Drake stole over a hundred thousand from the evidence room and that Deele's signature is on the form that booked that evidence. I have eyes everywhere," I said.

"What's your goal here?"

"It's real simple. We have several police reports that state four Alpha More men were attacked and that the Klovises need to drop the lawsuit filed against the university."

"That's not in my jurisdiction," said Bradshaw.

"You're right, but if you drop whatever you and your mystery partner are trying to pull, the case Internal Affairs has on you will disappear," I said.

"You expect me to believe that you can make that go away?"

"That all depends on you, Detective Bradshaw. You tried to make a fool of me once, and that got you investigated. Cross me again, and I'm sure you'll share a cell with Katheryn Klovis. Have a good night."

Bradshaw

After meeting with German, the previous night, I went to Valve's office and said, "He knows."

"We need to scale back," said Valve.

"What about the plan to keep my job?" I asked.

"I'll come up with a new plan, but right now, we need to go back to the investigation as I know how German Rigen operates. It won't be good."

"This is unbelievable," I said.

"You're telling me."

Markston walked into the office. "Agent Valve, Detective Bradshaw, funny you're here. I was just about to mention you."

"What's this about?" asked Valve.

"Apparently, Drake was involved in a blackmail scheme with German Rigen. Valve, I heard of your past with that person, so I'm going to take over with Bradshaw, and you can take Captain Deele effective immediately. Detective Bradshaw, I'll expect you in my office shortly."

Valve put his head down after Markston left. "I'll talk to her."

"I need to tell German Rigen you're the one I'm working with to take him down," I said.

"That's out of the question."

"No. Everything German said last night has just happened. I can't risk jail," I said.

"Let me guess. he told you that if you expose me, he'll make all of this go away?"

I was quiet; I didn't know what to do. All I could think about was how I'd gotten where I was in the first place.

"Do you what you have to, but understand that I know the truth and that should speak better volumes than someone trying to blackmail you, Detective."

"Drake started this by blackmailing him, and since he's gone, it's all on my shoulders," I said.

"Whoa, wait a minute. Did you mean gone or dead?" asked Valve.

"Dead. I meant dead," I said.

Valve gave me a look. "I better go talk with Markston." I leave the room as I knew what I just did made him suspicious of what German believes. I didn't know what to believe or how to move all I know is that I wanted out of this.

Donnie

I drove to the gym to work out. "Hey, Phil," I said to the guy working the counter.

"Donnie. Didn't think I was going to see you. It's been a ghost town since it's midterms."

"I can see," I said looking around.

"Did you ever consider personal training? I know you have your certification."

"I'll get back to you on that," I said.

"All right, man. Have a great workout."

"Thanks," I said. I headed to the bench press. I looked at my phone as my mind was corrupted with knowing Ginger and Paris were hooking up. I placed weights on the machine and did ten lifts. I saw Paris walking into the gym, and he looked excited.

"Donnie! I see you're working out, bro."

"I see you're still in town, P. Don't you have an important job or something?" I asked.

"I don't punch in or out. That's what happens when you become a boss. Let's see what you're pressing," Paris said as he went under the press. He struggled a bit. "Man, that's heavy. Let me do one more." He struggled with that lift too, and I helped him place the bar back.

"So you and Ginger?" I asked.

Paris smiled at me condescendingly. "What about me and Ginger?"

"Don't play with me, man. You know what the hell I'm talking about," I said.

Paris laughed defensively. "OK, man, you caught me. We're together now."

"The only reason she's with you is to get back at me, to have fun at my expense. It won't last long," I said and walked away. I knew that was harsh, but I was furious.

I went back to the house and went to German's room. "They're a couple," I said.

"Who?" asked German.

"Come on, G," I said.

"Oh, I knew about that already. It's just like Paris. You can't be that surprised."

"You knew?" I asked. I was taking the Ginger and Paris thing hard. "I need to talk to her."

"Donnie, not in your current state of mind. I know this is a hard thing to accept, but this will blossom or crumble. No matter the outcome, cherish the memories you have and honor her decision to choose someone else. If it makes you feel any better, you still have me. I still have a crush on you."

German was joking and trying to make me feel better. It worked. "I knew it! You can't resist me," I said as started poking him.

"Stop!"

"I love you too, man. See you later," I said. I went to my room.

"Hey, bro," I said when I saw Justin. "How's the studying going?" I asked.

"I'm almost done. You want to get something to eat soon?" Justin asked.

"You know it, man. Paris just told me that he and Ginger are together," I said.

"Pushed her into the arms of another man. That's karma, bro."

"Why can't you be like G? He gave me this nice speech and told me he still has a crush on me," I said.

"Forget it, bro. You're not my type," said Justin, and we laughed.

"All right, I'm ready," he said.

We left the room and saw Steven looking at us in the hallway. "That guy is such a creep," I said.

Adam came out of his room. "Where you guys going?"

"To get something to eat. I'm starving," said Justin.

"Cool. I'm hungry too," said Adam.

When we left the house, I saw Ginger getting out of her car. "Hang on a sec," I said. I walked over to her and said, "Hey."

"Hi," she said in a low tone.

"Congrats. He's a great guy. I'm sorry I couldn't be him," I said. I kissed her forehead. It was big of me to do that. German was right. I needed to let her go and be happy.

CHAPTER 17

WHOM TO BELIEVE?

Justin

AFTER MY EXAM, I walked to the quad and saw Brandon talking to Pip, which concerned me. They hugged, and then she turned and saw me. "How was your midterm?" she asked.

"As good as it gets. What was that all about?" I asked.

"I ran into Brandon in the library, and he walked me to the quad. We were just laughing about Ben, no big deal."

I looked at her, and she gave me an annoyed look. "You can't think I'd do that, do you?"

"When it comes to him, I don't know what to believe. I still don't know the relationship you had with Ben and if you're over it."

"That's not fair. We agreed to put that behind us, Justin."

"You're right. I'm sorry," I said. I leaned in to kiss her.

"I have to work tonight, so I won't make it to dinner," said Pip.

"I'll get something with the guys. What are you doing after?" I asked.

"You want to come over?"

"Do I?" I asked as I continued to kiss her.

Back at Alpha More, I went to my room, where Adam and Donnie were laughing and talking. "Justin! How were midterms?" asked Adam.

"Let's hope I passed them all," I said.

German came in. "Hey, guys."

"Don't you have a midterm in an hour?"

"Yeah. I left my laptop here. I came back for it," said German.

Donnie looked at German suspiciously "You need your laptop for a midterm?"

"Yes," said German.

We were quiet. We'd learned that if we did that, he'd eventually talk.

"Bradshaw told me that someone from my past was trying to reopen something that had been closed," he said.

"Who? And do you really believe her when we all know Drake's alive?" asked Donnie.

"Yeah, but do you think Bradshaw knows that?" asked Adam.

"It doesn't matter. However, a few things need to happen. We need to go back to Matthew Richards's farm to see if there are any other leads to Drake. I need to figure out who Bradshaw's working with, and I have a plan for the Klovises that might end the lawsuit," said German.

We had a lot of work to do.

Donnie

Adam and I pulled into the Richards farm. He stopped, and his engine started knocking. "Adam, you have to get rid of this truck," I said.

"Can't afford to. This truck is all I have. I don't even have a home."

We went to the front door and rang the bell. No answer. We heard a wood chipper, so we went to the backyard and saw the same guy we'd seen there before.

"Excuse me, sir," I said, but he didn't hear me because of the noise. I tapped him on the shoulder, and he turned around quickly and turned off the chipper.

"Can I help you?"

"Yes sir. We were here a while ago. We're students from the university hoping to do an experiment with Mr. Richards," said Adam.

"Yeah, I remember. Weren't there four of you then?"

"Yes. The other two are going to another farm. We figured we'd give Mr. Richards another try," I said.

"You just missed him. He was here, but then he left."

"He was here when?" asked Adam.

"Last Friday. The other farmers and I got our paychecks then."

"I'm sorry if this is a little personal, but how does receiving your paycheck indicate that Mr. Richards was here?" I asked.

"The checks were in our personal folders in the break room as normal. His signature was on all of them, and the checks cleared."

"I'm a little confused. If he were missing, wouldn't the police want to find out where he was and speak to him?" asked Adam.

"Maybe he already went to the police station to speak with them."

Adam and I looked at each other. I pulled out my card and gave it to the man. "This project is due in a few weeks. Would you ask Mr. Richards to call us when he gets back please?" I asked.

"You got it."

Adam and I walked back to his truck. He said, "That's odd. Richards signs for paychecks to pay his employees."

"Yeah, and I looked it up before we came here. He's still missing," I said.

"Something isn't right about this, Donnie."

"Let's get back and tell G and Justin," I said.

Adam couldn't get his truck started. "It's a bit of a process," he said.

"More like a delayed process. If Michael Myers was after us, we'd be dead," I said.

Adam chuckled as he tried to start the truck. He succeeded. "See? There we go."

We got back to the house and went up to German's room, where Justin was as well.

"What did you find out?" asked German.

"Apparently, Matthew Richards made an appearance," said Adam.

"Made an appearance?" asked Justin.

"Yeah. According to that same guy, they received their paychecks with Richards's signature," I said.

"He could have signed those checks before he went missing or died," said German.

"I looked it up. According to the newspaper, he's still missing," said Donnie.

"Then how were they paid?" asked Justin.

"Like G said, he could have done it before," I said.

"What do we do now?" asked Adam.

"I'll meet with Bradshaw in the morning. I may bring up Richards," said German.

Bradshaw

I pulled up to town square to meet Rigen. It took me forty-eight hours to build a case against Katheryn Klovis, but it was on the verge of suspension. I saw Rigen.

"Good evening," he said.

"Good evening," I said.

"Are you going to do what I asked, Detective?"

"How were you able to find that information on me?" I asked.

"That's not need-to-know information. Let's be clear. If you get Katheryn Klovis down for this, all of what you are experiencing goes away," he said.

"She'll be arrested within a week. You have my word," I said.

"Whom are you working with?" he asked.

"You seem concerned about that, German. You afraid that my accomplice might have something on you?" I asked.

German smirked. I couldn't tell if he was being condescending or if he was nervous.

"The question was rhetorical. I know it's Greg Valve. The only person who felt I was guilty in my late fiancée's crime spree," he said.

I was impressed that German knew that. Maybe I'd given him a clue in our prior meeting. "You're very clever, almost too clever to be twenty," I said.

"That comes from always searching for something that proves you're worthy. I've had to do that my whole life. I don't expect that to change."

"What do you hope to accomplish?" I asked.

"To get everything back to normal."

I nodded, and he left. He was caught up in catastrophic situations, and the only way he knew how to get out of them was to expose them to the light.

"One week, Detective Bradshaw. I'll be watching," he said and then walked to his car.

Adam

"Dammit!" I yelled. My truck wasn't starting.

Someone knocked on my window. It was Brody, who asked, "You all right?"

"Can't get this thing started, and I'm running late," I tell him.

"I can give you a ride. C'mon," said Brody.

I get in his car, and he asked, "Hey, man, no hard feelings for the other night?"

"I wouldn't say hard feelings, but I'm uncomfortable about why you did that," I said.

"If I tell you why, you wouldn't believe me," said Brody.

"Try me," I said.

"I cheated on a bio test. The instructor is Bradshaw's husband. He knew what I did, and he said that he'd keep quiet if I helped her with this case."

"He blackmailed you to turn on us?" I asked.

"Yes. Look, don't judge me. I'm not like you guys. I have no family, no money … I did what I had to do."

"You and I are more alike than you think. My mom's in a rehab facility, I never knew my father, and I'm broke too," I said.

"Yeah, but you four have each other. We're all brothers, but you guys actually show that to each other. It's a lot more than I have."

We got to school and started going our separate ways. He said, "Good luck on your midterms."

"Brody, if you ever want to hang out, we can," I said, and Brody nodded. I started thinking about how much Brody wanted to be included and how often we'd shut him out.

After my exam, I went to the cafeteria, got food, and sat with the others.

"I know I failed this midterm," Justin said. "I can feel it. My mind was on this situation."

"You're just being hard on yourself. I'm sure you did fine," said German.

"You did a lot better than I did," I said.

"What's wrong with you guys?" asked Donnie.

"For starters, my truck wouldn't start this morning. I was almost late," I said.

"I keep telling you get rid of that piece of junk," said Donnie.

"Can't afford a new one," I said.

"Why don't we find you a different mechanic?" asked German.

"I can't afford that either," said Adam.

"I'm not going there with you," said German.

"G, how'd it go with Bradshaw?" asked Donnie.

"I didn't show her the picture, not yet. I need her to arrest Mrs. Klovis."

"She's for sure going to arrest her?" Donnie asked.

"Within a week," G said.

"I think we should get out of town," said Donnie.

"And go where?" asked Justin.

"Fall is at its peak. Let's go to my parents' cabin on Willows Lake," said Donnie.

"Just us?" asked Adam.

"Do we want the ladies to come with us?" asked Donnie.

"I haven't spent much time with Jessica. I'd like to bring her," I said.

"Same with me and Pip," said Justin.

"I'm cool with that," said Donnie.

That surprised the rest of us, and G said, "Let me get this straight. You're OK with Pip coming up to your parents' lake house?"

"The place is nine thousand square feet. She and I can avoid each other," said Donnie.

"I'm going to invite Jessica. See you guys later," I said.

I left the cafeteria and walked to the culinary department to find Jessica. I saw her go into the storage room, and I went in. She turned, smiled, and said, "Hey!"

"Hi," I said, and we kissed.

"How'd you do on your midterm?" asked Jessica.

"OK, I guess. How about you?" I asked.

"I usually test well, so I think I did really well."

"Nice. Well, no pressure, but Donnie is getting together us guys and our ladies to go to his parents' lake house. Would you like to come?" I asked.

"Sure! I need to get away."

"Good. I have to go. I'm catching a ride with Justin. See you later," I said.

"Yep," she said.

We kissed, and I walked out of there happy.

German

I walked into the precinct office and into Valve's office, which was empty. I sat in his chair. I heard his voice. I just waited for him to walk in.

"Greg Valve," I said when he did. "Who'd have thought in Boston that you'd be Internal Affairs in Pendleton?" I asked.

"There was an opening," he said.

"Ironically, the same city I go to school in. How coincidental," I said.

"I take it this isn't a social visit, German."

"It's not. I came here to warn you that if you continue to work with Bradshaw to take me down, all that you thought was buried in Boston will be dug up in Pendleton," I said.

"Are you threatening me, German Rigen?"

"You can take this as a threat, a promise, or a revelation. Cross me and I'll expose you," I said as I put a folder on his desk and smiled.

He picked up the folder and opened it trying not to seem nervous, which I knew he was. He put the folder down and looked at me. "So you want to stoop that low?" he asked.

"You started this. There are no rules," I said as I stood. Valve was quiet. "Believe me, there's a lot more. Twenty years in the business and you didn't manage to stay clear in any of them," I said. I walked out of his office. I got in my car and pulled out the flash drives, the only things that stood in the way of my being found guilty. I needed to hide them, and I knew where.

CHAPTER 18

PARTY RAT

Donnie

IT WAS OCTOBER 31—Halloween and German's birthday. Alpha More's tradition was the tank of shame. Justin, Adam, and I prepared the tank with ice and water.

"Donnie, this is so cruel," said Justin.

"Yeah. I mean, I didn't have ice in mine," said Adam.

"Well look. He's the other single one who doesn't have somebody, so I'm sure he wakes up with morning problems," I said, and the others laughed. "Be quiet. He might hear us."

The other members of Alpha More came out in Greek masks and attire.

"OK, it's ready. Let's get him," I said.

We went to G's room, and I quietly opened the door. He was asleep. I counted down on my fingers three, two, one, and we all yelled, "It's your birthday! Prepare to be sacrificed!" Justin, Adam, Petey, Otto, and I picked up German, walked him outside to the tank, and sat him on the hinged plank over the tank.

"Donnie, why's there ice in the water?" asked German.

"Don't worry, brother. It won't be cold at all," I said as I laughed.

"All right, let's get going. Remember that if you miss, that's twenty push-ups because German is twenty. First up, Randall!" I said. Randall's throw missed the target. "A miss! Twenty push-ups for you, sir," I said. German looked cold and nervous.

"Next up," I said. The brother missed the target too. "That's twenty push-ups for you!" I said. I walked up to German sitting on the plank.

"That water's cold!" he said. "I just stuck my toe in it, and I swear there's no blood flowing to it now."

"Yeah, well, it could be worse. Someone could actually hit the target," I said.

McKinney threw and missed. "Twenty for you!" I yelled.

"All right, Adam, sink him."

Adam's throw went deliberately to the side. "Happy birthday, G!" He dropped to do twenty.

"You suck, Adam!"

Justin did the same, as did the others.

"Seriously? All of you missed? Let me show you how it's done," I said as I picked up the ball. I threw it and hit the target, and German fell into the ice water.

"Score! Happy birthday, G! That's how you do it," I said.

Justin, Adam, and I ran up to help German out. Adam gave him a towel. I snuggled him to warm him up. "All right, it's over. You were a good sport," I said.

Stuttering due to the chill, he said, "I'm going to kill you!" which cracked us up.

Alves walked up. "All right, gentlemen, let's get this cleaned up please. Happy birthday, German!"

Paris

I drove to Pendleton for German's birthday and to see Ginger. I checked in at Rita's Bed and Breakfast, and the clerk said, "Your room is already paid for. Here's your key."

I walked to the room and opened the door. There was Ginger in sexy lingerie.

"Hello, boyfriend!" she said.

"What are you doing here?" I asked.

"I figured we could have some alone time before Alpha More's Halloween party," she said.

"Forget the party. I just want to be here with you," I said.

We kissed, and we flopped on the bed.

"I spent a hundred bucks on my Halloween costume. I have to make an entrance," she said.

"Perfect. I'm supposed to me with my parents and G for his birthday, but we should be done by eight," I said.

She and I kissed some more, and then she took off her top revealing a black push-up bra.

"Damn! You're so sexy, babe," I said.

She turned on a radio and started doing a seductive, sexy dance; she dropped her skirt and walked up to me. I took off my shirt, and we kissed, got under the covers, and began to have sex, the best way I could come into Pendleton.

German

I pulled into the restaurant parking lot, gave the valet my keys, and walked over to my parents, who were waiting for me in the lobby. "Hey, Mom, Dad," I said.

"Happy birthday, German!" said Verna.

"Happy birthday, son!" said Chance.

I hugged Verna, and she kissed my forehead.

Paris walked in with Ginger and said, "Little bro, happy birthday to you!"

"Happy birthday, G," said Ginger.

"Son, who's this?" asked Chance.

"Mom, Dad, this is Ginger, my girlfriend and current member of Theta Monroe."

"It's a pleasure to meet you, Mr. and Mrs. Rigen," said Ginger as she shook their hands.

The host led us to our table, we settled in, and my dad said, "German, you're twenty now. If I had my twenties back, oh what a mess I would make of it."

Paris, Verna, and Ginger laughed, but I felt slightly out of place.

"Dad, so you don't think German makes messes?" asked Paris trying to make me look bad.

"I'm sure German gets his hands dirty," said Chance.

"That's enough both of you. Quit talking about my baby," said Verna.

"So Ginger, is Paris the first frat guy you've dated?" I asked.

"Yeah, he's the first," said Ginger; I just smiled at her.

"She did have a small fling with Donnie Diamante," said Paris.

"Really? Donnie? What made you not pursue that further?" asked Chance.

"He had commitment issues," Ginger said as she looked at me.

After dinner, I asked, "Can I be excused for the restroom?"

"Go ahead, son."

I walked from the table; Paris followed me and said, "I saw you giving Ginger those looks."

"You need to give her those looks too. She just lied to our parents," I said.

"Don't give her a hard time, all right? She used to be with Donnie, but she's with me now."

"Knock yourself out, bro. I just want to get through this dinner and go to the party," I said.

When I got back to the table, my dad was laughing more than he usually did. I sat, and he pulled out a small box. "Happy birthday, son."

"Thank you," I said. I opened the box and saw a key fob with the Lamborghini logo. I was shocked. I looked at my dad. "No way!" I asked.

"I helped Dad pick it out. It's out front," said Paris.

I got up and hugged my dad and Verna. We all walked out of the restaurant, and I saw my new red Lamborghini Urus with a bow on it.

"Have fun, son," said Chance as I got in my car and drove to Alpha More. The streets were crowded with students coming to the party. I parked in our lot, and someone yelled, "Nice ride!"

I walked in the back entrance to the kitchen, where Otto asked, "Hey, G, how was your birthday dinner?" I pulled out my key. Otto asked, "Is that a Lamborghini fob?"

"Yep. My dad bought me a new Urus," I said.

"Dude, you owe me a ride!" Otto said as I left the kitchen and headed to my room.

I walked in and heard the shower going. "Donnie, is that you?" I asked.

"Yeah, G. One sec," he said.

He came out with a towel around his waist. "I swear the water's hotter in your bathroom."

"The party's started. How come you're just getting ready?" I asked.

"We were setting up all day. Get dressed and meet me down there," said Donnie as he put on his shirt and pants and left the room.

I changed my clothes and went downstairs to the party, where the DJ gave me a shout-out. "Look who just walked in! Alpha More's very own birthday boy, German Rigen!"

Everyone was wearing a costume and was cheering me on. I went over to Donnie, who gave me a shot. I downed it, and everyone kept cheering me.

Justin

We pulled up to Jessica's apartment, and she came out and climbed in the back with Adam and said, "Hey, guys!"

"Hey, happy Halloween," said Adam.

"I'm excited to go to this carnival. I hear it's more like a fright fest," said Pip.

"I thought you didn't like that kind of stuff," I said.

"It's different when you're there to protect me," said Pip, which made us all laugh.

"Have you heard from G or Donnie?" asked Adam.

"G said he went out to dinner with his parents. Paris brought Ginger along," I said.

"Why?" asked Adam.

"I have no idea, but he said it was awkward," I said.

"Why would that be awkward? It's not like he doesn't know who she is," Pip said.

"The fact the she'd been with Donnie was the awkward part," said Adam.

"Define 'with Donnie,'" Jessica said.

"Right," said Pip.

"I don't think we should get into that now," I said.

"So you guys just say you don't want to talk about something if it's a difficult topic?" asked Jessica.

"No, it's just that whether or not Ginger and Donnie had a relationship that wasn't just sex, they had a chemistry that couldn't be denied," said Adam.

"We're not denying that they had chemistry. I've watched him disrespect that girl to the point that she'd cry herself to sleep. She finally gets a guy who treats her with so much grace, and the three of you are saying it's awkward because she's with someone else you know?" asked Jessica.

"You go, Jess," said Pip.

"Can we change the subject please?" I asked.

"Men," said Pip.

We got to the carnival, and Jessica and Pip walked together while Adam and I followed.

"That was the worst car ride ever," said Adam.

"Agreed," I said. "I'd almost rather go the party than defend Donnie."

We walked into the carnival; everyone was in costume.

"It's creepy here tonight," said Pip.

"The rides are over there, and there's a band at the south end of the carnival," I said.

"Where are the concession stands? I want a corn dog," Jessica said.

"It's by the Ferris Wheel," said Pip.

She and Jessica took over the planning; I felt that Adam and I were just there.

"How about asking us what we want to do?" asked Adam.

Jessica and Pip looked at each other. "Fine. That's fair. What would you guys like to do?" asked Pip.

Adam and I smiled and led the girls to the roller-coaster.

"I don't know about this," said Jessica.

"Don't tell me you're afraid of roller-coasters," Adam said.

"Afraid? No. Terrified? Yes," said Jessica.

"I'll be there to protect you," said Adam.

"I think it's a little beyond your control," said Jessica.

When we boarded the ride, Pip seemed apprehensive, so I took her hand. She smiled at me.

After the ride, we took a short break as Adam and I watched live feeds of the party at Alpha More. We felt slightly guilty because it was German's birthday and we'd chosen to be with our women.

Jessica and Pip rejoined us. "Did you guys order any food?" asked Jessica.

"Yep. We're number four thirty-two," said Adam.

"Jess, are you going to Donnie's parents' cabin?" asked Pip.

"Yes."

"As much as I don't like Donnie, I'm excited about going," said Pip.

"Four thirty-two!" we heard someone yell.

"That's us," said Adam.

He and I went to get the food, and he said, "This is going well."

"Yes sir, it is," I said. We grabbed the food and went to the condiment station.

"Hey, so the thing between her and Donnie?" asked Adam.

"I don't even want to talk about it," I said.

Back at the table, Jessica asked, "So who's all going to the lake house?"

"Us, G, Donnie, Otto, Petey, Brian, Adore, Derrek, Savannah, and Lollie," I said.

"Great! We're not going to be the only girls," said Pip.

"It's fine," said Jessica, and we all laughed.

When we finished eating, Adam and Jessica walked off to make out at a big rock, and Pip and I walked on the beach. "It's getting cold. Here's my jacket," I said.

"It's really nice out despite being cold," Pip said. "I'm glad that you decided to be with me here versus going to the party," she said.

"I really wanted to be there too but not just for the party. It's German's birthday," I said.

"You can make it up to him at the lake."

We just hugged and looked at the waves hitting the shore, a beautiful sight.

Sometime later, Adam and I headed to the house after dropping the girls off and walked into the party. It was about one in the morning, and the partygoers were dispersing.

German and Donnie were in the kitchen, and Donnie said, "Well, well, if it isn't the party ditchers of the century."

"Cut it out," I said.

"How was the party?" asked Adam.

"You should have been there," said Donnie.

"Did you guys see my new car?" asked German.

"That's your Lamborghini in the parking lot?" I asked.

"Yes!"

"We have a long day ahead of us. I'm going to bed," said Donnie.

"Goodnight," said German.

"I'm going to turn in too. Goodnight, guys," Adam said.

I sat at the table with German and said, "Sorry I wasn't here to celebrate with you."

"Don't worry about it, bro, I get you have a girlfriend, so you have to split up your time. That's cool."

Adore walked into the kitchen and got juice from the refrigerator. "Birthday boy! What's up, Justin? When did you get in?"

"Just now," I said.

"Shouldn't we be sleeping? We got a long drive ahead of us," Adore said.

"I'm going to bed now," German said.

"'Night, G," I said. They left the kitchen, and I began to clean up a little.

Alves came into the kitchen. "Hey, Justin, shouldn't you be in bed?"

"I'm going. I just wanted to clean up a little since we're leaving tomorrow," I said.

"Don't worry about it. German has a cleaning service coming in the morning. Justin, are you OK?"

"I can't believe that after this year, this place won't be here. To think that if we hadn't done what we did, we'd still have this place," I said.

"Everything happens for a reason, Justin. It's not your fault any of you."

"Thanks, Mr. Alves. Goodnight," I said.

"Goodnight, Justin."

CHAPTER 19

UNINVITED HOUSEGUESTS

German

IT WAS THE day after my birthday, and I wanted to take my new car out on the road.

"Hey, G, you about ready?" Donnie asked as he walked in.

"All packed and ready to get out of here. Where are Adam and Justin?" I asked.

"Justin's taking a shower and Adam's on the phone with his mom."

"Would you do me a favor when we get back and put this in your safety deposit box?" I asked showing him the flash drive that contained the video.

"Why my box?"

"I've painted a target on my back with Valve. Luckily, they haven't found the camera in the smoke detectors, but even if they do, nothing will point to me," I said.

Donnie nodded, and Justin walked in "Are we ready?" he asked.

"Yes, we're ready," I said.

We carried our bags out and put them in my new car.

"When are the girls coming?" Donnie asked.

"Pip has to work today. She and Jessica will drive up a little later," said Justin.

"Come on, G, start it up already!" an excited Donnie said.

We left Pendleton behind.

We got to Donnie's lake house first; the other brothers would be arriving in a few hours. We went in and saw that the place was dusty. "Damn, Donnie. When was the last time your family was here?" I asked.

"My high school graduation. I told my dad that he should rent it out," said Donnie.

"So what's the plan?" asked Adam.

"I figure we get the barbecue going, cook some burgers and dogs," said Donnie.

"We need to clean up in here a little first," I said.

"OK, G, you and Adam clean up. Justin and I'll go to the store."

I knew that was a way for Donnie to take my car for a test drive; when he said, 'go to the store,' he had a huge smile on his face. I didn't mind. Why not share a half-million-dollar car?

"The vacuum's in the hall closet, and there are cleaning supplies in the kitchen cabinets," Donnie said as I threw him the fob. "Be back in a jiffy!" he said.

"Adam, you want the kitchen or the living room?" I asked.

"Since I'm cooking, I'll take the kitchen."

"Good. I didn't want the kitchen at all," I said.

Donnie

My driving ninety mph in German's new car was making Justin a tad nervous. I pulled into a mini mart with a gas station. We got out, and I pulled a five-gallon gas can out of the trunk to feed the generator at the family place. "I pay, you pump?" I asked.

"Rock, paper, scissors," he said.

"Bro, you're ridiculous," I said. We pumped our fists three times, and I had rock while Justin threw scissors.

"Pump it up," I said, and I went into the store. I grabbed a cart and started loading it with chips and water. I asked a clerk, "Excuse me, sir. Do you sell burger patties and hot dogs?"

"Aisle three in the back there's a meat counter."

"Thank you," I said and headed there stopping for ketchup and mustard. I grabbed six packages of hot dogs and four pounds of ground beef. I happened to look out the window, and I saw the Greek god pointing his axe at me. Just then, someone tapped my shoulder, which made me jump.

"Whoa, bro!" said Justin.

"Sorry, bro. I thought …" I looked out the window again. The Greek god was gone.

"You thought what?"

"Nothing. Let's go," I said.

At the checkout counter, I kept looking outside. Justin saw that and looked outside too. "You OK, Donnie?"

"Yeah man," I said. I asked the clerk, "Does Mr. Jenkins still own that jet ski rental place?"

"It's fall, so most people are preparing for winter, but I can give you his card. Your total is eighty-four dollars and ninety-six cents."

I gave him my credit card, and Justin and I walked out. I looked where I'd seen the Greek god as Justin opened the liftgate. "OK, Donnie, spill it. What did you see?"

"The Greek god," I said.

"What?"

"He was standing over there by the window," I said and pointed.

"Are you sure that's what you saw?" asked Justin after looking over there.

"Maybe not. Let's just get back. Here, you drive," I said. I looked behind as we drove off.

We got back and saw Otto, Petey, Brian, and Adore in the kitchen with German and Adam. "Yo! You guys made it," I said.

"What did you buy?" asked German.

"It was a mini mart. There weren't many options to choose from," I said.

"More like we took all the meat they had," said Justin.

"I'm sure the owner thanks you," said Adore. We laughed as we put the groceries away.

"You want us to set up the grill and start cooking?" asked Petey.

"Yeah, but I have to put more gas in the generator. I'll meet you out there," I said.

I went up to my room, and I heard a car pull in. I looked out the window and saw Paris, Ginger, Pip, and Jessica. I put my head down as I didn't want to see Paris and Ginger at all. Matter of fact, I didn't want to see any of the girls. I'd known Pip and Jessica were coming, but I had no idea Paris and Ginger were coming. I headed outside and saw the guys talking to Paris.

"Donnie! I hope you don't mind me crashing. I was picking up Ginger, and the other girls told me about coming up here," said Paris.

"No man. You're family," I said as Ginger and I made eye contact. Paris and Ginger walked off as German and Adore were sitting at the table. "Did you know he was coming?" I asked.

"No," said German.

"Come on, man. It's Paris. He's good," said Adore.

"Paris isn't my issue," I said.

"What happened to this being my birthday getaway?" asked German.

"You're right, G. This is all for you," I said. I grabbed the football and yelled, "It's going down!" Adore, Otto, and Petey jumped up, and Otto held out his hands. I threw him the football, and Paris took the football from him and started running dodging Petey and Adore. I saw my chances. I ran at him and jumped on him, and we both went down. Everyone gathered around. I stood and asked, "You all right?"

"I'm good. Pretty strong there," he said.

"Yeah, maybe I was a little too aggressive," I said.

"Run it back!" he said and ran to the other side of the yard. German and Justin came up to me, and German asked, "What the hell are you doing?"

"Playing football," I said.

"Yeah, but why are you tackling each other like you're going pro?" asked Justin.

"Come on. Paris is used to this, right, G?" I asked, but German just shook his head.

After the football game, we were all at the picnic table waiting for dinner. Adam and Justin brought the hamburgers and hot dogs over. Paris and Ginger were across from me, and Ginger looked very uncomfortable.

"Are you OK?" I asked.

"Yeah, I'm fine, thanks for asking."

"So Donnie, what's the room situation?" asked Paris.

"I get the master bedroom. G gets my sister's room, Justin gets my brother Frankie's room, and Adam gets mine. If you'd like, you and Ginger can have the guest room," I said.

"I thought we were getting the guest room," Petey said.

"I'm cool with the couch," said Otto.

"That's the spirit!" I said.

"Hello! We made it!" Savannah yelled as she and Lollie came over.

Ginger looked very uncomfortable as she looked at Pip and Jessica, who also looked confused. Savannah gave me a big hug and said, "Hi, guys." She and Lollie hugged all the guys at the table except Paris, Adam, and Justin. Savannah said, "Ginger, I didn't recognize you at first. Your skin looks dry. Must be the outdoors."

"I didn't recognize you either, hon. Whore Street must not be poppin' tonight," said Ginger, and the group chuckled quietly.

"You're one to talk. I see at least three skeletons you've dealt with here," said Savannah.

"Excuse me," Ginger said. She got up and walked toward the house. Pip and Jessica followed her.

"Let's get this party started!" said Lollie as she and Savannah sat.

I went into the house quietly and overheard their conversation.

"I don't know if I can stay here tonight," said Ginger.

"Don't let those two run you out of here," said Jessica.

"Right. It's three of us against two of them. As long as they don't come for my man, we'll be fine," said Pip.

"I'm going upstairs," Ginger said. "Would you tell Paris to come up when he's done eating?"

"Sure," Pip said. She and Jessica went outside. I walked into the room. "Your room is upstairs, last door on the right," I said.

Ginger looked at me with guilt all over her face. "I didn't mean to come here."

"Yes you did. You've been looking for every reason to get back at me," I said.

"I'm going to bed. There's no reasoning with you, is there?"

"At least my dirt is on the rug instead of under it," I said.

Ginger walked upstairs, and Paris came in, walked past me, and followed her. This was going to be a long weekend I was sure.

Justin

"This is going to be an interesting weekend," I told Pip as we sat on the dock.

"I can't believe … Well, I can believe Donnie would invite Savannah and Lollie," said Pip.

"Go easy on him. You girls came with Paris and Ginger," I said.

"Yeah, you got a point," she said.

Pip and I started to snuggle. "It's really beautiful up here," she said.

"Yeah. We came up after finals last year before we left for the summer," I said.

Petey came up. "Guys, we're setting up the bonfire."

"Thanks, Petey," I said. Pip and I got up and walked over to the group around the bonfire—Adam, Jessica, German, Adore, Lollie, Otto, Donnie, and Savannah.

"You two seem like an amazing couple. How did you meet?" asked Lollie.

"We were doing community service, and from there, we just continued," said Pip.

"You look so familiar," said Lollie.

"I can imagine. Pendleton isn't a big campus," said Pip.

"You used to be with that other hot guy before he died," said Lollie.

"OK, we're going down a rabbit hole here. Let's tell scary stories instead," said Donnie.

"Petey, start us off," said German.

Petey

"Does anyone know why the Sorcerer represents the Greek system?" I asked.

"Oh great! Another frat boy cliché," said Savannah.

"Trust me. You never heard a story like this before," I said. "The first to join Alpha More were seniors. The younger classes were unable to join because fraternities were created to bond the seniors before they graduated and went off into the world.

"On graduation day, the four captains of the basketball, football, soccer, and volleyball teams came up with this game of sacrifice. They crushed some glass and put it in a red solo cup, poured Wild Turkey in it, and hid it among many other red solo cups at this party. Students showed up for the party, and no one knew who had this red solo cup until one partygoer started choking and spitting up blood. People were screaming as the student with a piece of glass sticking out of his neck ran up to a young blonde and decapitated her with his neck. The student disappeared, and they never found his body."

Justin

Petey's story was so creepy that the girls were holding onto us men. A chainsaw started up, and someone with a mask and a piece of glass pointing out of his neck jumped into the circle of light around the bonfire. The girls screamed until Paris took his mask off. The guys laughed, but the girls were angry.

"You guys are assholes!" said Savannah.

"You have to admit that was pretty good," said German.

Ginger came running out of the house. "Are you guys OK?" she asked.

"Oh yeah! Your boyfriend is hilarious," said Savannah.

We saw the lights in the house go off. "Justin, did you pour all the gas into the generator?" asked Donnie.

"Yeah. It was almost a full tank," I said.

Donnie and I went to the shed to look at the generator, and we saw that it had three-quarters of a tank. Donnie started the generator, and it came back on. "That's strange," he said. He looked around the shed as if someone might be hiding.

"What's wrong?" I asked.

Donnie quietly walked to a corner, grabbed someone, and pulled him out.

"Whoa! It's me!" said Brody.

"Brody, what the hell are you doing here?" asked Donnie.

"I saw that you invited some of the other guys, so I figured I'd crash too."

"Did you turn the generator off?" I asked.

"No. It was some dude in the Sorcerer's costume. Who was that? Petey?"

Donnie and I walked out, and Brody followed us.

"What's going on?" asked German.

"Brody showed up," I said.

"What's up, guys?" Brody asked.

"What are you doing here?" asked Adam.

"Just crashing the party."

"Looks like you guys are up to something," said Savannah.

"Like what?" Donnie asked as he sat next to Savannah.

"More pranks. I mean, your house is famous for them," she said.

"No worries. Other pranks are in the works," said Donnie.

"I'm sure," said Savannah.

"It's getting late. I think we're going to turn in," Adam said as he yawned.

German, Adore, Petey, and Otto left as well. That left Bryan, Donnie, Savannah, Lollie, Donnie, Pip, and me at the bonfire.

"Just, you want to help me put the fire out?" asked Donnie.

"Yeah," I said. We see Lollie and Brian making out.

"Damn, Brian," Donnie said, and they stopped.

"We're going in too. Goodnight y'all," said Brian.

After Donnie and I put the fire out, we went into the house.

Frankie's room was very interesting. He had posters of playmates on the walls, and some were very scary to look at in the dark. Pip walked into the room and cuddled next to me. "Wow. This room is something else," she said.

"Yeah. Frankie is a little obsessed," I said.

"I guess some things just run in the family," she said.

"How's Ginger?" I asked.

"She's OK. I just think it's really awkward for her to be here."

"Yeah," I said. Pip and I kissed, and she was coming off very seductive.

"The walls are kind of thin here," I said.

"I promise to be quiet," Pip said as she climbed on top of me. We engaged in a very intimate French kiss until we heard very loud moaning.

"What the hell?" I asked.

"Who's that?"

"It sounds like Savannah," I said.

The moaning got louder. I went to the door and looked into the hall. German had opened his door as was looking out as well. The moaning was coming from Donnie's room. German and I walked to Donnie's door. "Donnie!" yelled German as he banged on the door.

"What?" yelled Donnie.

"Bro, we're all trying to sleep here," I said.

Donnie opened the door in his underwear. "Donnie, put on some clothes," said German. "And keep it down."

Donnie grinned. "What? She was making too much noise?"

Just then, the lights went out again. German and I took out our phones to create some light.

"Dammit, Brody!"

Brody ran upstairs. "It wasn't me. I've been inside the whole time."

Adam came out of his room.

"Let's go check it out," said Donnie.

Adam, Donnie, German, and I get to the generator shed. As Donnie was checking out the generator, German said, "Damn. It's warm in here."

"Yeah. Keep the door open," I said.

"There's still three-quarters of a tank left. What the hell?" asked Donnie.

The door slammed closed. We turned and saw the Greek god holding his axe up, and we panicked.

Adam

We all backed up quickly after the Greek god slammed the shed door. "Uh, guys, now's the time to say something or at least do something," I said.

He charged us, but we all managed to dodge him. Donnie tackled him from behind, and we all jumped on him. German pulled his hood forward as he squirmed up and broke free from us. He pulled his hood back on right as Paris opened the door. "What's going on?" asked Paris.

Greek God shoved Paris aside and ran out of the shed, so we started chasing him, but he was too quick. He got in a car and drove off.

"Who the hell was that?" asked Paris.

"We don't know," said German.

The girls came outside, and Ginger asked, "What's going on?"

"Nothing, babe," Paris said. "Get your stuff. We're leaving."

"Paris, it's the middle of the night, man. Wait at least until morning," Justin said.

"I'm not sticking around here just to get attacked!" Paris said; he and Ginger headed to the house.

"I'll talk to him," said German.

Justin opened the door, and we heard Paris screaming, "I can't believe you, G! You set me up and had someone attack me!"

"Paris, don't be stupid. Trust me. If I wanted you to be attacked, it wouldn't be on my birthday in front of all these people," said German.

"Whatever. Let's go," Paris said to Ginger.

"What the hell's that about?" asked Donnie.

"He thinks I set him up to be attacked," said German.

"Who attacked him?" asked Brody.

"No one. It might have been a dog or something," said Donnie.

"Let's get back to bed," said German.

I was up at seven that morning even though I hadn't slept much during that crazy night. Jessica was asleep. I kissed her forehead and left the room. Downstairs, I saw Brian, Brody, Otto, and Petey asleep on the floor and couch. I went to the kitchen to start breakfast.

"Good morning," said Lollie.

"Good morning," I said.

"What happen last night?"

"Just a little misunderstanding," I said.

"I see," Lollie said as she gave me a flirtatious look.

"Would you like some breakfast?" I asked.

"I would, actually."

"Waffles? Bacon and eggs?" I asked.

"How about some eggs with a side of you?" Just then, Jessica cleared her throat. "Oh. I forgot about her," said Lollie.

Lollie walked out passing Jessica as she did. Jessica walked outside, and I followed her. I knew she was pissed. "Jess, wait," I said.

"What the hell was that all about?" she asked.

"I just offered to make her some breakfast as I would anybody," I said.

"You know she's a slut. She and that other wench who kept us up with her moaning."

"Nothing would have happened," I said.

"Just stay away from her, Adam."

She went back into the house, and I followed her. Justin and Pip were in the kitchen. Jessica grabbed Pip's hand, and they walked upstairs.

"What was that about?" asked Justin.

"Lollie tried to seduce me over breakfast," I said.

"Of course," Justin said as German and Adore came into the kitchen.

"What's this about Lollie trying to seduce you?" asked German.

"Don't ask," I said.

"You can blame Donnie for inviting them," said Justin.

Adore, German, and I started making breakfast. Brian asked, "What's the plan for today?"

"You'll have to ask our fearless leader when he wakes up," said German.

Donnie came downstairs with Savannah on his arm. "Good morning, everyone," she said.

"Speak of the devil," said Justin.

"What's up?" asked Donnie.

"We were waiting on you to see what you have planned for us today," Petey said.

"I chartered a boat so we could go tubing," said Donnie. "Let's eat."

Donnie, Justin, and Adore left the kitchen, and German started helping me with breakfast. I asked him, "Have you talked with your brother?"

"No. He ignored my calls this morning. He must be still pissed."

"How did Greek God know that we were here?"

"Someone here is connected, its strange that Brody would show up randomly."

"You don't think Brody bought him here?" I asked.

"I feel like that's too easy considering we already busted Brody for working with Bradshaw."

"Breakfast is ready!" I yelled.

After breakfast, the girls decided to stay at the house and let us go tubing. Donnie and I were getting instructions from the captain of the boat. "You push the throttle forward to accelerate, place it in the middle to stop, and pull it back to reverse. It's top speed is fifteen miles per hour."

"That's all?" asked Donnie, and we chuckled.

"If you have to stop the boat for any reason, put this orange flag in the holder to ensure that the other boats stand clear. Any questions?"

"No sir. Thank you. We'll return it in one piece," said Donnie.

The captain left, and German, Adore, Brian, Petey, Otto, and Justin walked up to us. Justin kissed Pip. Jessica hadn't come out of the house.

"We ready to go?" asked Donnie.

"Yeah," I said as we got in the boat. Donnie started it up and headed to the middle of the lake as Justin and I held onto the tube. "Who's going first?" I asked.

"Me and the birthday boy," said Donnie as he and German put on life vests. They jumped into the water and swam to the tube, which Justin and I had pushed overboard, and the got on it.

When Donnie yelled, "Go!" I pushed the throttle forward and got up to fifteen mph quickly. I looked back and saw German and Donnie hanging onto the tube.

"Adam! Stop! G fell off," said Justin.

I slowed down and turned around. German swam to the boat, got aboard, gave his vest to Adore, and told me, "Donnie sucks."

"Why? What happened?" I asked.

"He pushed me off," German said, and I chuckled.

"What's up with you and Jessica?" he asked.

"Jessica walked into the kitchen right when Lollie was coming on to me," I said.

"She'll get past that," said German.

"I hope so," I said.

"All right, Adam! I'm on!" yelled Adore.

I pushed the throttle forward with my mind on Jessica and what she thought about me.

Pip

Jessica and I walked to the dock. It was getting warm. We lay down.

"Are you still mad at him?" I asked.

"No. It's just that I was the other girl in my last relationship and seeing those two in the kitchen reminded me of that." said Jessica.

"Adam is a great guy, I don't think you have anything to worry about" I said.

"Yeah, well everyone talks about Fraternity men and how there never faithful.,"

"Before we were an official couple, Ben, my last boyfriend, was dating another girl. I made him choose between me and her, and he chose me," I said.

"Why do you think he chose you?"

I was a little thrown off by her question. I chuckled out of nervous. "I have no idea. Why would you ask me that?" I asked.

Savannah and Lollie came over. "Hello, ladies," said Savannah. Jessica and I turned back to face the water

"Hi," I said quietly.

Savannah and Lollie sat behind us. "Listen, ummm … Jessica," said Lollie, "I know what you saw might have been inappropriate. I'm a big flirt, and sometimes I don't know how to turn it off."

"Maybe you should practice doing that," said Jessica.

"Well, look. I don't want it to be awkward. We're spending one more night here, and we can at least be cordial," said Lollie.

"I'm not interested in that. Excuse me," Jessica said as she stood and walked away.

"Well, I tried," said Lollie.

"You call that trying?" I asked.

"What more could she have done?" asked Savannah.

"Try apologizing," I said.

Savannah and Lollie laughed at that, and Lollie said, "Look. All I wanted was breakfast, not marry the guy. If you two are going to be that sensitive about it, I'm fine with pretending you or she aren't even here."

"What a bitch," I said.

"Be careful, honey. She said 'pretend.' I can make it permanent," said Savannah.

I got up and left them. It was going to be a long day and night with those two there.

Adam

We got back from the boat ride and wanted to celebrate our last night there. Things between Jessica and I were awkward. She signaled me to walk outside. We went out and sat on the stoop.

"Look, I know I've been distant all day. It's just that girls like her always stand in the way of my happiness with a guy I'm with," she said.

"What do you mean?" I asked.

"The guy I was with before you cheated on me and left me for the other girl. She was vindictive and knew he had a girlfriend."

"I'm not that kind of guy," I said.

"Neither was he," Jessica said. When she walked away, I didn't know what to do or how to help her with this. I went back inside as everyone was packing up.

"Hey, Adam, can you give me hand?" asked Donnie.

As I helped him clean up the kitchen, he asked, "What's wrong, bro?"

"Nothing, man," I said.

"C'mon, bro. I know you, and you're going through a lot as it is."

"She was worried about me cheating on her," I said.

"Jessica?"

"Who else am I with?" I asked.

"Damn bro, don't shoot! Come on. She has nothing to worry about. You're not that type."

"You want to tell her that?" I asked.

"Sure. Where is she?" asked Donnie, and he and I chuckled.

German walked in. "The other guys just left, and I called a car service for the girls."

"Yes. I refuse to ride back with those two playmates," said Pip.

German, Justin, and I chuckled at that.

"Thank you," said Pip.

German's phone rang, and we heard a car honking. "Your car's here," I said.

"Where's Jessica?" asked Pip.

"I'll get her," I said, and I walked outside. Jessica was at the dock. I took a deep breath and said, "German ordered a car service for you and Pip. It's here."

Jessica turned to me. "I'm sorry, the last guy I was with made it hard for me to trust again."

She walked toward the house, and I did too. I saw Justin and Pip kissing. Jessica and Pip got in the car and left. I walked up to German and Justin as Donnie was hugging Savannah and Lollie. The two girls got in their car and left.

"Well, gents, let's get our stuff and head out too," Donnie said.

CHAPTER 20

THE NEW DISCOVERY

Donnie

I WOKE UP IN a hot sweat. The temperature in the room was seventy-nine. I got out of bed and went to the bathroom. As I was urinating, I felt pain sharp enough to make me tear up. "Damn!" I said as I flushed the toilet.

I went to German's room and saw him at his desk and Adore reading on his bed.

"Yo, Donnie. Where are your books, man?" asked Adore.

"I'll get them in a sec," I said.

"You all right? You look like you've been sweating," German said.

"I'm good, man, just a little tired," I said.

"I'm hungry. I'm going to kitchen. You guys want anything?" asked Adore.

"No, I'm good, man," I said.

"Pop in a hot pocket for me, pepperoni pizza please," German said, and Adore left. German scooted his desk chair next me as looked at me intently. "What's wrong with you?"

"I woke up in a cold sweat, and when I peed, it burned like hell," I said.

"Did you have unprotected sex with Savannah?"

"Yes," I said. I knew where he was going.

"We need to go to the emergency room, bro."

I couldn't move not because I was in pain but because I was embarrassed.

"Donnie, come on," said German. He grabbed my arm and led me out of his room.

"Hey. Where you guys going?" asked Adore when he met us on the stairs.

"We'll be back. Start chapter thirteen. I'll follow up with you," said German.

We got to the ER and were waiting for the doctor to call me into an exam room.

German put his hand on my forehead. "You're burning up."

"I just peed again, and this hurts, bro," I said.

"Damn, man. I'm sorry, let's just hope it's a UTI and nothing more serious."

"Donnie Diamante," the nurse announced. When German and I walked over to her, she said, "I'm sorry. Only family and significant others can come into the admissions area."

"No worries. This is my boyfriend. Wherever he goes I go," I said, and G looked confused.

"Very well. We'll need a urine sample," the nurse said and gave me a cup. "The bathroom's the second door on the right."

The nurse walked away, and German asked sarcastically, "Do you want me to hold it while you pee?"

"Yeah, c'mon, dumplin'," I said.

"You serious?"

"No. I'll be right back," I said.

I knew this was going to hurt, and it did. The pain seemed to have gotten worse. I washed my hands and left the restroom. "Here it is," I told German.

"Why are you showing it to me? Give it to the nurse," German said, which made me chuckle.

The nurse came up, took the cup, and said, "Right this way."

She led us to a bed in the ER. I sat on it while G took a chair. I started have shortness of breath, which made G ask, "You OK?"

"No. I'm in pain," I said.

He went to the sink, soaked a paper towel, and put it on my forehead.

"Thanks man," I said.

A doctor walked in. "Mr. Diamante, I'm Dr. Cavell. You're in pain when you urinate?"

"Excruciating pain describes it better, a complete ten," I said.

"All right. I'll step out. Disrobe and put on this smock. I'll be right back."

When German got up, I asked him, "Where you going?"

"I'm stepping out to let you change."

"But I need you to fold my clothes!" I said.

He sat and started folding my clothes as I took them off. When I took off my underwear, he said, "Damn, Donnie! No wonder girls go crazy over you!"

I chuckled and donned my smock, and the doctor walked back in and said, "We examined your urine sample. You need to drink more water, but it's not a UTI. Have you had unprotected sex within the last seventy-two hours?"

"Yes," I said getting nervous.

"We're going to test you for STDs. I'll send a nurse to draw your blood."

My heart sunk. I didn't know what to think or do.

The nurse came in and drew my blood. When she left, German said, "I'm going to the cafeteria. You want some coffee?"

"No. I need a drink," I said.

"I'll be right back," G said. After he left, I pulled out my phone and went on my social media page. I scrolled down and liked one of Adam's posts, and I did the same with Justin's and Pip's posts. I continued to scroll and came across a picture of Ben and Brandon, so I went on to Ben's page and saw the picture of him and Pip and a comment from Jessica: "Justice is coming for both of you." I was confused about that.

German came back. "No matter how much cream and sugar I put in this coffee, it's still horrible."

"G, look at this," I said as I gave him my phone.

German read it. "What does she mean by justice?"

"It makes sense. The Greek god attacked us at the lake house, and she was there," I said.

"The Greek god attacked us at the party, and she was there as well," said German.

225

We looked at each other. "We need more proof that it's her," said German.

"Like what? G, c'mon. We keep going in circles here. We have Mrs. Klovis to worry about as well as the Greek god," I said.

"That's what I need," said German.

"What?" I asked.

"Mrs. Klovis. She might not know who the Greek god is, but she knows what he told her."

I was confused about what he meant, but just then, the doctor walked in. "Mr. Diamante, I'm going to keep you here for a few hours as we run your results. We'll let you know as soon as we know something. If you have an questions or need assistance, please use your nurse call button."

"So I have some time," G said. "I'm going to pay Mrs. Klovis a visit. Be back soon."

German

I heard Donnie calling my name as I left the room, but I kept going. When I got to Klovis's flower shop, I saw her behind the counter.

"German, what are you doing here?"

I pulled out my phone. "I came to ask you some questions. Do you know who this girl is?" I asked as I showed her a picture of Jessica.

"Isn't that your friend's girlfriend?"

"The irony is that she knew Ben. She commented on his social media, and we can place her at every scene where the Greek god attacked us," I said.

"What does this have to do with me?"

"What did the Greek god tell you that would make you partner up with him?" I asked.

"I have no idea what you're talking about."

"Mrs. Klovis, cut the whole innocent positive mom junk. I'm not buying it. I know you're mad as hell about losing a child and rightfully so. Instead of settling with me and moving on with life, you've chosen the most unethical way to handle this," I said.

I knew she was getting angry. What I had said was very harsh; maybe I shouldn't have gone to that extreme.

Her demeanor changed as she squinted at me. "That's the problem with you rich kids. You think throwing money at something will make it go away."

"Yeah, yeah, yeah. That's why your husband's filing a lawsuit. Skip the antics. I asked you a question, and you can't give me an answer," I said. I looked out the window and saw Jessica talking with Steven. In a second, every encounter we had with Steven flashed before my eyes. He was the Greek god.

I walked out of Klovis's shop and watched them walk away. I didn't follow them; instead, I went back to the hospital to tell Donnie what I'd seen.

When I entered his room, he was in tears. "The doctor said I have chlamydia," he said.

"I'm sorry, bro, but at least it can be treated," I said.

"I'm ready to get out of here. I just need my prescription."

The doctor came in. "All right, Mr. Diamante, this is the antibiotic I'll inject you with. This will make you a bit drowsy, so I recommend rest. Here's some information on protected sex."

The doctor gave Donnie the injection, and we checked out of the ER. Outside, I got a call from Paris. "What's up?" I asked.

"Bro, where are you?"

"On my way home. What do you want?" I asked.

"Why didn't you tell me the university was going to close down Alpha More?"

"Because I have it handled," I said.

"How?"

"Don't worry about it," I said.

"I'm calling Dad. I need you to be here when I call him, G."

"I can't talk to him right now. Can we call him in the morning?" I asked.

"Yeah."

"Goodbye," I said.

I drove back to the house and walked Donnie to his room, where he lay down and went to sleep.

Justin

German called Adam and me to his condo; he said he needed to talk to us.

"Hey, G, what's going on?" Adam asked when we got there.

"I paid Mrs. Klovis a visit. Our conversation let me tie up some loose ends. Drake is alive, and she knows exactly where he is. He has something on her that if it got out would make her look just as guilty."

"What's going to happen from that?" I asked.

"Bradshaw has enough evidence to arrest her for the murder, which we all know she didn't commit. Drake isn't dead, but this might be what we need to get her to confess where he is," said G.

"What about the Greek god?" asked Adam.

German opened a thick folder. "Donnie and I saw a comment on Ben's profile that concerned me. I did more research. Adam, I hope you don't hate me because of this."

He pulled out a photo of Steven and Jessica. The look on Adam's face said he was disappointed to the max. "I really am sorry," G said. The way I figure it, Steven is the Greek god and Jessica is his accomplice."

Adam started pacing. German and I knew he was on the verge of a breakdown. We tried to comfort him, but he grabbed the picture and stormed out of the room.

When Donnie got there, I filled him in on what had happened. German called Adam, but his call went right to voice mail.

"What did you expect? I'd ignore your calls too," said Donnie.

German was at his screen watching Bradshaw arrest Klovis.

"Well, your plan worked G, Bradshaw arrested Mrs. Klovis and we know who Greek God is." said Donnie.

"I'm just hoping she tells the truth. We know he's alive," said German.

"Do we?" I asked. I got frantic. "I'm just saying, what if we're wrong?"

"She didn't deny it. Since this is taken care of for now, let's call Adam again," G said.

"I'll try," Donnie said.

Adam

I pulled up at Jessica's house and saw that Donnie was calling. I sent him to voice mail. I went to her door and knocked. She opened it, smiled, and hugged me. "Hey! I've been thinking about you all day," she said.

"Same here," I said. She waved me in and went to her kitchen, where she stirred something on the stove. "What are you making?" I asked.

"Ginger mango shrimp with white wine and seared garlic. I have this ladies' luncheon interview at a church, and this is my presentation dish."

I pulled out the picture but hid it behind my back. "We haven't had a chance to talk about what happened at Donnie's lake house," I said.

"Yeah, and I think it's for the best. Maybe we should talk about something else."

"How about talking about you and Steven?" I asked and put the photo on her table.

Jessica looked at me; she didn't seem guilty about being with Steven. "I was really happy with him," she said. "He carried on the best conversations, and he was a great listener. Living in that fraternity was his downfall because it took away who he was."

She turned to the stove, grabbed a pan, and threw hot water on my face. She ran off. I was in pain. I couldn't see a thing. I felt a shock go through my body, and I fell to the floor. I didn't know what had happened, and I couldn't see or hear anything, but I knew I was alive. I blacked out …

When I opened my eyes, my vision was blurry, but I recognized Steven looking at me. "What the hell? Where am I?" I asked as I realized I was tied to a chair.

"Adam, Adam, Adam … What happened? You were supposed to have my back," he said.

"Untie me!" I yelled.

"Or what? You're going to take away my eyesight too?"

"Look, man! It was stupid prank that I'm really sorry for," I said.

"A prank that cost me my hearing. That's the problem with you four. Tonight is the ultimate payback."

Donnie

German, Justin, and I knew for sure where we'd find Adam—at Jessica's and confronting her. Justin called Pip for Jessica's number and got it. "Thanks, babe." He put the number on German's phone through his Bluetooth, and G called her.

"Hello?" Jessica asked.

"Hi, Jessica, it's German. Donnie and Justin are with me. Have you talked to Adam?"

"Yeah. He's here, and he seems very upset."

"Yeah, I know. Can we talk to him please?"

"He's in the shower. I tell you what. I think you three need to talk to him. I'll text you my address. Come on over."

We looked at each other thinking that was odd.

"Uh, are you still there?" she asked.

"I am, and we'd be happy to come over," I said.

"Great. See you soon."

She hung up, and I asked, "Is it just me or did you think that was odd too?"

"It was definitely strange," said German.

Jessica sent her address to G, who put it in his GPS. We drove there. It turned out to be an old, abandoned sugar mill.

"What the hell is this?" asked Justin.

"Is this the old sugar mill Why would this be her address ?" I asked.

"Its not, this is the set up," said German.

"I have a bad feeling about this, shouldn't we call someone?" asked Justin.

"I'll call Bradshaw, in the meantime lets go in Adam could be in trouble," German said.

After I made the call to Bradshaw, we got out of the car and went to the door. German knocked but got no answer.

"Guys, this isn't right," said Justin.

German turned the doorknob. It was unlocked. We all looked at each other, but then I went in followed by German and Justin, who closed the door. I saw that the lights were on in the warehouse part of the building. A furnace was making the place warm.

"It's hot in here," said German.

"G? Is that you?" asked Adam.

"Adam!" German said as we walked in farther and saw him tied up.

"Jessica's in on this with Steven. They knocked me out and brought me here," Adam said.

A door flew open, and the Greek god approached us. We gathered around Adam, who was struggling in the chair. The Greek god pulled his hood back. It was Steven.

"So you really are the Greek god!" I said.

"I'm not alone in this," said Steven.

"What does that mean?" asked German.

Another Greek god came up on our right. This one had the axe.

Justin

"So there are two of you?" I asked.

"Look. I have nothing to do with this," Steven said. "I just put on a costume because I thought it would be fun. The other Greek god here wants revenge in a different way."

"Untie me!" said Adam.

"Go ahead, untie him," said Steven.

German started on the knots just as Jessica came into the room pointing a gun at us.

"I knew her crazy ass was in on this," said Donnie.

"Shut your mouth!" Jessica yelled.

"Steven, come on. You don't have to do this," I said.

"Of course I do. I'm the Greek god who gets the luxury of killing you so he won't have to. I'd feel much better knowing I got to you first," said Steven.

The Greek god began signing to Steven while Jessica kept the gun pointed at us.

"G, what's he saying?" asked Donnie.

"Shut up!" said Jessica.

The conversation got intense. Jessica didn't know what was going on either. "Baby, what's going on?" she asked.

"He's saying that he needs us alive and Steven is saying no way, we're his," German said.

Jessica fired a warning shot. "I said shut up!"

The Greek god grabbed Steven by the neck and started strangling him.

"Damn!" said Adam.

"Let him go!" Jessica screamed.

Steven was wrestling with the Greek god; we didn't know what to do because Jessica looked very unstable with the gun.

"Shoot him!" said Donnie.

"Shut up!" she yelled at Donnie. "Let him go!" she yelled at the Greek god, but he snapped Steven's neck, killing him instantly. Jessica, enraged, started shooting at the Greek god. We ducked until she stopped firing.

"Damn! That bitch is crazy," said Donnie.

"Shut up, Donnie," said Adam.

Jessica pointed her gun at us. "Get up!" We all did. "Call him out here now!" said Jessica.

"How? We don't even know who he is!" said German.

Jessica shot above German's head and started crying. "I swear I'll kill all four of you!"

The door burst open. Bradshaw and four cops rushed in. "Put the gun down!" said Bradshaw.

Jessica pointed her gun at Adam, and Bradshaw shot her twice.

"No!" Adam said as he fell to ground.

German

We gave our statements about Steven and Jessica. We told Bradshaw that they had kidnapped Adam and had come down on all of us.

"I have your statement. I'm sorry this had to happen. You're free to go. German, can I have a word with you please?"

She and I walked toward her car. "Katheryn Klovis was arrested this evening for Drake's murder. I don't know if what you and your friends started is truly over, but in her warehouse, we found surveillance bugs in her smoke detectors. Right now, we don't know who put them there, but we figure whoever it was may be still out there."

I simply nodded and went to my car. The others got in, and we drove off.

"What did Bradshaw say?"

"They found the cameras in the smoke detectors and are investigating where they came from," I said. I pulled the flash drive from the console. "As long as she doesn't find this, they'll never find out," I said.

"I feel real sick about all this," said Adam.

"You couldn't have helped her. She was a sick woman," said Donnie.

In the rearview camera, I saw a truck coming up fast on my tail. It rear-ended me and then passed me.

"What the hell?" asked Justin.

I drove faster and passed the truck.

"Who the hell is that?" asked Donnie.

"Who do you think?" I asked.

I pressed my phone to call Bradshaw as the truck came up and hit us harder. I lost control and crashed into a ditch.

I woke up. My head was hurting. I looked in the console. The flash drive was gone. I got out of my car and looked in both directions. I didn't see anyone. I realized that the proof I had had that Drake was alive was gone … and that I might end up in more trouble if it got into the hands of the law.

Bradshaw

I drove out to an abandoned shack on the lake as I got out of my car. I walked inside as I see the Greek Hooded man walk up to me as I smile. The man removed his hood as its Detective Drake.

"Our plan worked." Drake said as he held of the flashdrive.

"It certainly did, now all we have to do is leak this evidence and German Rigen goes down for good.

Another Greek Hooded man comes out holding an Axe as Drake and I look over at him and smile.

To be continued……

Printed in the United States
by Baker & Taylor Publisher Services